BURNING
For Him

Trident Security Book 13

SAMANTHA COLE

Copyright ©2025 Samantha Cole

All Rights Reserved.

Suspenseful Seduction Publishing

Cover Design: Samantha Cole

Photographer: Paul Henry Serres

Models: Melissa & Mathieu

Editing: Alyssa Nazzaro

Burning For Him is a work of fiction. Names, characters, businesses, organizations, places, events, and incidents either are the product of the author's imagination or are used fictitiously. Any resemblance to actual persons, living or dead, events, or locales is entirely coincidental.

AI RESTRICTION: The author expressly prohibits any entity from using any part of this publication, including text and graphics, for purposes of training artificial intelligence (AI) technologies to generate text or graphics, including, without limitation, technologies that are capable of generating works in the same style or genre as this publication. The author reserves all rights to license uses of this work for generative AI training and the development of machine learning language models.

No part of this book may be reproduced, scanned, or distributed in any printed or electronic form without permission. Please do not participate in or encourage piracy of copyrighted materials in violation of the author's rights. Purchase only authorized editions.

AUTHOR'S NOTE

**(I'm sorry it's so long!
Feel free to skip to Chapter One.)**

My dearest readers,

I know you've been waiting for Jenn "Baby-girl" Mullins' story for what seems like forever. At first, she wasn't old enough, being only nineteen when she was introduced in *Leather & Lace*, two years after both her parents were murdered, and she went to live with her godfather, Ian Sawyer. She needed to mature, go to college, and figure out her future before committing herself to a man for life. However, during that time, she fell in love with Doug Henderson, but that love was unrequited, at least for the time being. Doug was in denial. Hey, it happens. He's human (okay, *fictionally* human), and sometimes they can have the best thing staring them in the face, and they can't see it. But since this book has a happy ending, you know Jenn didn't give up without a fight.

Now, here's the second reason you're just getting their story. My personal life got in the way of my writing. Between my mother's health issues and my own, moving because my rent skyrocketed (they wanted people to move out so they could renovate and get higher rents), COVID, and dozens of other real-life issues that would take forever to mention, I found it challenging to focus on my writing. I was a mess for a bit because my characters wouldn't talk to me, and trust me, that's unnerving for a writer. The stress of that makes it worse too.

In addition to the events unfolding in my personal life, during the summer of 2023, I decided to remove all my books from KU and list them on other platforms. I'd already made several smaller series available on other sites at the end of 2022, but now it was time to take the Trident Security series and its spin-offs out of KU. It was scary, terrifying even, but I felt it was the right thing to do at that point in my career.

Several things factored into my decision: 1) In 2023, Amazon's payout for KU pages read had dropped to an all-time low. It didn't help that AI-generated books were flooding the market. 2) Kobo Plus, an alternative to KU, was introduced to the US and UK markets around the same time. 3) I had author friends

AUTHOR'S NOTE

who had their Amazon accounts shut down, by no fault of their own, and suddenly found themselves without an income while they fought to get the accounts back. Some did. Some didn't and had to start from scratch on other book sites. I couldn't risk that happening to me.

Since ninety-nine percent of my books would be available on sites like Kobo, Apple, B&N, and more, I chose to update my brand first and dropped the middle initial "A" from my pen name. In doing so, I could make my name bigger on the book covers, which would be easier for my readers to spot. That meant updating the covers, blurbs, and back matter for over fifty titles, in e-book, print, and audio formats. Then I had to upload them to the various websites—five for e-books, four for audiobooks, and two for print books. If you lost count, when combined, I had to update or create over 550 listings for all my books and their available formats. Yes, that's a lot, and yes, it took months to complete everything. I also updated my logo. My website is currently undergoing a makeover, and it's not yet entirely up to date. But hopefully, the designers will have it finished soon.

Now, I know this all sounds like a lot of excuses for why it took me so long to write Baby-girl's story, but as most of you already know, real life throws you curveballs when you least expect them. Real life didn't care that I'd written Jenn and Doug's prequel short story for the *Trident Security Field Manual* **SEVEN** years ago. I was shocked and devastated when I realized that's how long you've been waiting for their whole story. I sincerely apologize for that—it was never my intention to keep you in suspense for that length of time. Many of you often asked when the book would be out, and unfortunately, I couldn't give you an exact release date until I was almost finished writing it. For much of that time, I hadn't even started it.

Over the past two years, the only books I released were short stories from anthologies that I expanded into novellas, and writing them took a lot out of me. I was worried that I could no longer write a full-length novel—a worrisome thought. At any given time, I have approximately twenty-four manuscripts open, some of which are half-completed or have several chapters, while others are just basic outlines. I want to tell these stories so badly, but I can't force the words if they won't come. If I try to do that, I won't be happy with the results, and neither will my readers.

I was so excited yet anxious when I finally had the chance to sit down and start *Burning For Him*. Would I get a few chapters in, only to have the characters stop talking to me? It's happened to me before. (Yes, I'm calling you out, Brian Malone!) And if I did finish it, would it be the book you've all been waiting for so patiently? Would I feel that I had done my best to give Doug and Jenn the happily-ever-after they deserved

AUTHOR'S NOTE

after all this time? Would you, my dear readers, love it, think it was so-so, or hate it?

I hope you enjoy it, but I'll understand if you're not happy with the results. Not every reader is pleased with every book they read. It's what makes us all unique and diverse. But I promise you, if I didn't think this was the best way to give Doug and Jenn their HEA, I wouldn't have released the book. I would have rewritten it over and over until I was finally happy with the story. When I finally typed "The End," it was a huge relief, and I celebrated with a bottle of wine.

One last thing I need to mention. The Trident Security series and some of its spin-offs contain elements of the BDSM lifestyle. Up until now, the only book in the original series that didn't was *Whiskey Tribute*. It just didn't fit in with Curt and Dana's story, and my readers understood that. I knew before I started to write *Burning For Him* that this would also be the case for Doug and Jenn, and I realize some readers might be upset or disappointed about that. However, in earlier books, it was mentioned several times that Jenn was not interested in the lifestyle, so it would be odd for her to change her mind suddenly. Additionally, I would have needed another club, one that her uncles approved of, because there was no way any of them would be comfortable playing at The Covenant while Jenn and Doug were there, or vice versa. The "ick" factor was too strong. However, that doesn't mean the sex scenes aren't steamy because they are, and Doug and Jenn have a fun conversation about the lifestyle too. So, I hope you understand why the book is written in this manner.

I know this was a long "author's note," but I felt you deserved a detailed explanation. And, now, my dear readers, I give you *Burning For Him: Trident Security Book 13*, the story you've all been waiting for.

Sincerely and with all my love,

Samantha

INTRODUCTION

A prequel short story for Jenn and Doug, titled "Burning Embers," is included in the *Trident Security Field Manual*. If you're following the best reading order for the original Trident Security series and its spin-offs, you've probably already read it. While it's not necessary before continuing with the whole story, it does include their first kiss, what led up to it, and what happened immediately afterward. *Burning for Him* takes place almost a year later.

The Who's Who of Trident Security and The Covenant can be found at the back of this book.

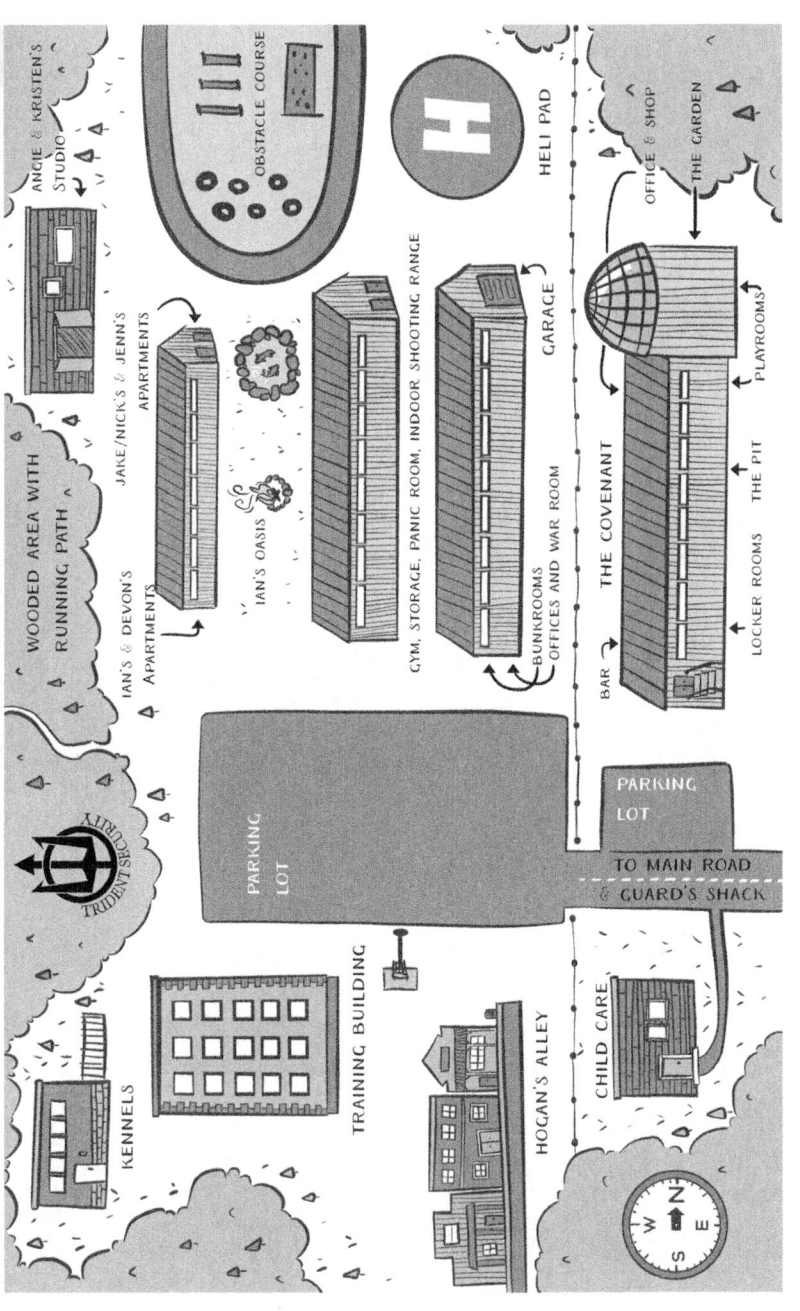

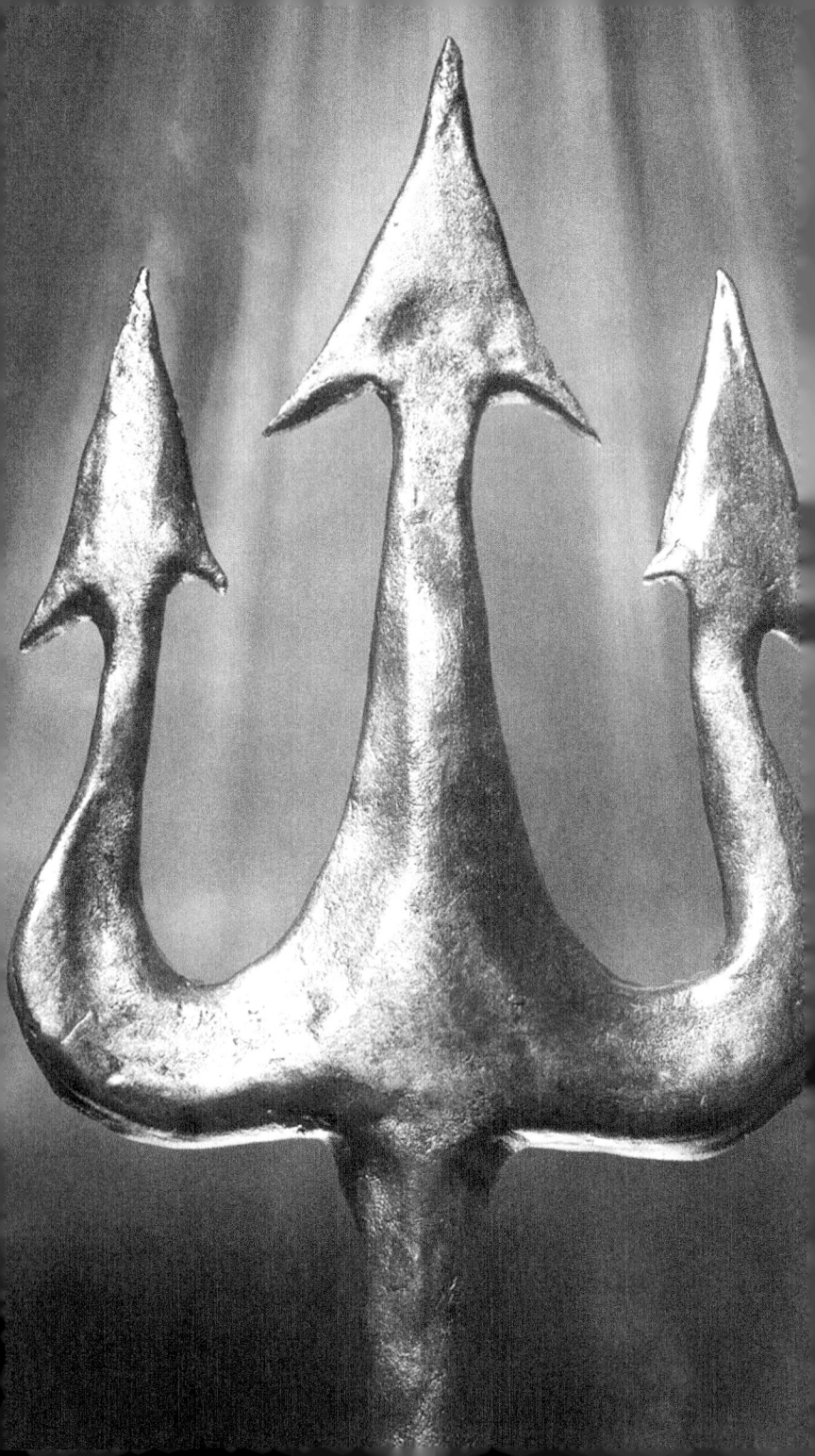

CHAPTER ONE

"I'm still not happy about this," Angie's husband, Ian, grumbled while staring across the backyard at his goddaughter, Jennifer Mullins, excitedly chatting with a few friends. Her large surrogate family and many others had gathered for her going-away party.

Angie turned her head to the side so Ian couldn't see when she rolled her eyes for the third time in less than an hour. She wasn't in the mood to rack up punishments, which usually resulted in Ian's hand making hard contact with her ass. Since they were in the BDSM lifestyle, spankings were normal for them, but she preferred erotic ones over the others.

"We've had this conversation dozens of times over the past two months, my love. She's a grown woman now and allowed to make important decisions like this on her own. You can't confine her to this compound for her entire life."

The well-guarded, fenced-in complex, situated on dozens of acres on the outskirts of Tampa, Florida, was owned by the Sawyer brothers: Ian, Devon, and Nick. They bought it at an auction, years ago, after the government discovered it was used to run an illegal drug operation disguised as an import/export company and seized it. At the time, retired Navy SEALs Ian and Devon wanted the place for their new company, Trident Security. Then, their cousin Mitch approached them with the idea for an elite BDSM club, The Covenant, which now occupied the first of four warehouses when anyone entered the compound. The next two buildings housed the Trident offices, bunk rooms, a firing range, training areas, a gym, and a vehicle garage.

The fourth and final warehouse was converted into four penthouse-size apartments. On one end, Ian and Angie lived below Devon and his wife, Kristen, while at the opposite end, Jenn had her own three-bedroom apartment, with Nick and his husband, Jake Donovan, occupying the one above hers. In between the last two warehouses was Ian's Oasis, the backyard Angie designed for him as a birthday gift a few years ago. Then, after Kristen and Devon's son, JD, was born, the brothers had a cottage built for their wives where the two women could focus on their respective careers

—Kristen was an author, while Angie was an artist. The building had plenty of room for each of them to spread out and a play area for the kids, which now included Ian and Angie's ten-month-old daughter, Peyton.

"Why not?" Ian asked.

Shifting Peyton to her other hip, she glared at her idiotic husband—not that she'd call him that to his face. Alpha men could be so damn stubborn sometimes, but the ones like Ian made up for it in so many other ways. "She's twenty-three and a college graduate with a great career ahead of her. She just wants to do this first. You can't control where she goes, what she does, and who she dates anymore."

His gaze whipped to hers. "Who she *dates*? Who the fuc—fudge is Baby-girl dating?" Like all the other retired-military Trident Security men and women, he made an effort not to curse in front of Peyton, their nephew, and their friends' little ones, but he was still a work in progress. Too bad it was after Marco and Harper's daughter, Mara, learned to say twatwaffle, which probably wouldn't go over well when she started preschool soon.

"Ugh." She fought the urge to roll her eyes again. "No one. At least, not that I know of. My point is that you have to let her live her life the way she wants to. Jeff and Lisa raised her right. And after they were killed, you stepped up and finished the job for them.

They would be so proud of her, and you should be too."

"I am, but—"

"But nothing, Ian. I know you're worried, but you have to let her go. You gave her the watch with the tracking device in it, a backup satellite phone, pepper spray, a collapsible baton, and probably a dozen other weapons and doohickeys. You've met Dr. Sanchez before, and Carter knows her well. You told me her place is guarded by expats, and nothing has ever happened to any volunteers who stayed there. Jenn's also not going alone, and you investigated everyone who will be with her. And Carter, Jordyn, and your teams put an end to that drug and sex trafficking cartel that operated nearby."

Carter and Jordyn were friends and members of the club, as well as undercover agents who worked for a highly classified government organization that most Americans were unaware of.

"The cartels are like rats—you destroy one colony, and dozens more are waiting to take over."

"But Dr. Sanchez told you there's been no new activity at Diaz's old estate down there."

"Once they found out he was dead, the Colombian *federales* seized everything they could and then let the jungle take the rest. It doesn't mean the area is safe, though."

She handed him Peyton when the baby reached for

her Da-Da, and then she kissed him on his rigid, stubbled jawline. "Jenn will be fine. You and the teams trained her to think like an operative. She'll have protection there and the self-awareness you instilled in her. Let her spread her wings."

"I still don't like it." His intense gaze remained pinned on the young woman he loved as much as his own daughter, but it softened a little as Peyton patted his cheek.

Angie glanced around the party and spotted someone else glaring and frowning at Jenn while trying to hide from her. She knew better than to say anything to Ian, though.

You're not the only one, my dear husband.

Why the hell is Ian letting her go to fucking Colombia for three months? Is he out of his fucking mind?

Doug Henderson kept his feet rooted to where he stood for the past hour, fighting the compulsion to demand that his boss lock Jenn in her apartment. Better yet, Doug should drag her in there himself.

No, you shouldn't, you asshole. You've gone over this time and again. She's too damn young for you, and she's got a hero complex since you took a bullet for her.

As he repeated that last line over and over in his

head, like a mantra, he absentmindedly rubbed the puckered scar on the right side of his chest under his T-shirt. It was a reminder of how he fucked up nearly four years ago, while guarding the then nineteen-year-old, and almost got her killed. It was bad enough that she was kidnapped, but Doug also had to deal with the murder of his partner during the same incident. With his own injury, he hadn't been able to save either of them. Thankfully, her surrogate uncles, the six original Trident Security team members, and some of their associates rescued her along with Angie, who'd also been taken hostage.

"You're gonna go nuts while she's in Colombia, aren't you?"

Doug turned his glare to Jason "Tuff" Tanner and his massive brown and white pit bull, Meat, who snuck up on him while his mind wandered. Tuff worked for another company, Blackhawk Security, which had a strong relationship with Trident, despite the two being technically competitors. The owners of both were retired military—most of their employees were too—and they often helped each other out with personnel and equipment. In fact, Doug initially worked for Chase Dixon at BHS, and it was then that he was assigned as one of Jenn's bodyguards to escort her to and from her college classes because of an ongoing threat against Angie. On their way home one afternoon, they were ambushed, and Jenn was taken by crooked DEA agents and a few gang members they'd hired.

After it was all over, he expected Ian to finish killing him. Instead, once Doug had fully recovered, the man shocked him by offering him the supervisor position for Trident's new Personal Protection Division. Had he known how often he'd run into Jenn on any given week, Doug might have turned down the job. He'd been attracted to the younger woman, eight years his junior, but despite his best efforts, his captivation had only grown stronger. It didn't help that she had a crush on him and kissed him eleven months ago. It was also fucked-up that he kissed her back before his brain overrode his body. Since then, he tried to avoid her, but when he worked in the same compound she lived in, it wasn't always possible.

"No, I'm not gonna go nuts, asshole. What are you talking about? Jenn is—she's my boss's goddaughter and a friend. Nothing more," he said, knowing it was a lie. "Like everyone else here, I'm just worried about her safety, that's all."

He couldn't stop himself from glancing toward the stunningly beautiful blonde woman. When he first met her, she had strawberry blonde hair, but about two years ago, she started adding highlights to it, making the color more blonde than red. Even with the distance between them, he could see her brilliant blue eyes sparkle as she laughed at something one of her friends said.

Tuff chuckled and slapped Doug on the shoulder. "Yeah, you keep telling yourself that, dude. Maybe someday you'll convince yourself that's all it is. C'mon, Meat. Let's grab a beer."

Doug didn't follow the man and his dog. He wasn't in the mood to be teased by, hopefully, the only person who'd figured out his attraction to Jenn. Tuff made subtle comments about Jenn to him on a few rare occasions, but Doug never took the bait. Her godfather would throw him out of the company's helicopter at five thousand feet above the Earth if he suspected anything. Since Doug was still alive and employed, he'd obviously done a good job of hiding his feelings. Too bad he couldn't get rid of said feelings altogether. He tried dating other women over the past several years, but none had sparked more than a passing interest from him. After a few dates and a roll in the sack a time or two, he was ready to move on. But when alone in his bed or the shower, and the need for release overtook him, it was Jenn his mind always conjured up to send him over the edge. Then the guilt and shame kicked in, and he felt miserable afterward.

He glanced around. Over seventy people had come to wish the young woman a bon voyage. They filled the landscaped yard, which featured numerous seating areas, a fire pit, an outdoor kitchen, a large grill capable of holding a whole pig, and a koi pond. A few shade trees and a misting system helped keep everyone cool when Gulf coast temperatures soared, and two areas on the far end were set up for cornhole and horseshoes. It was often used for parties or as a gathering place for when the Trident employees needed a little downtime. However, for a crowd of this size, they'd needed to set up tables and chairs in the parking lot beside it to accommodate everyone.

Laughter and raised voices caught Doug's attention. He turned to his left to see three of his division's bodyguards approach him, undoubtedly intending to drag their supervisor into the friendly argument they were in the middle of. Taking a sip from his half-empty beer bottle, he decided to let them, hoping whatever it was about would keep his attention away from Jenn.

Fat chance.

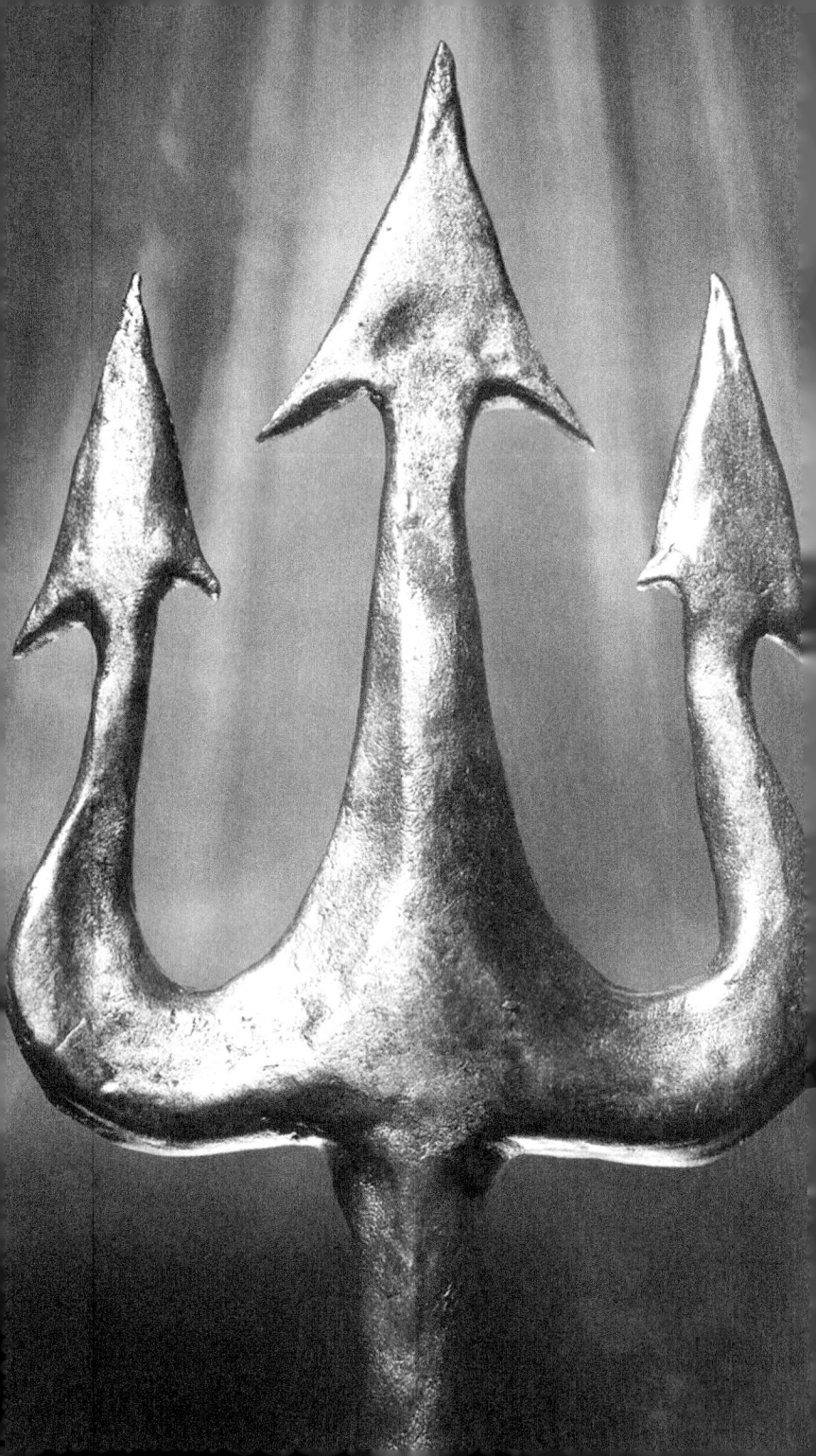

CHAPTER TWO

As she chatted with her friends Daniella Mavis and Yardley Adams, Jenn did her best to ignore Doug's glare from where he unsuccessfully tried to blend in with the shrubbery. She didn't know what his problem was, but she wouldn't make it hers. He made it perfectly clear he wasn't interested in her romantically almost a year ago, after she practically threw herself into his arms and kissed the ever-loving hell out of him.

"Stop staring at him," Yardley chastised. She and Jenn met in college while taking many of the same classes together and became BFFs. "He had his chance, and you deserve better than him."

Jenn didn't realize that she was staring and ripped her gaze away from the man. She confided in both women about her humiliating experience back then and asked them to help her get past it. They offered shoulders to cry on while gently telling her that it was time to move on and find someone else to love. There was no point in yearning for a man who didn't want her in return. She even let her friends set her up on a few blind dates, but they all failed. Her heart and body still yearned for Doug, despite his rejection. However, he avoided her like she was a predator and he was the prey she wanted to eat alive. She almost groaned aloud—that was not a good analogy when she was trying to forget the man.

Doug was one of the reasons she was flying to Colombia tomorrow to spend the next three months working at a medical commune. She'd wanted to volunteer in an undeveloped area of another country after being inspired by two friends who'd done that during a summer break before entering their third year of college. However, she decided to wait until she earned her bachelor's degree in social work, during which time she researched where she wanted to go. Grandpa Chuck and Grandma Marie Sawyer, who loved her as if she were their own granddaughter, were involved in many charities and helped her explore several volunteer programs. Jenn's biological grandparents all died before she started kindergarten, and she didn't remember any of them, so she was grateful for the relationship she had with her godfather's parents.

After talking to several other people, Jenn narrowed it down to two places. One was an Argentinan orphanage, and the other was a commune run by Dr. Ramona Sanchez, located near the small settlement of San Justino, just an hour northwest of the bustling city of Bogotá, near the foothills of the Andes Mountains.

After researching both places and contacting the women who ran them, Jenn decided to go to Colombia, which she knew her uncles weren't thrilled about, even though Carter had known Dr. Sanchez for years and often sent her supplies to help the underprivileged native Colombians that she aided. Although she doubted they would've been happy if she had chosen Argentina instead. If the alpha men in her life had their way, she'd stay cocooned in their well-guarded compound until she was an elderly spinster virgin. Well, they weren't getting their way this time, and she definitely wouldn't be the one to tell them the virgin thing was no longer an issue.

Before Doug was assigned as her bodyguard and her attraction to him began, Jenn quietly dated a nice guy she met at the University of Tampa. "Quietly" because she didn't want her uncles to go ballistic and investigate and interrogate Cole. He was her first real love, but after six months of dating, they realized they weren't meant to be together. Their dreams and aspirations were vastly different from one another. Jenn knew she wanted children someday, and that didn't blend in with Cole's plans. His parents' nasty divorce and neglect of their three kids had jaded him. He also wanted to move to California after graduation, and Jenn didn't want to be on the other side of the country from the only family she had left. So, in the end, she and Cole went their separate ways but remained friends, staying in touch through social media. He was now in a stable relationship with a woman who also wanted to remain child-free, and Jenn was happy for the couple.

While she'd dated a few other guys since then, she hadn't slept with any of them. Her heart, mind, and body compared every man to Doug, and they all fell short. Someone else had to be out there who could meet the high standards she'd set. After observing the deep love and affection her parents and her uncles had for their spouses, Jenn refused to settle when it involved giving her heart away to someone for life.

Daniella stepped between Jenn's line of sight and Doug, then skillfully steered the conversation in another direction. "I still can't believe Ian and the rest of them are letting you go."

"Trust me, it wasn't easy to convince them."

"How did you?"

Jenn smirked. "I got my aunts, Grandpa Chuck, and Grandma Marie to back me up. And Nick too."

Only a few years older than her, she never considered the youngest Sawyer brother to be an uncle. In fact, she even had a brief crush on him in junior high. Now, he was more like the older brother she never had.

Daniella laughed. "I bet that didn't go over well with his brothers and Jake."

Though eleven years older, the pretty brunette and Jenn had clicked last year when Jenn trained her to take over her job at Donovan's Pub so she could start a social work internship. Since then, Daniella had gotten to know Jenn's extended family well since they often hung out at the pub, which was owned by Mike Dovonan, whose younger brother, Jake, was a Trident operative and Nick's husband. Uncle Jake was on the same SEAL team as Jenn's dad, Ian, and Devon, and came to work for the brothers when they all retired from the military, along with their teammates Marco DeAngelis, Brody Evans, and Ben "Boomer" Michaelson. Nick had also been a SEAL before retiring from the Navy, but on Team Three in San Diego.

"I don't even want to think about what his punishment was." She knew all about the BDSM club on the other side of the compound—how could she not? Her uncles and their spouses were in the lifestyle, but it wasn't something she was interested in. However, because of her long-time exposure to everyone being so comfortable in their sexuality, she wasn't embarrassed by it. As long as she didn't observe them being too intimate, she didn't mind hearing about it sometimes. She even got a kick out of some of the conversations her aunts had about sex.

"But Kristen, Angie, Nick, and the others all knew what doing this meant to me. We've talked about it a lot over the past two years. I think Uncle Ian and Devon hoped I would forget about it, but this is why I went into social work. I want to help people." A family friend, Kayla London, was a social worker, and it was through her that Jenn became interested in the field as a career. "It's only for three months, and it'll look good on my resume, even though I already have a job in Kayla's office when I get back. I just wish my uncles would stop calling me Baby-girl and see that I'm an adult now. Hopefully, this will help."

Uncle Ian was at the hospital the day Jenn was born and the first person to call her what would become her nickname among the Navy SEALs on her father's team—thirty-three of them who came and went over the years. While she'd loved the moniker for a long time—it made her feel special as a child—now that she was twenty-three, with little nieces and nephews, it only made her cringe. They would never see that she was a grown woman until she proved it to them, and the way to do that was to step out on her own.

"I think it will. And then when you get back, we'll find you a man." Yardley hooked her arms around Daniella's and Jenn's. "In the meantime, c'mon. Let's get some more wine and toast the new and improved grown-up Jenn Mullins."

Doug couldn't remember a funeral or any other event where more tears flowed than they did as Jenn said goodbye to her extended family. Although everyone gathered for the party yesterday, most had returned to hug and kiss her before she left for the airport in a few minutes. Because she was taking several items that Ian had insisted on, which might get flagged by TSA, he offered to fly the small group of volunteers down to Colombia in Trident's private jet. Jenn accepted on one condition—that Ian and everyone else stayed behind instead of giving the group an armed escort to Dr. Sanchez's ranch.

Damn, this was killing him. She'd be on another continent for fuck's sake. Whether he wanted to admit it or not, having her close by and not being able to claim her like he wanted was torture, but the next three months, not knowing if she was safe every minute, would be ten times worse. While he didn't see her every day, when they did cross paths, she lit up his world, even for just a brief moment.

He knew she was embarrassed about their kiss and pissed about how he rejected her and then left—the most challenging thing he'd ever done in his life—but it was the best thing for her. Jenn was an intelligent, warm, generous young woman who could have any guy she wanted, and for some stupid reason, she thought that guy was Doug. She deserved someone better than him. Someone closer to her own age. Someone who could protect her better, rather than almost getting her killed because she was a beautiful distraction. And someday, he'd have to remain in the shadows and watch her find that man.

It'd been a while since Doug relived that horrible day in his nightmares, but last night, after he left the party and went home to sleep, he woke up in a cold sweat. His chest ached and burned where the bullet had torn into his flesh and ripped a hole in his right lung. Jenn's screams for him to save her as she was dragged out of the SUV echoed in his head, and Doug barely made it to the bathroom before vomiting up everything he had eaten and drunk only a few hours earlier. He knelt over the toilet for close to half an hour, retching long after his stomach was empty.

His head throbbed, and he couldn't think of putting anything into his stomach yet. It still churned as he watched Jenn hug Marie and Chuck Sawyer. It took him a minute to realize she was making her way down the long line of people, and only Brody Evans, his wife, Fancy, and their young son, Zane, were left before she reached Doug, who was last. He should step back or crouch down and call Ian's dog, Beau, over for a belly rub—anything to avoid the awkward moment that was only seconds away. But he remained frozen until she side-stepped and stopped in front of him.

Her beautiful blue eyes brimmed with tears, and her cheeks were wet from those that had already fallen. Her chin quivered. Doug tried to tell himself that she was emotional because she was leaving her family behind, and it had nothing to do with him. But she stared at him a bit too long as if trying to memorize his face. After taking a deep, shaky breath, she wrapped her arms around him, squeezed, and then let go, not giving him time to return the embrace. "Goodbye, Doug."

His stomach threatened to revolt again at the finality in her voice. It wasn't goodbye for now. It was forever.

He swallowed hard, then cleared his throat. "Goodbye, Jenn. Stay safe."

She nodded as she turned away and waved at the small crowd. "Goodbye, everyone. See you in a few months. Don't forget to email me pictures of the kids every day so I don't miss them too much." Beau stood at her feet and barked, causing Jenn to let out a burst of laughter. She gave the lab/pit mix an ear scratch. "And all the dogs, too."

While Beau was trained as a protection dog, he was also considered a pet and Trident's mascot. He had a key fob on his collar, which opened the flapped doors leading into each of the compound's four apartments and the two TS buildings. Sometimes, he would hang out in the security company's garage with the dogs that belonged to the TS mechanics. Tempest "Babs" Van Buren, who was also Trident's helicopter pilot, adopted FUBAR, a Belgian Malinois that failed protection training, while Jagger, a Rottweiler, was Russell Adams's PTSD dog. The other four TS protection K9s were on leashes while working or training and stayed in a temperature-controlled building with comfortable kennels and doggie doors to an outdoor play area when off-duty.

Doug knew Jenn loved all the compound's dogs and spoiled them like crazy as long as it didn't interfere with their training. He wondered if she would adopt a pet of her own someday. She would make a great mother—of a fur-baby, that is. He didn't want to think of her having human babies with someone else. That just made unwanted jealousy course through his system.

Minutes later, Ian's SUV left the parking lot with Jenn and her luggage. When they were out of sight, the group broke up, with some heading back home while others went to work. Doug didn't know how long he had stood there before he glanced around and noticed that only he and Beau remained in the now-empty lot.

The dog peered up at him and whined. Doug could only manage a weak smile. "I know, buddy. I'm going to miss her too."

CHAPTER THREE

"*Hola*, Jenn!"

She smiled warmly at the lively ten-year-old boy and his more reserved seven-year-old sister when they dashed toward her as she emerged from the dining hall, arms full of a large basket of corn. The Spanish classes she took in high school and college were extremely helpful in communicating with the local people. Fortunately, several of them knew some English, which was great when she couldn't remember specific words or phrases. "*Buenos días*, Matteo and Elena. *¿Cómo estás?*"

"Good," Matteo replied, switching to the English he learned in school at Dr. Sanchez's commune. "Can we help you?"

"Sure, if you want to." She had to shuck the corn, which would then be dried and ground into cornmeal.

Two weeks had passed since she and seven others from all over the United States arrived in San Justino. The commune was much larger than she expected it to be—approximately forty acres. It was once a grand estate in the 1800s, but it was eventually abandoned in the 1950s after the government seized it. About thirty years later, Dr. Sanchez's predecessor, her uncle, who was also a physician, had purchased the land and created a haven for the impoverished. After completing medical school and gaining some ER experience in a Chicago hospital, she came to work with him. Side by side, they helped the underprivileged people of the region for three years until his death. He left her the property in his will so she could continue his charitable work. Donations from various sources helped fund items such as medical and school supplies.

The doctor and her primary staff lived in the main house. The volunteers shared two bunkhouses, which reminded Jenn of ones she'd stayed in when she went camping with her Girl Scout troop as a girl. A third bunkhouse had small one-room apartments with a shared living room area for the guards who protected the place—mostly expats from the US and Canada. The property's other buildings included a clinic with room for a few overnight patients, the schoolhouse, the dining hall and kitchen, a chapel, and several storage units. Along the north perimeter were over a dozen small cabins, occupied by local families, including Matteo and Elena. About five acres of the property were sectioned off for livestock, and another seven for a large garden—both providing most of the commune's food. Several men and women who lived in the cabins helped care for the livestock and tended to the garden in exchange for their children's education and the security provided by the guards. Others worked various jobs in the town of San Justino or on nearby coffee bean farms and contributed what they could to the commune.

Jenn dumped the corn atop a rustic picnic-style table and set the basket on the ground beside it for the ears after they were shucked. Matteo and Elena got to work, peeling the husks from the corn. It was Saturday, so the school was closed. All around the compound, other children played or helped the adults with chores and repairs. A few volunteers were fixing a hole in the chapel's roof, while others assisted in the clinic, garden, or kitchen. It was a sunny day, with the temperature hovering around sixty, which was normal for the summer here. However, the heavy humidity had Jenn's T-shirt and cargo shorts sticking to her skin. Rain was expected later in the day, but from what she had already learned, it wouldn't change the humidity level by much.

"Hey, everyone. Mind if I join you?" Tony Barone, a twenty-six-year-old high school Spanish teacher and hockey coach from Hazard Falls, Kansas, set a basket filled with carrots on the table.

"*Sí!*" Matteo responded while grabbing two ears of corn and handing one to his sister. He was a good big brother, always including Elena when possible, and very protective of her. She was shy and didn't talk as much as the other children, but she loved to read. Even though she was only in second grade, Elena had read everything available in the small school library up through the fourth-grade level several times. Last week, Jenn emailed Uncle Ian a lengthy list of supplies and other items she wanted him to send to her, including more books for the younger ones in both Spanish and English.

Tony pulled a paring knife and a carrot from the basket, then sat across from Jenn, giving her a smile and a wink. The dark-haired man was handsome and friendly, and Jenn had taken an immediate liking to him. On the flight to Colombia, they chatted for over an hour before getting into conversations with the other volunteers. This was his third summer volunteering at the commune. While the rest of them would be there for three whole months, he had to cut his time short by two weeks to be home in time for the start of his school year.

"*Matteo, ven a jugar con nosotros!*" one of his friends called out, waving him over to play *fútbol* with them, or soccer as Jenn knew it.

The boy looked at Jenn with a silent plea in his eyes. She smiled at him. "You don't need my permission to go play. Thanks to you and Elena, the corn is almost done, and I can finish the rest. *Gracias.*"

"*De nada.*" He glanced at his sister, and his brow furrowed. "*Pero Elena...*"

"She can stay with me. But before you join your friends, could you run and get a few of her favorite books?"

Matteo jumped up, grinning from ear to ear. "*Si! Gracias*, Jenn!"

He returned in less than two minutes with several books for Elena. As her brother went to play with the other boys, the little girl climbed onto a wooden rocking chair on the dining hall's porch, not far from Jenn and Tony. Opening one of the books, she got lost in the story.

"They're great kids," Tony said while peeling another carrot. "I miss them so much by the time I get home. And then, when I come back down nine months later, I can't get over how much they've grown."

"What made you choose to volunteer here?"

"My first year, I came with one of my colleagues. Jeff was a social studies teacher, about ten years older than me, who wasn't married and had no kids of his own. He volunteered here for almost a decade. By the end of that first summer, I knew why he loved it so much and swore I'd be back. Unfortunately, Jeff was diagnosed with cancer about a month into that school year. It was aggressive, and we lost him in the middle of the third semester. I like to think I'm carrying on his tradition by coming here."

While Tony talked, Jenn felt the blood drain from her face. When his gaze lifted, and he saw how pale she was, his eyes narrowed. He dropped the paring knife and carrot and reached for her trembling hand, covering it with his own strong one. "Jenn, what's wrong? Are you okay?"

She shook her head and used her free hand to swipe at her watery eyes. Her heart ached, but she couldn't blame that on Tony. "I'm sorry. You just caught me off guard when you said your friend's name. Jeff was my dad's name too."

"Was? He's gone?"

His voice was filled with compassion and sympathy. Most people who weren't part of her extended family didn't know what happened to her parents, and usually she just told others that they were dead, without giving them any details. But something about Tony gave her the courage to explain further. Over the past two weeks, they had become friends, and she felt comfortable telling him the whole story. "Both my mom, Lisa, and my dad are gone. They were killed...murdered actually, in a home invasion when I was seventeen."

Tony's eyes widened. "Oh my God! Jenn, I'm so

sorry. That's horrible. I-I don't know what to say." He stood, circled the table to her side, and sat beside her. For a moment, she thought he would put his arm around her, but instead, he clasped her hand and squeezed. "You told me that you lived with family in Tampa, and I just assumed..." He shook his head. "I'm sorry. That must have been so hard for you."

"It was. And it was even worse knowing I could've been killed with them, but I was at a slumber party that night. A neighbor saw the open front door the next morning, and the police were already there by the time I got home." She took a deep breath and shifted to face him. Understanding filled his dark hazel eyes, and another squeeze of her hand urged her to continue.

"They called my Uncle Ian—he's my dad's best friend and my godfather. They were Navy SEALs together." The corners of her mouth ticked up slightly, and she shrugged. "I sorta have a lot of quote, unquote uncles who were my dad's teammates—and *a lot* is an understatement—but Uncle Ian is the closest to me. I don't know what I would've done without him. I was an only child, and so were both my parents. All my grandparents passed away either before I was born or while I was still really young. So, Uncle Ian stepped up and took care of the funeral arrangements, life insurance policies, my parents' wills and probate, and everything else I was too young to handle. He stayed with me in Virginia so I could finish out my senior year, then packed up and sold our house, and brought me to live with him in Florida. And on top of that, he found me grief counselors in both Virginia and Tampa who helped me get through it all."

"Your uncle sounds like a great man."

She gave him a watery smile. "He is. The absolute best." A chuckle escaped her. "He's sarcastic and protective as hell, but I couldn't ask for a better godfather. And now, I'm *his* baby's godmother. His wife, Angie, gave birth to their little girl, Peyton, last year. The only thing that sucks about being here is that I'm going to miss her first birthday in a few weeks. But thanks to the satellite internet, I can Skype the party."

"Thank goodness for the internet."

"Yeah, I miss my nieces and nephews something fierce." She pulled out her cell phone, tapped the photo gallery icon, and turned it so he could see the screen as she swiped through several images. "This is Peyton with JD, who is Uncle Devon and Kristen's son. These are Uncle Marco and Harper's two little ones, Mara and Luca. Zane is Uncle Brody and Fancy's. And these two cuties are my friends' boys, whom they adopted from Argentina, Franco and Victor. They're both eight years old but not blood-related. Shelby and Parker flew down there to get Frankie, and when they found out the boys were best friends, they adopted both so they could be brothers."

"Cute kids. And that's cool that they adopted his friend too—instant family. I don't have any nieces and nephews yet, but I want to do that someday—adopt, I mean. So many kids need homes."

"I think you'd make a great dad."

"Thanks. I have a good role model. My dad is one of the best. My mom, too."

"That's awesome. They probably can't wait to become grandparents."

"Oh, yeah. Mom's been dropping hints about it for the past few years, but she'll have to wait a bit longer. I'm not ready yet, and neither are my two younger sisters—none of us are married—but someday."

Smiling, she tucked her phone in her back pocket, and they resumed preparing the carrots and corn. A few moments of silence passed before he asked, "So, did they…um. If you don't want to talk about it, I understand, but did they ever find out who was responsible? Who killed your parents?"

Concern eclipsed curiosity in his tone, and Jenn was glad she opened up to him. Just from observing him over the past two weeks, she knew he was a great teacher. His students in Hazard Falls probably loved him as much as those at the commune did, and many of the high school girls most likely had crushes on him. Maybe some of the boys did too.

"Yeah, they did. It had to do with my dad seeing something while on a SEAL mission, so I don't know any of the details. All I know is that the guy murdered two more of my dad's former teammates before someone in law enforcement killed him." That was a slight exaggeration, since Uncle Ian's friend T. Carter was a US government spy, something she wasn't allowed to disclose to anyone, for her safety, his, and Jordyn Alvarez's, who worked with him.

"Wow. That's...that's crazy. I keep up with news all over the world and don't remember seeing anything about Navy SEALs being killed on US soil a few years ago."

She shook her head. "You wouldn't have. The connection between my parents' deaths and the other two SEALs, whom I also knew, was never made public. And the three of them were already retired from the Navy at the time."

"God, Jenn. I'm so sorry. I can't imagine going through something like that as an adult, much less as a teenager. But thanks to all the help you got, you seem to have survived and thrived. Your parents would be proud of you."

Before she could say anything more, they were interrupted when two other male volunteers wandered over to join them. They'd finished repairing the chapel roof and were taking a break. Releasing her hand, Tony stood and went back to peeling the carrots, while Jenn breathed deeply and pasted on a smile.

Despite the heavy conversation, she was glad she told him her story.

Fiddling with the watch Uncle Ian gave her on her left wrist, she sighed inwardly and studied Tony's face as he laughed at something one of the others said. He was a nice, attractive, compassionate, and attentive man. Why couldn't she fall for someone like him? Why was the man who invaded her dreams night after night the one who didn't want her in return? And why was she counting down the days until she could see him again?

Damn it. So many "why" questions, and she didn't have or like the answers to any of them.

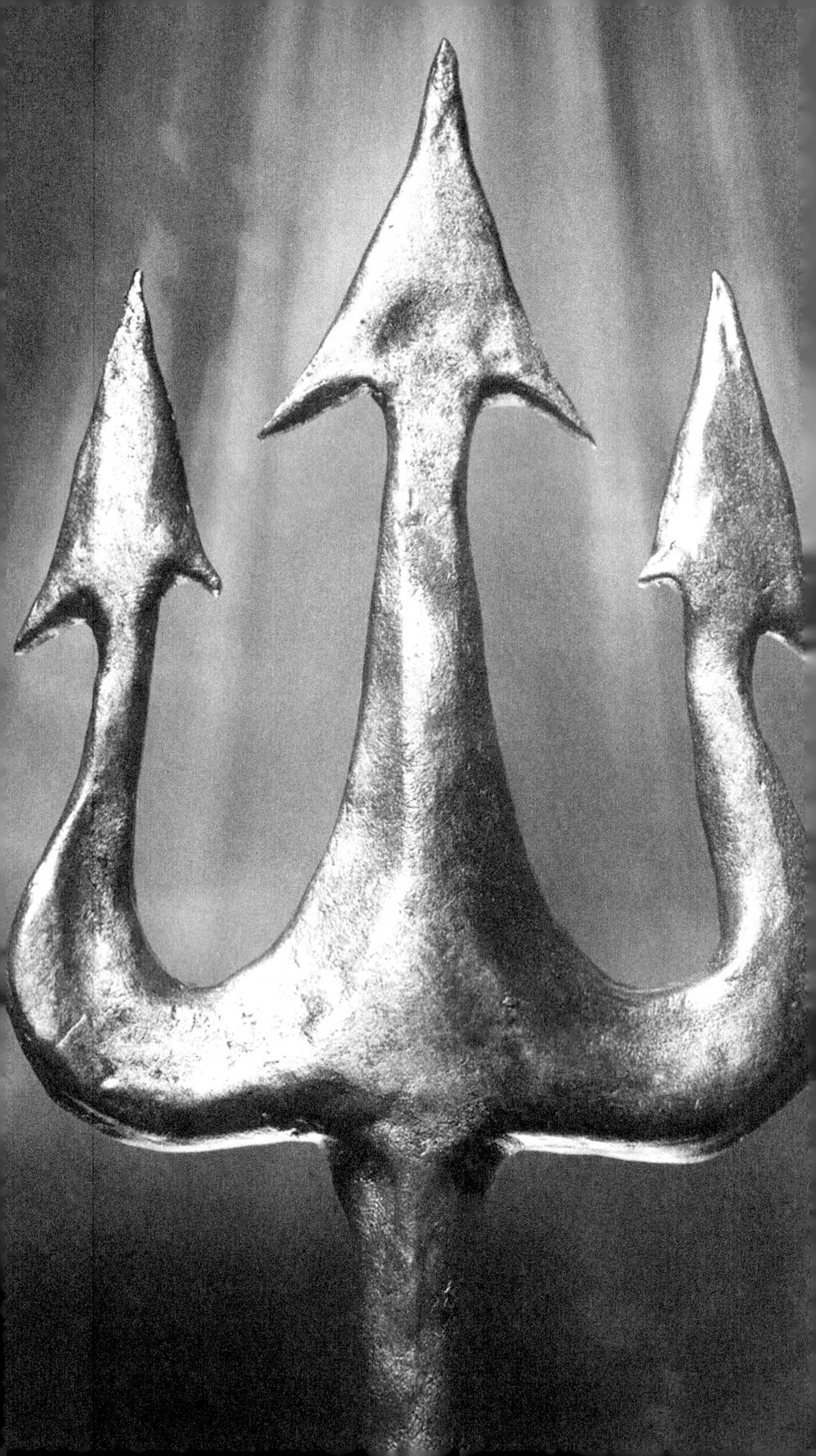

CHAPTER FOUR

Doug breathed a sigh of relief when he stepped into the Trident Security offices and the cool air conditioning hit him full blast, sending goose bumps skittering across his overheated skin. It was the middle of July, and one hundred two degrees outside, twelve above average, but the humidity made it feel even hotter. His Trident Security polo work shirt was drenched with sweat, and he was grateful for the spare ones he kept in his office. Showers were available in several of the bunk rooms upstairs and also in the gym located in the adjacent building. He undoubtedly wouldn't be the only person using them today.

He had just returned to the compound after having lunch with his grandmother at the assisted living facility where she resided. While the octogenarian was still active, she couldn't drive anymore due to slower reflexes, so Doug stopped in at least once a week to share a meal with her.

Before he had a chance to get further than the reception area, Colleen McKinley-Helm, the company's office manager, stopped him. "Hi, Doug. Ian wanted to see you as soon as you got back."

Instead of going right, he made a left toward his boss's office. The door was open, but he still knocked softly and waited for Ian to wave him in. The man sat behind an impressive mahogany desk, talking to someone on the landline phone. "Thanks for the update. I'll talk to you later."

Disconnecting the call, Ian gestured for Doug to take a seat in one of the guest chairs in front of the desk. "Bullseye, sit down."

He did as ordered. "What's up?"

"I need you, Romeo, and Costello to head down to Colombia for a quick trip in a few days."

His heart rate spiked as he tried not to leap out of the chair. "What? Is Jenn okay?"

If Ian had noticed Doug's near panic, he didn't acknowledge it. He simply held up a hand while using the other to search through some files on his desk. "Baby-girl's fine. At least she was as of last night, when she emailed me to find out when I was sending all the supplies she asked for."

The tension eased from Doug's body, and he wiped a drop of sweat from his brow with the back of his hand. It wasn't leftover from being outside, but instead, it appeared the moment Ian mentioned Colombia. "The stuff you shipped last week still isn't there yet?"

Jenn had sent her godfather a long list of things she wanted to gift to the poor people who lived at the commune. All the clinic's medical supplies and medication were acquired through donations from pharmaceutical companies, hospitals, charities, and philanthropists. However, sometimes basic or non-necessities were hard to come by. Jenn warned him not to send anything expensive that could make the commune and its residents targets for thieves.

Between the brothers' wealth and that of their parents, the Sawyer family paid for everything Jenn asked for and had it shipped to Bogotá, where it was supposed to be delivered to the commune.

"It never arrived. It disappeared somewhere between the airport and Ramona's place. No trace of it." He sighed and finally met Doug's stare. "So, this time, you three will be at the airport, waiting for the next shipment to arrive, and will escort it to the commune. One of Ramona's guards will meet you at whatever hotel you stay at."

"What? Why me?" When Ian's eyes narrowed, Doug scrambled for something to say that wouldn't raise any red flags with his boss. "I mean, I have an interview with a new client scheduled for Monday. I won't be back in time, will I? Can't we send a couple of my guys down there?"

Ian shook his head. "No. The guys in PPD don't have enough training for a detail in Colombia—it's a fucking different world. And I can't send Nick or anyone Jenn considers an uncle. She'll think we don't trust her and are just down there to check on her. You, Romeo, and Costello are the only other people I can spare right now who won't piss her off."

Doug wasn't so sure about that—in fact, he was pretty confident Jenn would flip out when he showed up, but he couldn't tell his boss that. Ian would push for details until Doug finally broke down and confessed to kissing the man's beloved goddaughter. Since he didn't feel like dying today and having his body tossed into the Gulf of Mexico, Doug made one more attempt to get out of the trip. "What about my interview on Monday? I also have to finish the schedule for the next few weeks. And who's going to check in with my guys?"

"Give Jake all the info for the interview, and he'll take care of that. Start the schedule, and whatever still needs to be worked out, Devon can take over. As for the check-ins, Marco and Boomer can do those. You'll only be down there two nights—I want the three of you there the night before the shipment arrives and at the airport when the cargo plane lands. Clinton will fly you down and bring you back the day after you drop everything off at the commune." Clinton Howe became the primary pilot for the company's jet after C.C. Chapman retired a few months back. "This shit isn't going to get stolen a second time. I'm just waiting to hear back from the shipping company to find out when it's supposed to arrive. As soon as I have that, I'll have Clinton file the flight plan."

Doug racked his brain for another excuse not to go, but only drew a blank. The thought of seeing Jenn in a few days both excited and terrified him. He was so fucked.

Standing in the open doorway of the bunkhouse, where she and three other female volunteers slept, Jenn stared out at the rain coming down in buckets. They were waiting for it to let up a little before making a mad dash to the dining hall for dinner. Several strong storm systems blew through over the last few days, forcing everyone to work inside for the most part.

Large mud puddles dotted the commune's landscape. According to the weather reports from a Bogotá news station, they'd already received five inches of rain in the past seventy-two hours, which was a lot considering the region's average was a little over nine inches for the entire month. Lightweight waterproof ponchos and boots had been on the volunteers' list of suggested gear to bring, but even those were no match for the current torrential downpour. The fat raindrops hitting the building's metal roof were almost deafening.

Earlier, she used the satellite internet to check her emails after changing out of her wet, dirty clothes for dinner. She only turned on her iPad for short periods to answer emails, scan the weather and news reports, and occasionally post images or stories about her trip in her family's private Facebook group. Then, she shut the device down again to conserve the battery. The commune had several solar-powered generators for electricity that Carter had donated a few years ago, allowing everyone to charge their satellite phones and other devices when necessary, but they tried to limit their usage. The power was needed more for the clinic and the kitchen.

She was still pissed about all the supplies that Uncle Ian had shipped to her in several large crates that had been lost or stolen—most likely the latter— after arriving at Bogotá's El Dorado International Airport. The list she sent him was long, but she didn't feel guilty about it. He and his family always donated to good causes. Of course, Ian told everyone it was for the tax write-offs, but Jenn knew it was because underneath his tough exterior beat one of the biggest and softest hearts ever. Aside from her father, Ian was the most incredible man she had ever known.

According to the email he sent her a few hours ago, he had ordered a new shipment of supplies and made arrangements for it to be escorted to the commune by armed guards upon arrival at the airport. Jenn wished she could have seen the expressions on the thieves' faces when they opened the crates and found nothing of great value, like electronics. They probably would still sell or use most of the items, though.

Margie Kimball sidled up next to Jenn and eyed the rain. "I think this is as slow as it's going to get for a while, and I'm starving. I say we make a run for it."

The sixty-two-year-old retired school principal, who looked ten years younger, became a widow last year. She and her late husband often volunteered at various charities in their hometown near Albuquerque, New Mexico. With their wedding anniversary, their birthdays, and the anniversary of his death coming up, she didn't want to spend the time moping around her house. All four events fell within the same three-month period over the summer. Through one of the charities, she discovered Dr. Sanchez's commune and signed up as a volunteer. She reminded Jenn of Grandma Marie—outgoing, friendly, caring, and full of life.

Jenn glanced over her shoulder to see if the other two women, thirty-year-old best friends Rachel Cho and Lexie Miller, agreed with Margie. When they both nodded, Jenn pulled the bright yellow poncho's hood over her head. She wore a black and red University of Tampa T-shirt, tan cargo shorts, and her rain boots underneath it. "All right. Let's do this."

Squealing and laughing, they ran across the commune, doing their best to avoid the bigger puddles as the rain pelted them. Mud still splashed against Jenn's legs that were partially exposed between the bottom of the poncho and the top of her rain boots, but she didn't care. It wasn't like she was out to impress anyone there. Everyone else was a mess too.

A strong gust of wind blew everyone's hoods off, and the women gave up trying to stay dry and hurried as fast as possible to the dining hall. They burst inside, dripping and giggling.

Jenn pushed her sopping wet, long blonde hair from her face. "If we walked, I think we would've gotten just as soaked but not as muddy."

"The rain gods have it out for us today," Margie said, taking off her poncho and hanging it on a hook by the door. The other women followed suit. Their boots stayed on to prevent them from getting splinters in their feet from the old wooden planks that made up the floor.

Jenn spent the first week at the commune adjusting to things she had often taken for granted while living in a comfortable home in the States. Now, she couldn't go barefoot anywhere and always shook out her clothes and checked her boots, sneakers, and shower shoes for scorpions, snakes, or spiders before putting them on. Taking preventative malaria pills was a daily practice she started a week before arriving in Colombia, as recommended. Mosquitoes were unavoidable, even though she'd gone through several cans of bug spray already.

Glancing around, she noticed most of Dr. Sanchez's staff were already there, enjoying their dinner. Three of the five male volunteers sat together at a table. She knew one of the missing men, a nurse practitioner named Roland Elrod, had gone with the doctor and a guard to check on a patient in a nearby village earlier, and it looked like they weren't back yet. Jenn frowned when she noticed Tony sitting by himself at another table in a corner, away from everyone else. His gaze was downcast as he used his fork to push the food around on his plate aimlessly. That was unlike him. She'd never seen him alone before—he was a bit of an extrovert.

After filling a plate at the small buffet the kitchen staff had set up for dinner, she grabbed a fork and napkin, then strode across the room. Her boots made a squishing sound with each step. The muddy water that splashed against her legs had rolled down them, soaking her formerly dry socks.

"Mind if I join you?" she asked Tony, not waiting

for an answer as she set her plate down, pulled out a chair, and sat.

When he didn't acknowledge her at all, Jenn ducked her head to get a better look at his face. His eyes were red and watery. Reaching over, she placed her hand on his on the table. "Hey, what's wrong?"

Tony shook his head. Dropping the fork onto his still-full plate, he swiped at his eyes. "It's nothing."

Worried about her friend, she scooted her chair closer to him while keeping her hand on his. "Hey, Tony. Talk to me. Please. I'm a great listener, I promise."

She waited patiently as he seemed to collect himself. After inhaling deeply, he let out a shaky breath. "I...um. I got a Dear John email—well, actually a Dear Tony one."

"What? How awful. What kind of woman breaks up with someone through an email?"

He gave her a sad smile. "I wouldn't know. It was a guy. My boyfriend."

"Oh."

Since she'd moved closer, her arm was in an awkward position, and it cramped. She pulled her hand back, and Tony must have misinterpreted the move because he frowned at her. "Do you have a problem with me being gay?"

"What?" she nearly shouted before lowering her voice. "No, not at all."

Despite everything they talked about over the past few weeks, for some reason, they never discussed each other's significant others or lack thereof before, so she didn't know he had a boyfriend until a moment ago.

"My Uncle Jake is gay, and he's married to Uncle Ian's younger brother Nick. I don't call Nick an uncle because he's only a few years older than me. He was a surprise baby. And their cousin Mitch is in a full-on menage marriage. You know, a threesome where everyone loves everyone?" She had no idea why that came out as a question and not a statement. "Oh, and my social work mentor, Kayla, is married to a woman. So, no, I don't have issues with anyone in the LGBTQ+ community. I know a lot of people in it."

She knew she was babbling but couldn't help it. The last thing she wanted was for her new friend to think she was bigoted or homophobic, and that he couldn't discuss his broken relationship with her. At least she hadn't blurted out about the BDSM club that was only three buildings down from her apartment. "What I have a problem with is people who don't have the guts to break up with someone face-to-face, or even over the phone, and instead do it through emails or texts. I'm so sorry, Tony. That really, really sucks."

He shrugged. "It is what it is."

Picking up her fork, she stabbed a piece of green pepper. "How long were you together?"

"Almost two years."

She fumbled the fork, catching it before it clattered against the plate. "Seriously? Two years? What the hell changed in the three weeks since you left that made him decide to break up with you over a freaking email? What, he suddenly decided it was over between the two of you? I don't buy that at all. I bet he knew before you left and was too chicken to tell you. And if that's the case, then he never deserved you. You can do so much better than someone like that."

A small smile appeared on Tony's handsome face, a little lighter than the earlier depressed one. "You're very passionate about this, aren't you?"

"You're darn right I am!" She touched his arm. "Trust me on this. My parents were so in love that it was almost nauseating. The same goes for my uncles. They might have taken a few wrong turns before they found the love of their lives, but they did and couldn't be happier. And I couldn't be happier for them. I just hope I don't have to wait as long as some of them did to get my happily-ever-after."

Tony sat up straighter, wiped his eyes with a napkin, and then took a sip of water. "You haven't found him or her yet?"

She let out a sigh. "Him. And I thought I did, but…"

"But?"

She didn't want to talk about Doug, but if it gave Tony something to focus on instead of how his now ex-boyfriend dumped him, she would. "He thinks I'm too young for him—I'm twenty-three, and he just turned thirty-one. I don't think it's that much of a difference, do you?"

He shook his head. "Justin was almost eight years older than me too."

"See? Most people wouldn't have a problem with it. Uncle Devon is ten years older than his wife, Kristen, and Uncle Jake is nine years older than Nick." Her shoulders sagged. "But Doug thinks it's a big deal. He also thinks I have a case of hero worship when it comes to him."

Great. Now she was the one pushing the food around on her plate, feeling bummed.

"Ouch. How did that happen? The hero thing."

As she spent the next five minutes or so explaining what occurred back then, leaving out a few critical but confidential details, Tony's eyes grew wider and wider. Then, when she told him about last year's kiss and Doug's rejection, he frowned. "What a jerk! I mean, he took a bullet trying to save you, but still…What a jerk!"

He leaned over and nudged her elbow. "Aren't we a pair? Falling for the wrong guy and getting our hearts broken."

"Yup."

"Well, you were right about one thing—I deserve better. We both do." He held out his hand with the fifth finger extended. "Okay, pinkie-swear time. We're going to forget about what's-his-name and my jerk-faced ex, and when we get home, we're going to find our true loves. And we're going to stay in touch to make sure we both get our happily-ever-afters. Deal?"

A broad grin spread across Jenn's face, and she linked her pinkie with his. "Deal."

CHAPTER FIVE

Four days later

Scowling, Doug stalked back and forth inside a hangar at the cargo terminal complex at El Dorado International Airport, waiting for the shipping company's plane. It took off half an hour late from Mexico City for some stupid reason, and according to his watch, the crew had also lost some time in the air. At least the damn rain stopped.

Late yesterday afternoon, Clinton landed the company jet at the start of a storm, getting them safely on the ground at a small private airfield outside Bogotá before it worsened. The retired air force pilot was armed and stayed with the jet to ensure nothing happened to it. With comfortable couches to sleep on,

TVs, internet access, a stocked kitchenette, and a full bathroom with a shower, it was like a mini-apartment with wings. Meanwhile, the others called for a taxi to take them to a hotel near the much larger airport, where they were currently awaiting the shipment.

After checking in and having dinner with Valentino "Romeo" Mancini and Lindsey "Costello" Abbott, the lightning and thunder kept Doug up past midnight. He awakened about three hours later with a hard-on and the phantom taste of Jenn's mouth on his lips. Since he shared the hotel room with Mancini, he hadn't even been able to jerk himself off with hopes that an orgasm would let him drift back to sleep. He'd been wide awake ever since, fighting the images of a scantily-clad Jenn that randomly popped up in his mind, causing his dick to stir. While he'd never actually seen her naked, one time, he caught sight of her sunbathing in a strapless bikini in the compound's yard, trying to get an even tan for the dress she wore as maid of honor at Jake and Nick's wedding. Thoughts of her almost-nude body fueled his masturbation sessions for months afterward, no matter how hard he tried to erase the memory.

As he continued to pace like a caged lion, his two teammates chatted with Rich Parsons, one of Dr. Sanchez's guards. The forty-six-year-old expat had retired from Joint Task Force 2, the Canadian Armed

Forces' elite counter-terrorism unit. Like Doug, Abbott was a retired Marine, while Mancini served in the Army Special Forces before joining the FBI and being assigned to their Hostage Rescue Team. Now, Mancini and Abbott were part of Trident Security's Omega Team—a job that paid much more than the military or any of the alphabet agencies. The special-ops/private security company had grown tremendously over the years, and with its government contracts, they'd needed more operatives.

All four were dressed similarly, wearing combat boots, cargo pants, and black, tan, or olive green T-shirts. Their weapons were concealed by their clothing or hidden in their vehicles. They didn't blend in with the uniforms of airport personnel, but they didn't exactly stand out either, since Colombian soldiers patrolled there.

Parsons had picked them up at the hotel earlier in an old Jeep and then driven to an industrial area of the city. There, they obtained a utility truck big enough for the five large crates of supplies that Ian arranged for them. How the boss had obtained Aerocivil-approved passes at the airport, allowing them to bypass metal detectors and avoid being patted down, so they could meet the plane, was a mystery to Doug. The truck and Jeep hadn't been searched either. But Ian had contacts worldwide, so it wasn't too surprising. It was either that, or someone high up had been bribed to make sure everyone looked the other way.

Next to their two vehicles, parked beside the hangar, was a forklift to off-load the crates from the plane and load them into the truck. At the commune, they would have to open the heavy crates in the truck and empty them that way.

"You're going to create a trench in the concrete if you don't stop pacing like that," Abbott said as she approached him. "Something on your mind?"

The striking brunette was the last person anyone would suspect of being a bad-ass sniper capable of taking down a man twice her size in hand-to-hand combat. Doug knew better. He'd seen her in action during training and on several missions and details. She'd knocked him on his ass a few times during sparring sessions, and he wasn't ashamed to admit it. He loved to put her in the ring with newly hired bodyguards without giving them a warning. When Ian got wind of that, he demanded that Colleen be informed of the sessions so she could put them on his schedule. He wanted to watch them get their asses kicked. After that, it hadn't taken long for both the Alpha and Omega teams to start showing up and making bets.

Stopping in his tracks, he shook his head. "Nope. Just bored waiting on this stupid plane."

Abbott eyed him as if she knew he hadn't told the complete truth, but thankfully, she let it go.

"This looks like ours." Parsons gestured toward the Boeing 747-400F with the shipping company's logo on it, slowly taxiing toward them. A quick check revealed that the tail number matched the one they'd been given. Several aircraft marshals, wearing reflective safety vests, helmets with acoustic earmuffs, and gloves, hurried into position to guide the plane into its assigned spot. Doug and the others hung back just inside the hangar for safety's sake and so they wouldn't get in anyone's way.

As the plane's engines wound down, the ground under Doug's feet shook. If he hadn't been standing still, he might not have noticed it. He glanced around, searching for something that could have caused it. "What the fuck was that?"

"The ground shaking?" Parsons asked. When Doug nodded, the man shrugged. "Earthquake. Not even a three-point-oh. We get little barely-noticeable quakes once or twice a month, and probably dozens more that you don't even feel. It's no big deal."

Mancini narrowed his eyes. "How often do you get one that's really noticeable?"

"We get a quake registering between four-point-oh and seven about once a year or every two years. Above a seven—once every ten years or so."

"When was your last one over seven?"

Parsons thought about it for a moment. "Ten or eleven years ago, I think? Right after I moved here. But that was all the way out on the West Coast—about twelve hours by car from here."

"Great," Doug mumbled. "So, you're due for a big one."

"I wouldn't worry about it."

The man's nonchalant response didn't make Doug feel any better. While Florida was known for its hurricanes and even a few tornadoes, earthquakes weren't on its major catastrophe list. They experienced some slight tremors every few years, which he never felt and only learned about when they were reported in the news. The largest earthquake felt in Florida occurred in 2006, when a five-point-nine struck approximately two hundred and fifty miles west of Tampa, in the Gulf of Mexico. People in the five states bordering the Gulf noticed the tremors, but no damage or injuries resulted from them. And the largest quake to ever originate *in* Florida was a four-point-four magnitude in the late 1800s. The only reason Doug knew that was because he'd researched it years ago for a high school project about natural disasters in the Sunshine State.

Well, it wasn't like he could do anything about it. Maybe Parsons was right, and there was nothing to worry about. Regardless, they had work to do now that the plane's turbines stopped rotating and the cargo hold ramp was lowered. Doug pulled out the paperwork to claim the five crates they wanted and handed it to a guy with a clipboard. His Spanish was rusty, but he must have gotten his message across because the guy nodded and said, "*Un momento*."

"Un momento" turned into *fifteen momentos* before the crates were located among all the other cargo, and it was another twenty minutes before all five were loaded into the truck. Mancini went with Parsons and hopped into the passenger seat of the Jeep, while Doug settled into the driver's seat of the truck with Abbott riding shotgun. Once they drove out of the airport gates, she called Nathan Cook at Trident Security to let him know they were en route to the commune. Cook was a former National Security Agency computer hacker whom Ian and Devon hired a while back. He was the Omega Team's contact and support in the TS war-room, keeping track of them, gathering any intelligence they needed, and reporting the status of their missions to the bosses.

Doug was grateful when Abbott finished the call and didn't try to coax him into a mundane conversation or ask what was bothering him again. Instead, she turned on the radio and somehow found an English-speaking music station, playing classic rock. As they followed the Jeep through the city toward the outskirts, butterflies took flight in his gut, and they multiplied with each mile passed. Excitement and dread waged a battle within him, and he had to force his hands and fingers not to squeeze the steering wheel too hard.

What would Jenn say when he showed up at the commune? Would she look at him with annoyance and distrust? Or maybe she'd be happy to see a familiar face? After thinking about that for all of two seconds, he doubted it would be the latter.

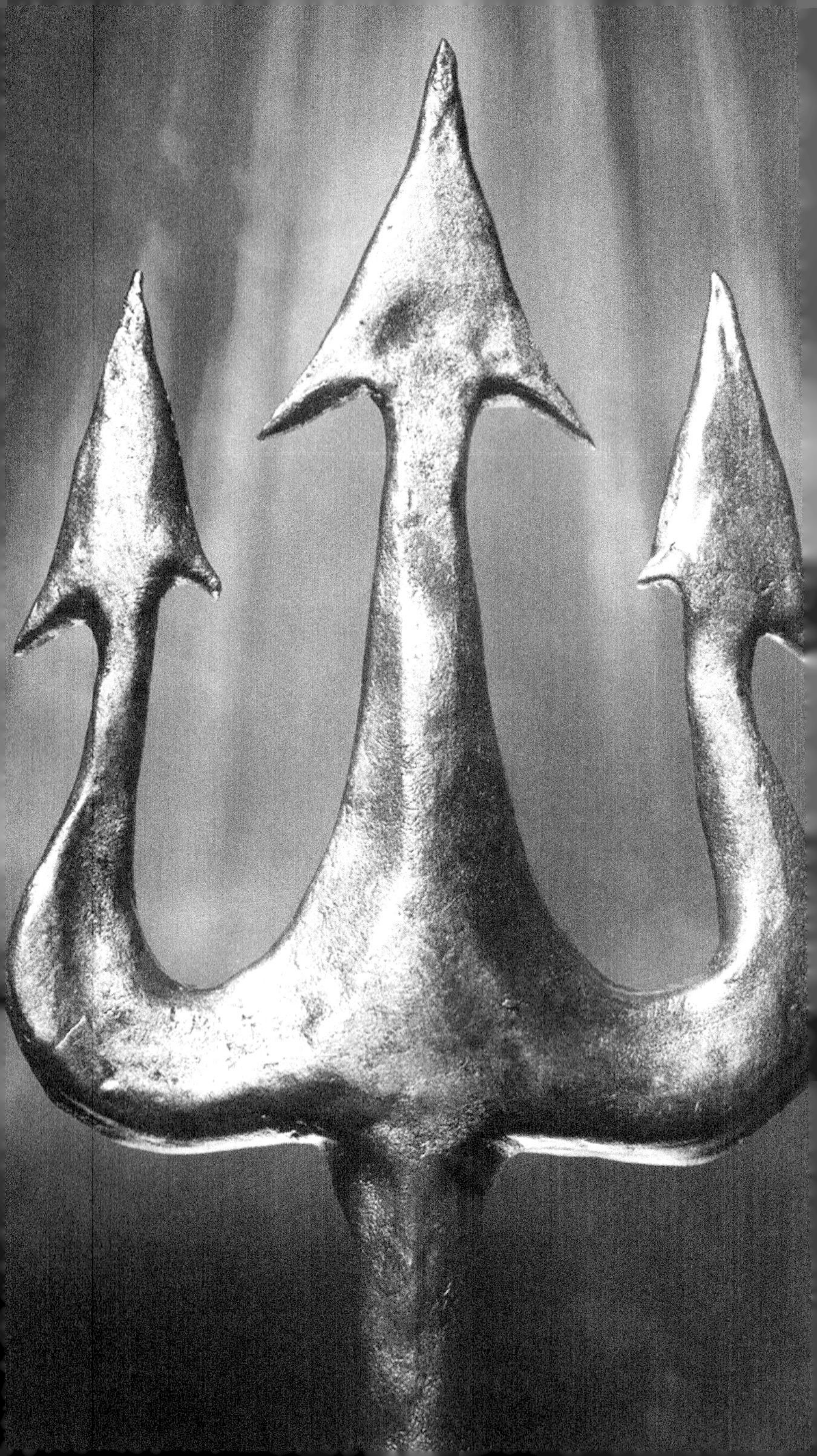

CHAPTER SIX

Jenn froze as the ground underneath her shook again. It was the second earthquake in the past hour, something she'd never experienced before. Everyone who lived full-time at the commune didn't seem shocked or bothered by them. Neither did Tony, nor three of the volunteers who'd been there in previous years. However, it was the first time for Jenn, Margie, Rachel, and Lexie, so the four women were a little freaked out. Dr. Sanchez tried to assure them that the quakes were normal and almost always benign. It was the "almost" part that Jenn found disconcerting.

When the mild tremor stopped after no more than ten seconds, she breathed a sigh of relief. Hopefully, that was the last of them. It was the first day all week that rain wasn't in the forecast, and she relished the sun shining down. She'd missed getting her natural vitamin D for a few days. However, the humidity was back in full force again. Her T-shirt was already stuck to her. At least during the storms, the winds accompanying them cooled the temperatures to something more bearable.

She wished the shipment of supplies would arrive soon, as she was excited and couldn't wait to see the children's faces when she gave them the books and toys. Uncle Ian had sent her an email yesterday morning explaining that a replacement order was on its way, and this time, it would have an armed escort from the airport to the commune. She knew that Rich Parsons had driven down to Bogotá to help with the transport.

Dropping her head and shoulders to the ground, she tightened her core and restarted her sit-up count. While the commune lacked the gym equipment and obstacle course she had access to at the TS compound, she found alternative ways to maintain her physical fitness routine. Her uncles had taught her how to defend herself, and staying in shape was part of that training. While she wasn't overly buff, her muscles had definition on her slender frame. On most days at home, she either ran three miles on a treadmill or the compound's track around the O-course or used an elliptical machine. That was usually followed by any combination of calisthenics, weights, Nautilus, yoga, kickboxing, or sparring with someone in the boxing ring at the gym. And by someone, she meant any of the TS operatives, men and women, who all came from military or law enforcement backgrounds. While they would never seriously hurt her, they didn't take it easy on her either. Not that she wanted them to. After her parents' murders, being kidnapped with Aunt Angie, having a sniper attack the compound, Aunt Harper's kidnapping, Uncle Brody almost being murdered—twice—and Grandma Marie's abduction in the Philippines, Jenn swore she would never feel helpless again.

Wow, she hadn't really thought about it before, but her extended family had been involved in a lot of kidnappings and attempted murders—and that wasn't even all of them. No wonder Uncle Ian kept threatening to insert tracking devices under everyone's skin. Instead, his extended family and the Trident employees all had electronic tags that Brody designed and installed in their cell phones and key rings. The men also had trackers in their military-style watches, while the women were given watches and pieces of fashionable jewelry, allowing them to wear whatever they wanted. Jenn had chosen to wear her leather bracelet to Colombia, so no one would be tempted to snatch it whenever she went into town.

Meanwhile, tracking tags were hidden in every pair of shoes the kids in the family wore. They could only be traced by the six Trident co-owners or Nathan in the event of an emergency. No one else had access to the program. Yes, it sounded like they were all paranoid. Still, the devices had proven invaluable on several occasions over the years, and the men refused to take any chances with the safety of their employees and their families.

Last year, she was grateful for all the training the Alpha and Omega teams put her through when two gangbangers accosted her and tried to sexually assault her in the parking lot outside Donovan's. When Doug ran over and confronted them, the duo turned on him, attacking him with their fists and knives. Instead of cowering, Jenn retrieved the expandable baton she kept in her vehicle's driver door pocket and whacked one guy's arm with it, causing him to drop his weapon before the next strike broke his kneecap, incapacitating him. In the meantime, Doug took down the other guy.

At first, she'd been terrified, but after her training kicked in and paid off, she was thrilled and triumphant. Those feelings quickly soured, though, when Doug yelled at her for putting herself in danger instead of running inside as he'd ordered. As if she would've left him there, two against one, when she had the strength and courage to try to even the odds against him.

Later, after Uncle Ian took her to the police station to give her statement, she was alone in her apartment when the adrenaline crash hit. Just as her tears started to ebb, there was a knock at her door. Doug stopped by to make sure she was okay. They ended up in an argument, and she stupidly blurted out that she loved him. To make matters worse, she threw herself into his arms and kissed him. Initially, he was shocked, but after a moment, he melted into the kiss. It was the most glorious thirty to forty seconds of her life. However, he then ripped his mouth from hers and told her it never should have happened and wouldn't ever again.

Like she told Tony, Doug thought he was too old for her and that she had a case of "hero worship." She knew in her heart that idolization was the *last* thing she felt for him. She wasn't fifteen years old with a case of puppy love.

Once done with her sit-ups, she stood and headed for a nearby twenty-five-foot tree sturdy enough for her to climb three-quarters of the way up. Two trips would complete her workout. Then, she would take a quick shower, have breakfast, and tackle her assigned chores for the day. The first one was to take inventory in the clinic's supply room with Tony—a task they'd done before. It usually took about an hour to ensure there was enough of every item and medication that the doctor and nurses might need. A long checklist and an organized supply room made the mundane but necessary job a little easier.

An hour later, showered and fed, she followed Tony into the supply room. Surprisingly, nothing had fallen off the shelves during the mini earthquakes. But that changed drastically before they were even halfway through the inventory. The next quake that hit was much stronger than the first two. Tremors reverberated through her body, and she lost her balance, bumping into Tony and then one of the shelf units.

The shock intensified. Boxes and packages flew off the shelves, pelting the two of them before hitting the ground, as the overhead light fixtures swayed wildly. She kept waiting for the quake to stop as quickly as the earlier ones, but it continued. A shelf tower tipped toward her, sending everything still on it tumbling down onto the floor. Tony snagged her arm and yanked her out of the way before she could be crushed beneath the heavy metal.

"Let's get out of here," he yelled over the rumbling and crashing chaos, pulling her toward the door as another storage unit toppled over. They were like two drunken college kids trying to walk a straight line and failing miserably. Jenn was thrown against the door jamb, and pain flared in her right upper arm and shoulder, but she ignored it as Tony grabbed her around the waist and kept her moving out of harm's way.

Once outside, they met others in the middle of the

commune, away from any trees or structures. It felt as if they were on a Tilt-a-Whirl, and a wave of nausea hit Jenn. Wide-eyed, everyone squatted or sat, clutching each other, since it was impossible to stay balanced while standing upright. Their gazes darted around, searching for signs of danger. Jenn prayed the earth didn't open up, creating bottomless canyons, as she'd seen in several natural disaster movies. Hopefully, those were just exaggerations created by Hollywood and didn't happen in real life.

After what seemed like hours, but in reality had only been a minute or so, the earth stilled. On her knees, Jenn breathed a sigh of relief. Her heart still pounded as if she'd run several miles, and she tried not to hyperventilate. The others weren't faring much better. Rachel and Lexie were in tears, and so were several of the children. Jenn sat and pulled a hysterical Elena onto her lap, trying to soothe her, while Tony wrapped his arm around Matteo's shoulders. All around them, people started to calm down and reassure the children that they were safe.

Dr. Sanchez stood on wobbly legs. "Is everyone okay?" When not everyone replied, she repeated the question in Spanish. It seemed they'd lucked out because no one claimed to be injured other than a few bumps and scratches. Two of the men who lived in the cabins with their families got to their feet and ran to check on the animals. Everyone else stood slowly, as if waiting for another quake to hit.

"Let's check the buildings," one of the armed guards, an expat from Texas, said to three other men. "Make sure they're all safe before we let anyone else go back into them. Everyone, stay here, okay? There might be some strong aftershocks, so keep away from anything that can fall on you."

Of course, everyone who understood English looked up, searching for anything taller than them that could come down and squash them.

Over the next fifteen or twenty minutes, two smaller aftershocks shook the ground, causing several people to yelp, but they only lasted a few seconds. Once the structures were deemed safe, Dr. Sanchez began issuing assignments. Every building was a mess, from the kitchen and dining hall to the clinic, chapel, classroom, bunkhouses, and individual cabins. Almost everything that wasn't a large piece of furniture or bolted down had been knocked to the floor. It would take all day to get it back to normal. Outside, several trees and large limbs had fallen, but thankfully, they hadn't caused any damage or injuries.

Jenn, Tony, and Margie were assigned to begin cleaning up the clinic and redoing the inventory, starting from the beginning again, since some supplies might now be damaged and unusable. However, they stopped in their tracks when a familiar Jeep, followed by a large utility truck, pulled into the commune. Jenn was shocked to recognize the man in the passenger seat of the Jeep. Val Mancini, otherwise known as Romeo, was the last person she expected to see.

Um. Scratch that. Doug was the last person she expected, but sure enough, he and Lindsey Abbott climbed out of the truck.

What the fuck?

Relief at the familiar faces quickly changed to anxiety and anger. Uncle Ian said the shipment would get an escort, but he failed to mention who would provide it. She assumed it would be someone who lived in Colombia whom he could trust, like the expats working at the commune. She hadn't expected two members of the TS Omega Team and *Doug*!

Okay, she didn't mind Lindsey and Romeo being there, but *Doug*? She was going to kill Uncle Ian when she got home in nine weeks—not that he would have a clue why. She would've preferred any of her uncles to show up. She still would've been pissed, thinking they were checking on her, but one of the main reasons she was in Colombia was to get away from the man who'd rejected her. And now, there he was, racing toward her. Wide-eyed, his gaze raked her from head to toe and back up again.

"Jenn! Are you okay?" He grasped her shoulders and looked her five-foot-eight frame over once more. "Are you hurt?"

Her heart thumped hard against her rib cage when she realized his husky voice was filled with concern.

"Jenn?" he repeated.

Finally, she nodded. "Y-yeah. I'm good. No one was hurt." She gestured haphazardly toward the buildings. "Everything is a mess inside, but we all got out in time."

"Thank goodness," Lindsey said as she and Romeo joined them. Elena moved closer, attached herself to Jenn's hip, and eyed the newcomers warily.

"What are you doing here?" While Jenn addressed the three of them, her gaze remained on Doug's worried expression. He still hadn't released her shoulders, and the heat she felt under his touch was not only comforting but distracting. Her nipples tightened, and her pussy clenched. She wished they were alone so she could beg him to touch her all over. Unfortunately, that only happened in her dreams.

She gave herself a mental slap and forced her attention to focus on Romeo, who gave her elbow a quick, reassuring squeeze before letting go. The man crossed his arms and stood with his feet shoulder-width apart, a stance that every TS operative tended to adopt, thanks to their military or law enforcement training. "Ian wanted to make sure your supplies got here this time, so Clinton flew us down yesterday, and we met the plane this morning. Other than the earthquake, we had no trouble getting here." He hitched a thumb toward the road leading to the commune. "Just missed getting flattened by a boulder that rolled down a hill and across the road. That's something new for my 'You won't believe what happened' list. I felt like I was in an Indiana Jones movie." He smiled and winked at her.

The man was so handsome, people often wondered if he was a model or an actor. However, Jenn preferred Doug's rugged good looks to Romeo's pretty-boy face. She did like him, though, as a friend. The same went for Lindsey and the rest of the Omega Team. They treated her more like a friend than the boss's goddaughter or the Alpha Team's niece, which she appreciated. None of them called her Baby-girl, either.

As if he had suddenly realized he was still cupping her shoulders, Doug pulled away and stepped back. Jenn immediately felt the loss but tried not to let it show.

A trill filled the air, and Romeo pulled out a satellite phone from a side pocket of his cargo pants and looked at the screen. "Speak of the devil." He answered the call, but barely got out "Hey, Ia—" before he was apparently cut off. He rolled his eyes at whatever her uncle said. "She's standing right next to me, and she's fine. Not a scratch on her." After a short pause, he handed her the phone. "He wants to talk to you. He heard about the quake on the news and doesn't believe me that you're okay."

It was her turn to roll her eyes as she brought the phone to her ear. "Uncle Ian, I'm fine. Like Romeo said, I don't have a scratch on me."

"You're telling me the truth?"

"Of course. You know I would tell you if I were hurt, but I really am fine. Just a little shaken up. Excuse the pun."

"Thank God." The relief in his voice was palpable. "Is anyone else hurt?"

She glanced around. "Not here at the compound. We don't know about any of the villagers in the area, though. The guards and some of the workers here are checking on them by radio or will drive out to see if they need help."

"Pack up your things. I want you on the jet with Romeo and the others and back home as soon as possible."

Her blood began to boil, and she saw red. Stepping away from the group, she emphasized her one-word response. "*No*."

"What do you mean, *no*?" he shouted.

"Exactly what you think I mean." Somehow, she kept her tone calm and firm as she paced back and forth. She had never defied her uncle before—he never gave her a reason to—but right then, she was putting her foot down. And to do that, she needed to speak like the intelligent adult she was, not a whiny preteen who wasn't getting her way. Her godfather deserved respect, but she would demand the same from him in return. "I came here for a reason, Uncle Ian. To prove to myself and everyone else that I'm strong enough to stand on my own two feet and do something like this. My being here has helped a lot of people, and I'm not going to abandon them because of an earthquake that caused a little damage. If I were Nick, Jake, Brody, Marco, Devon, or anyone who works for you, this conversation would never happen. They would all stay and help, and you wouldn't have a problem with it."

She stopped treading and stared up at the sky, hoping she could convince him not to argue with her. "I can do this, Uncle Ian. Over the past six years, everyone has helped to train me how to protect myself in case something bad happens. Whether that's being kidnapped again, God forbid, or getting accosted in a parking lot, getting lost in the woods, or ending up in a natural disaster. What I'm doing here makes a difference. Please don't make me choose between obeying your order and doing what I know is right. You won't like my answer."

The prolonged silence on the other end of the call made her think she lost him, but then there was an exasperated sigh. "When did you grow up to be such an amazing young woman?"

"When you blinked?" The tension in her back and shoulders eased a bit, but he hadn't given in yet.

He let out a wry chuckle. "I guess so." Another sigh erupted from him. "Okay. I'm not going to be the ogre you think I am at the moment. I won't demand you come home. On one condition."

Relief coursed through her. "Anything."

"There will probably be aftershocks, and some can be as strong as the six-point-four that already hit the area." It didn't surprise her that he already knew the strength of the quake before she did. The man could obtain any information he wanted within seconds from Brody and Nathan in their computer war-room. "I want Romeo, Lindsey, and Doug to stay there for a few more days to make sure everything is okay. They can help with whatever needs to be done."

What? Oh, no. Anything but that!

Of course, that's not what she said to him. He was letting her stay, trusting that she was making the right decision. If having the two Omega Team members and *Doug* with her for a few days made her uncle feel better, she would suck it up and accept it. "Okay. Thank you for not forcing me to go home."

"I'm just worried about you, Baby-girl. It's been my job to worry about you since the day your dad asked me to be your godfather. But it's also my job to trust you and know when I need to let you go and be who you want to be. Just stay safe. Peyton will need her godmother to guide her when she gets older."

She smiled. "I will. I promise."

"Good. Let me talk to Romeo again."

Rejoining the group, she handed off the phone but didn't say anything. She wouldn't be the one to break the news to Doug that he was stuck there with her for the next few days—especially when he probably wished he were anywhere else.

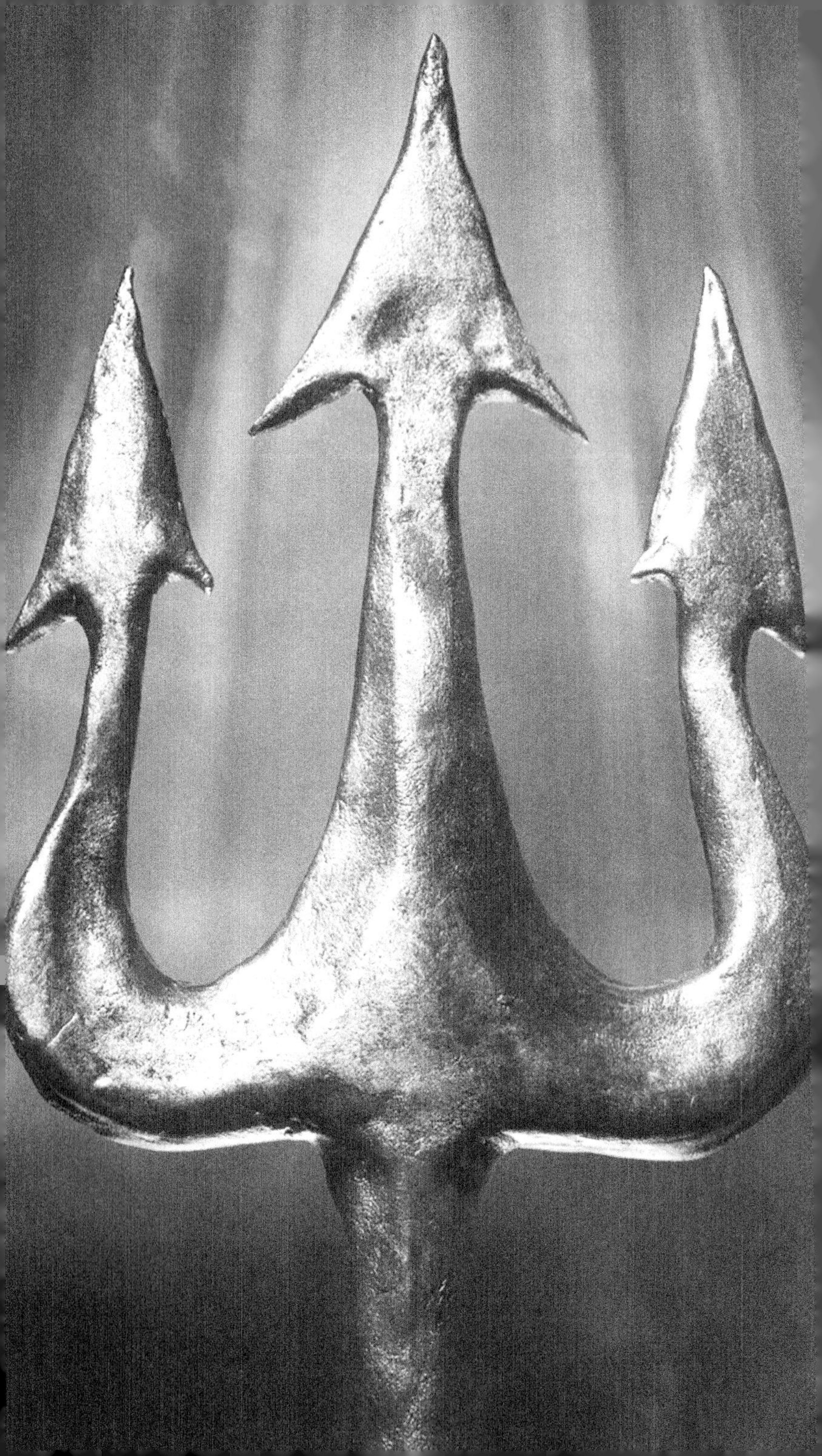

CHAPTER SEVEN

Doug had never been so relieved to see Jenn standing there in one piece, insisting she was okay. The fear that surged through him during the massive earthquake—while they were still miles from the commune—might have even outweighed what he'd felt when those two assholes tried to attack her in Donovan's parking lot. It came damn close to what he'd experienced when she was kidnapped, but this time, he was still in a position to rescue her. Although as he studied her, he realized she didn't need rescuing. She was unharmed and safe. Thank fuck.

His heart still galloped as if he were a racehorse coming down to the finish line at the Kentucky Derby, but the gripping fear that constricted his lungs slowly dissipated while he stared at her. Clearly, the quake had frightened her and everyone else, but she seemed to be holding it together—probably for the children's sake. He glanced down at a little girl, around six or seven, who eased over and leaned against Jenn's hip, wrapping her arm around the woman's thigh like it was a security blanket. The girl's cheeks were stained with tears that had stopped falling, but an occasional sob shuddered through her while Jenn petted her hair reassuringly.

As Romeo explained why they were there, it suddenly registered that Doug stood way too close to her and still had his hands on her shoulders. He quickly removed them and stepped back, giving them both space. He needed it because all he wanted to do was wrap her tightly in his arms and inhale her scent —just over three weeks without seeing her had felt like a lifetime.

Guilt over his lust for the younger woman flooded through his veins as she took the satellite phone from Romeo to talk to Ian. While she tried to reassure her godfather that she and everyone else were unharmed, she tapped the little girl's shoulder to get her attention, then pointed toward a woman in her thirties exiting a nearby building. The girl ran over to the woman, presumably her mother.

Unexpectedly, Jenn moved away from the small group, but even with the short distance, Doug could still see and hear her. From her fiery exchange with Ian, he gathered that her boss had ordered her to get on the company jet and head back to Tampa as soon as possible. Doug wanted that, too, until her words sank in.

It suddenly hit him how much she'd grown and matured over the past four years, not just physically but emotionally, even though he still felt the significant age gap between them. Well, eight years wasn't exactly major, but it was enough that he thought he was too old for her. Most twenty-three-year-olds were out partying with friends, traveling the world, and doing stuff they wouldn't have time for in a few more years when careers, marriages, and kids took over their lives. Doug's party days were long gone. Getting shot and almost dying tended to put one's priorities into perspective. He dated here and there, spent time with friends and family at their homes more often than in bars, loved his job, and enjoyed some quiet downtime. His favorite thing to do on his off hours was fishing in the Gulf on the twenty-five-foot used boat he had bought the previous year.

He also wanted to settle down with the right woman and have kids someday. His three sisters, one older than him and two younger, were all married with children, which meant Doug had six nieces and nephews between the ages of four and thirteen, with another on the way. His youngest sister's second child was due in six months. Rowan and her husband, Wes, wanted to be surprised, just as they were when their son, Cayden, was born, so they opted not to learn the baby's sex.

Doug loved doting on his nieces and nephews. They all lived within a twenty-minute drive of his condo, and he saw them often. The children weren't just cousins but friends, too, and Doug hoped his own kids would have a similar relationship with the others someday.

A vision of Jenn, her belly round with a child—his child—popped into his head, and he swayed on his feet. For a moment, he thought another earthquake had hit, but it was the unexpected thought that knocked him for a loop. She'd be beautiful pregnant and a fantastic mother. He'd seen her with all the kids she considered her niblings—a gender-neutral word for nieces and nephews that he'd never heard until recently. They adored her, and it was evident to anyone who watched her with them that she loved each of them as if they were her own.

"Well, looks like we're staying for a few days."

Romeo's statement brought Doug out of the fog he was in. Glancing at Jenn, he realized she was no longer on the sat phone that his teammate now held and was staring at her feet as if they were the most interesting things she'd ever seen. "Huh?"

"Ian wants us to stay and help out here."

Of course he did. Shit.

It wasn't as though Doug didn't want to stay and

assist with the recovery—there had to be damage to the commune and nearby villages, and people who were injured or, God forbid, dead from the quake. He was a fourth-generation retired Marine—helping people in need was ingrained in his DNA—but he'd rather get Jenn back to the States for her welfare. However, it seemed she convinced Ian to let her stay, and so Doug would glue himself to her side to ensure her safety until he was certain she was no longer in any danger. She wasn't going to like it, but too fucking bad. He could never forgive himself for letting her be kidnapped four years ago, and he'd be damned if he wouldn't protect her now when he had another chance.

"By the way, Tony and Margie, this is—" Jenn started and gestured to a man and woman standing nearby, but before she could complete the introductions, another female voice interrupted.

"Lindsey, is that you? What in heaven's name are you doing here?" a slender woman in her early-to-mid-sixties asked in slightly accented English as she strode toward the group. She was approximately five feet eight inches tall, with long, gray hair pulled up into a bun. If Doug guessed correctly, she was the doctor who ran the commune.

Costello had been there once before while on a mission with Ian, Carter, Jordyn, and a few others, and she stepped forward to hug the other woman. "Hey,

Ramona. It's good to see you. We came to make sure the supplies Jenn wanted got here this time." She pointed at the two men the doctor hadn't met before. "This is Val Mancini, but everyone calls him Romeo, and this is Doug Henderson. Guys, this is Doctor Ramona Sanchez."

"Call me Ramona, please." She shook hands with Romeo and then Doug. "You picked a heck of a time to visit."

Lindsey chuckled. "That seems to be an understatement. But you're in luck. Boss-man just told us to stick around for a few days and help however we can."

"I never turn down volunteers or *voluntolds*."

"Volun-what?" Doug asked, his brow furrowing.

The doctor laughed at him. "You've never heard of a voluntold? It's when someone else, like your boss, Ian—God bless his sarcastic soul—tells you that you're volunteering whether you like it or not."

Actually, he knew that from his time in the military. His brain just hadn't caught up with the conversation yet. It was still stuck on the earthquake and the fact that he and the others were staying to help, which meant being in close proximity to Jenn for the next few days, longer than he'd anticipated. Ever since Ian ordered him to fly down to Colombia, Doug prepared himself to see Jenn for a few hours, at the most. Now he had to figure out how to keep his distance yet ensure her safety until he could get the hell out of there.

"Ah. Yeah, he does that often." He scratched his temple. "In fact, that's how we all ended up down here to begin with. We were voluntold."

"I'm not surprised." She placed her hands on her hips and glanced at the cargo truck. "Well, we've got a lot of work to do before we can even think about unloading whatever you have in there."

Romeo raised his hand holding the sat phone. "I'll call Nathan and have him extend the rental agreement. I'll also give our pilot a heads up and tell him to find something to do for a few days."

"Perfect. Lindsey, you remember where the women's bunkhouse is, right?"

"Yes, ma'am."

Ramona frowned and lightly swatted Costello's shoulder. "Don't 'ma'am' me. You know I hate that. I know it's a military thing, but it makes me feel old." The two chuckled. "Anyway, you go get settled in there. Do you need anything? Clothing? Toiletries? I can't imagine you brought much if you didn't know you were staying."

"Our go-bags are in the trucks." Most of the time, they took them wherever they went, in case plans changed at the drop of a hat, as was often the case, like today. Lindsey turned to Romeo, who was already on the phone. "Call Colleen, too, and have her check us out of our hotel rooms."

"Got it," he said before returning his attention to whoever he was talking to.

Ramona clapped her hands once. "All right. Gentlemen, Tony can show you where the men's bunkhouse is. Toss your bags on an empty bed, and then let's get to work.

"Tony, when you're done, can you get started on that inventory in the clinic with Jenn, please? I'm sure we lost some supplies during the quake, and we'll need to replace them ASAP. Lindsey can give you a hand." The doctor could rival most of the military officers Doug had known during his career, as she quickly assigned tasks to the group. "I need Margie to help Roland and me check the medical equipment. Hopefully, nothing's damaged. And Doug, I'd appreciate it if you and Romeo would join the other men, making sure there's no structural damage to any of the buildings, including the roofs, and doing the heavy lifting. A few of them are also trying to round up some livestock that got loose when a section of the corral fencing fell."

"No problem," Doug said. Romeo echoed the response a second later after finishing his call, which had been to Clinton.

As Jenn joined the doctor and another woman as they walked toward one of the buildings, the man she and Ramona had called Tony stepped forward, smiled, and extended his hand to Romeo. "Tony Barone."

"Val Mancini or Romeo."

"Is there a story behind that nickname?"

"Ha! Yeah, I got it in the Army. I'll take it over some of the other nicknames from my old unit, though."

He shook hands with Lindsey next. "Tony Barone. Nice to meet you. Lindsey, was it?"

"Yes, Lindsey Abbott. You may hear one of these two call me Costello, though."

The man's grin grew wider. "'Who's on First?'" When she smiled and nodded, he added, "Nice. Is that also a military nickname?"

"Yup. Marine Corps."

"Really? Awesome. My cousin, Dara, is currently in boot camp at Parris Island. She's halfway through and loving it, according to my aunt."

"Oorah! Good for her. That's where I got my training too."

Tony turned to Doug, but despite holding out his hand, the man's smile disappeared while his eyes narrowed. And there was a little more pressure than necessary in his handshake. "Tony Barone. I'm a friend of Jenn's."

Doug studied the man who appeared to be only a few years younger than himself. Tony was a couple of inches shorter, physically fit, with dark hair, hazel eyes, and a firm jaw. If Doug were gay or bi, he might even think the guy was handsome. But what the fuck? *A friend of Jenn's?* Tony hadn't stressed that to Lindsey or Romeo, but it seemed he wanted to make a point with Doug. Had Jenn mentioned him to this twit? Or fuck! Was Jenn romantically involved with him?

Squeezing the other man's hand harder, Doug waited until he saw him wince slightly before easing up. "Doug Henderson. Pleasure to meet you." It wasn't in the least.

He let Tony's hand go, and satisfaction rolled through him when the guy stepped back, flexing and closing his fingers several times, as if trying to assure himself that no metacarpals or phalanges were broken. From his left, he heard Romeo let out a snort, and Doug glared at him. With a smirk, his teammate held up his hands in surrender and then hit a button on the satellite phone before putting it to his ear.

While Romeo called Nathan and Colleen, Doug retrieved their go-bags from the truck and Jeep, then followed Tony to the bunkhouse they'd been assigned. Lindsey took her bag and headed toward the building next to theirs.

The bunkhouse was as basic as Doug suspected. It reminded him of his old boot camp barracks. There were twelve cots, each with a brown one-drawer nightstand, a footlocker, and a small wardrobe cabinet, which all looked like they came from IKEA—probably acquired through donations. Portable camping lamps were on the nightstands along with the occasional book or two and a few personal items. Near the door stood a rustic table and four chairs, accompanied by another lamp, a well-used deck of cards, a large plastic container filled with sourdough pretzels, and another one containing individual packages of peanut M&Ms. Doug did a double take on those, as they seemed out of place in the rudimentary commune.

Tony pointed to four cots on the far end of the room. "Those are all available. Toilets and urinals are in there. Showers are in the next building over. Keep them short."

The man's terse tone grated on Doug, and after tossing his and Romeo's go-bags onto two empty cots, he said, "Hey, man. What's your problem with me? With my teammates, you were smiling and joking. With me, it's like you got a stick up your ass."

Crossing his arms, Tony took a step forward. "Jenn and I have become friends. I've heard all about you, and let's just say I'm not a fan. You hurt her, and you'll have to deal with me."

Friends? Jenn made friends easily, so that wasn't surprising, but Doug still wondered if more was going on between the two. The thought of Jenn romantically involved with anyone made him sick. *Damn it.* He was stuck in a mindset that, even though he shouldn't be attracted to her, no one else should either—a walking contradiction. He couldn't have his cake and eat it too

—and he didn't want to share said cake. Jenn was a beautiful, vibrant woman. Of course, she would garner interest from any guy who met her or even saw her from across the room. But this fucking twit certainly didn't deserve her.

Growling, Doug closed the distance between them and glared down at the man, who surprisingly stood his ground. "I don't give a shit who you are. I'm here for two reasons—to help out and to make sure Jenn stays safe and returns to her family unharmed. So stay out of my way, and we'll get along just fine."

With anger flaring in his eyes, Tony opened his mouth to say something else, but he was interrupted when the door swung wide and Romeo stepped inside. His gaze shifted between the two men, and then he shook his head and snorted. "Wonderful. A gunfight at the O.K. Corral. Or is it a dick measuring contest?"

"Shut it, Mancini," Doug warned as he moved around Tony, intentionally bumping the guy's shoulder hard as he passed and strode toward the door. "Let's get to work."

CHAPTER EIGHT

It took Jenn, Tony, and Lindsey three hours to get the clinic's supply room back in order and complete the inventory. Most of the supplies and medications were salvageable, but some were crushed under the weight of heavier items and fallen shelf units and had to be discarded.

Dr. Sanchez, Margie, and Roland had spent about the same amount of time restoring the exam rooms and medical records in proper order. Thankfully, they only reported two pieces of equipment needed to be replaced, and those were readily available at a supply company in Bogotá and weren't too expensive. As soon as they could confirm the business hadn't sustained any damage and was open, one of the guards would drive down and get what was needed. Right then, regular cell and landline phone reception was spotty, with only a few calls getting through to various parts of the city and surrounding towns.

Everyone else at the commune had been busy too. The wayward goats, sheep, chickens, and two donkeys were safely back in their respective enclosures. The buildings were all inspected and suffered only minimal damage. Things could've been much worse—at least all the structures there were only one-story, and no trees had fallen. Rachael and Lexi had helped the kitchen staff clean up in there and the dining room, which were now in working order again.

Reports came in of heavily damaged areas and a few deaths in the region—at least one apartment building had collapsed in Bogotá. Several injured people—none of whom were critical—arrived at the commune shortly after the clinic was operational again, and Dr. Sanchez and the nurses got to work tending to them.

The cooks threw together a simple lunch of empanadas and chimichurri rice. All the hard work had made everyone hungry, and they took a break, wolfing down their meals. Except Jenn. She ate a little, but her stomach was in knots just being in the same room as Doug. The next few days would be her own private hell until he left. As she sat with Tony, Lindsey, and Adam McKee, one of the other male volunteers, she tried to ignore Doug, who was sitting one table over with Rachel, Lexie, and Romeo. The two women shamelessly flirted with the male newcomers, but didn't seem to be making any progress with them.

Jenn knew Romeo wasn't the manwhore some people thought he was just because of his handsome face, well-toned body, and outgoing personality. In fact, she didn't think he dated much at all. He seemed hung up on renowned country singer Summer Hayes, who was a member of The Covenant and friends with Jenn's extended family. She didn't know what was going on between the two but thought they'd make a cute couple if they ever hooked up. Unfortunately, just because two people looked good together didn't mean they belonged together.

Romeo did a good job of deflecting Rachel's and Lexie's advances while keeping things light and friendly. The women weren't capturing Doug's attention either. He kept glancing over at Jenn and glaring at Tony. She didn't know why and was afraid to ask. Tony hadn't mentioned anything to her earlier—they hadn't had a moment alone while working in the supply room—but she didn't miss the dirty looks he sent Doug's way too. It was apparent the two men didn't like each other. Tony probably recalled their conversation about Doug and was being overly protective. But she had no clue why Doug seemed to want to pummel Tony like a punching bag.

The door to the dining hall swung open, and Rich and a short older man Jenn didn't recognize hurried in. "We need help," Rich announced. "The village of Anjama suffered heavy damage." He tilted his head toward the man standing next to him. "Luis said they've got numerous people injured and some trapped in buildings that collapsed."

Everyone got to their feet, and Doug asked, "How far away is it?"

"It's remote—about forty minutes up into the mountains. Home to about eighty to a hundred people. It took Luis a while to get his old truck started. Otherwise, he would've been here sooner. I've notified the federal authorities, but they don't know when they'll be able to get anyone up there. They've got their hands full with the damage and injuries in the larger towns and the city. We're all the people of Anjama have right now."

"Then let's go."

They quickly gathered in the center of the commune, stocking several vehicles with the necessary supplies—ropes, chainsaws, tarps, shovels, work gloves, first aid and emergency kits, boxes of medical supplies, a few collapsible military-style stretchers, blankets, water jugs, and more. Not everyone could go —some had to stay behind and help Dr. Sanchez and her staff with the injured people already there as more had arrived in the past hour.

Since Doug, Lindsey, and Romeo had medic training from their time in the military, they could assist Roland with triage in the village. Rich and two other guards would drive the vehicles, while Jenn, Tony, Margie, and Adam offered to help as well. When the vehicles were nearly stocked, the volunteers took a few moments to change into jeans and their hiking boots before grabbing sweatshirts. Lindsey, Doug, and Romeo also retrieved their go-bags. It would be a bit cooler up in the mountains, especially if they were still there after dark.

Doug told Jenn several times that she was to stay at the commune, but she ignored him, refusing to get into an argument in front of everyone. She was going whether he liked it or not. When she returned from getting changed, Doug stepped in front of her and opened his mouth, most likely to order her to stay behind again. Her eyes narrowed, and she didn't give him a chance to say more than her name before pointing at him. "Enough! I stood up to Uncle Ian, and now I'm standing up to you. I'm going, and that's final. Get over it."

He clamped his mouth shut and scowled at her while Lindsey and Romeo tried to hide their smirks and laughter. She skirted around him, marched over to one of the pickup trucks, and climbed in the passenger side before sliding to the middle of the bench seat. Tony got in beside her, slammed the door shut, and tapped her thigh. "So...would it be okay if I laughed at his expression when you told him off?"

"Yup." She popped the P in aggravation before glancing at him. The look he gave her made her chuckle, and then she sighed loudly. "Why, out of all the men in the world, did I have to fall in love with a grumpy, domineering jackass?"

"Well, personally, I can see the physical attraction—girl, he's hot and definitely all alpha. But you're right, he *is* a grumpy, domineering jackass. But don't worry—I've got your back."

"You two had words earlier? I saw you both giving each other death glares at lunch."

He shrugged. "A few. No big deal. I do get the feeling he just wants you safe, and so do I. It's not that I don't think you can't handle yourself—you already proved that to me these past few weeks—but that doesn't mean I can't worry about you. You're my friend—a good one—and I care about my friends."

Smiling, she nudged her shoulder against his. "I care about you too."

They dropped the subject when a guard got into the driver's seat and started the engine.

A half-hour later, Doug's jaw had been clenched so tightly since they left the commune that it ached, and he wasn't sure it would unlock anytime soon.

Tension had seized his entire body, and he rubbed the bullet wound scar on his chest. At some point over the past few years, that had become an unconscious habit. Most of the time, he didn't realize he was doing it until his fingers had rubbed off a layer or two of skin around the area, causing it to become sore.

They left the flatlands behind about fifteen minutes ago and were on a well-traveled dirt road heading up into the mountains. The higher elevation brought with it lush vegetation, and they passed the occasional tapir, deer, and armadillo along the way.

He was in the passenger seat of an older model Chevy Suburban, which he swore was held together by nothing but duct tape and grease, following the pickup truck Jenn was in. Parsons was driving, and Lindsey and Romeo were in the back seat. Conversation flowed between the three, but Doug hadn't listened to a word they said. He was pissed and worried about Jenn. Why couldn't she just stay back at the commune where it was safe? She wasn't trained for situations like this, which put her at risk, and in turn, put Doug at risk because he'd be too distracted while trying to keep her out of danger.

Damn that woman! She was stubborn as all hell. Doug never knew her parents, but from what he'd heard, her dad was a lot like her godfather, which was probably where she got her tenacity.

Lindsey smacked his shoulder. "Hey. What's with you and Jenn?"

"Nothing," he bit out too quickly. "She should've stayed at the commune, that's all. She's gonna get hurt or worse."

"Seriously? Do you really think Ian would've let her come down here and now stay after an earthquake if he didn't think she could handle herself? You don't give her enough credit, Doug. She's a strong woman, physically and mentally. She'll be fine."

He huffed but didn't respond. Lindsey was right. He wasn't being fair to Jenn—he knew that—but the urge to protect her was so powerful that he didn't always think rationally when it came to her.

"Don't worry," Romeo said. "We'll all keep an eye on her and each other. Just like any other detail. Think of her as the newest member of our team."

"She doesn't have the training we do."

"She's gone through a ton of training—maybe not military grade, but damn close. Ever since her kidnap—" There was a long pause, but Doug knew what was coming. "Oooh. That's what's going on here. Jesus." Romeo leaned forward. "Doug, man, listen. Lindsey and I weren't at Trident then, but we know all about it. You were fucking ambushed. I'm sorry you lost your partner, but from what I heard, there was nothing you could've done differently—especially with a hole in your goddamn chest. Bad shit happens to good people

—we all saw it over in Iraq and A-stan. If that weren't true, none of us would've lost anyone over there. But we did, and it wasn't anyone's fault but the enemy's. Ian doesn't blame you for what happened. None of her uncles do. Hell, Jenn doesn't blame you ei—"

"Shut up! Would you—" He ran a shaky hand through his hair. "Just fucking drop it, all right."

Romeo let out a heavy breath and tapped Doug's bicep lightly. "All right. I've got one more thing to say, and then I'll back off. You've got to get past what happened. It's been four years. Jenn survived and is thriving. Let it go, and take a good look at her now. You might be surprised by what you see."

That was the last thing he wanted to do. If he let the past go, he might forget why he wasn't good enough for her. The more he thought about it lately, the more he realized that the age thing wasn't the big issue. Hell, the fact that she was his boss's goddaughter wasn't it either. It was because he had failed her once and never wanted to be in that situation again. If that happened, he might lose her forever.

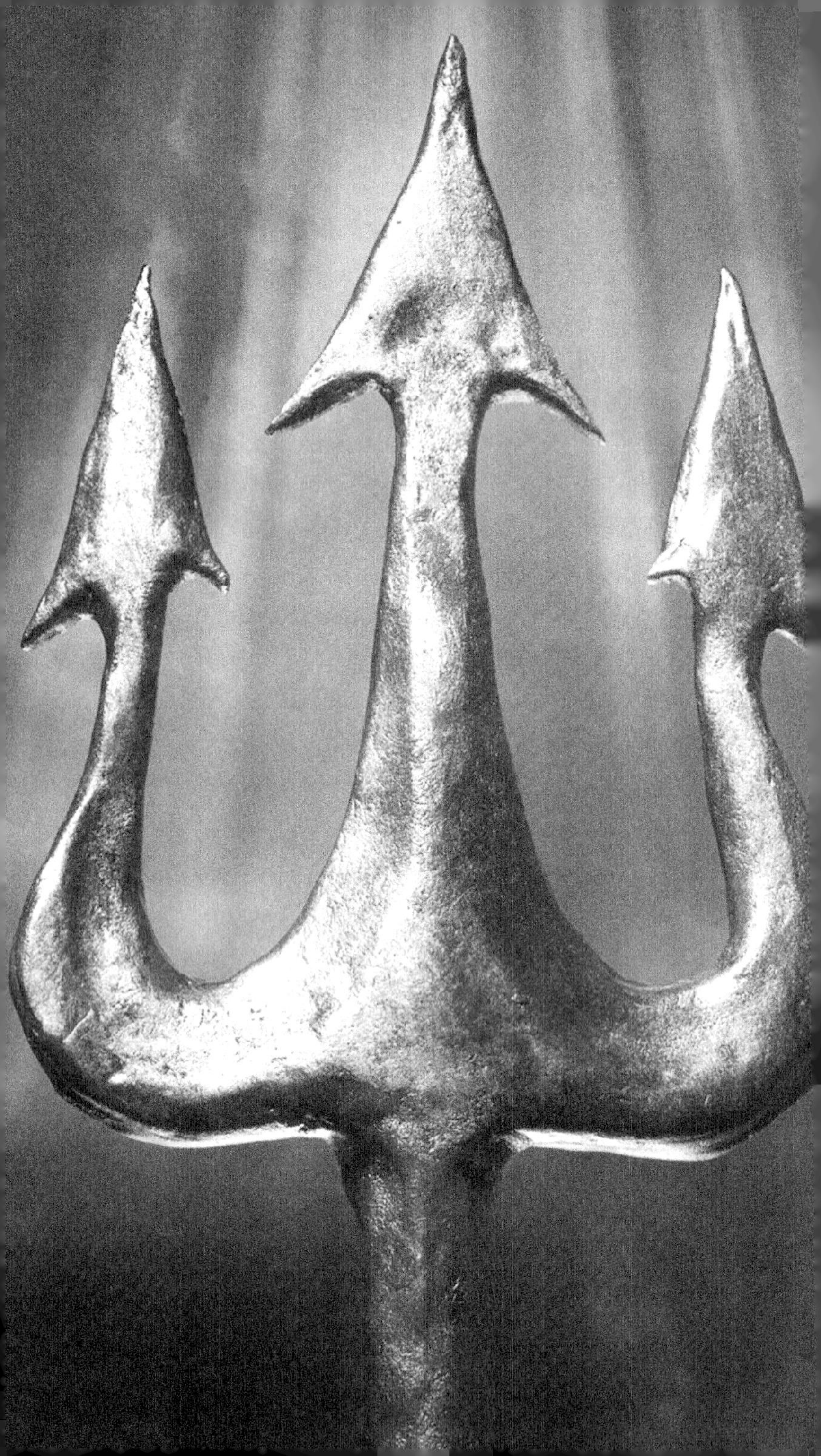

CHAPTER NINE

"Oh, my God!" Jenn exclaimed when they arrived at Anjama. The village had been transformed into a hellscape of shattered homes and broken lives. People, young and old, were scattered throughout the area. Some lay on the ground, writhing in pain, while others tried to comfort them. At least two didn't move at all, and Jenn feared they were dead. Towering trees blocked pathways where they'd fallen, their roots torn from the earth, while numerous buildings had pancaked into piles of debris. Two large boulders, that must have rolled down from the hill above, sat off to the side of the main dirt roadway. One landed partially on top of a hut, and she hoped no one was inside when it hit. Men frantically dug in the piles of rubble, pausing only to call out in Spanish if anyone could hear them underneath the wreckage.

The village was similar to the commune, with a combination of large buildings and smaller huts or cabins. However, instead of being built on acres of flat land, they sat on multiple natural outcroppings protruding from the hillside, with well-worn paths zigzagging to connect those above and below the main road, if you could call it that. Some structures were constructed with wood and metal sheets, while others were made of concrete. Livestock—sheep, goats, cows, and chickens—and several dogs roamed free.

Everyone piled out of the four-truck caravan, including the one Luis had driven to get help, and Rich started issuing orders. He knew this area better than any of them and was a natural leader. Doug, Lindsey, Roland, and Romeo immediately began triaging the wounded. At the same time, Tony, Adam, and the other guards grabbed the chainsaws, ropes, and shovels and joined forces with the men searching for victims. Rich pointed toward a nearby building with a wooden cross above the front entrance. "Jenn, Margie, I'm going to check out the chapel. If it's stable, we'll move the wounded in there for treatment. Start unpacking the medical supplies. I'll be right back."

They got to work, and a few minutes later, Rich returned. "It's safe. I pushed some benches out of the way. I'll help the others with the victims who can be moved in there."

"Got it," Jenn replied as she picked up two boxes and carried them into the chapel.

She spent the next two hours contributing however she could—organizing the provisions on the chapel's altar and several benches, bringing victims inside, getting them settled, treating minor injuries, and grabbing supplies for whoever needed them. She kept an eye on a group of young children who were more scared than anything, but she couldn't do much to comfort them because the wounded were everyone's priority.

The impromptu medical staff did their best, but outside, a row of bodies slowly grew. They were beyond help, lined up on tarps with their faces covered by clothes. Several relatives stood or knelt near their loved ones, wailing in grief. So far, fourteen hadn't survived, including a teenage mother and her three-week-old infant. Jenn tried not to think about them or look at the corpses, but it was difficult not to do so. Somehow, she managed to hold herself together. There would be time later to mourn the dead and deal with the horrific experience. She wasn't naive enough to think she wouldn't escape the natural disaster unscathed. While she wasn't physically injured, mentally and emotionally, she would suffer, as would the others working beside her.

No one had taken a break—they were too busy—but when the urge to urinate became unbearable, she grabbed Margie. "I need to pee really, *really* bad, and you need to stand guard so I can go behind a tree." The village probably didn't have much in the way of plumbing before the quake, and she didn't want to look for an outhouse or whatever might be available. A tree would do just fine.

"I was just thinking the same thing—I have to go too. I'll guard you, and then you guard me."

Exiting the chapel, they glanced to the left and right. The building was one of the first when you entered the village from the direction they'd come. They turned left, walked a dozen yards or so past the commune's haphazardly parked vehicles, and found an area that would provide enough cover to tend to their personal business. While the other woman ensured her privacy, Jenn squatted behind a tree first, sighing as the pressure in her bladder was relieved. She then switched places with Margie.

While waiting, her gaze went to the makeshift morgue again, and a shiver went down her spine. It was times like that when she realized she often took things for granted. Yes, she'd lost her parents to the hands of a brutal murderer, something that would haunt her for the rest of her life. But she had her extended family who loved her to pieces, and she loved them in return. She had an apartment with electricity, plumbing, cable, and internet, a soft, warm bed, a full refrigerator and pantry, a new car she had bought the previous year, clothes that weren't in tatters, a good job, and wonderful friends. These people had so little, and thanks to the earthquake, they now had even less. Not only were lives lost, but many of the survivors' homes and livelihoods were gone too.

As they headed back toward the chapel, Doug stepped outside, stretching his arms over his head and cocking his head from side to side, probably working out some kinks. Jenn's breath caught when his T-shirt lifted just enough for her to catch a glimpse of his washboard abs. Beside her, Margie sighed. "Oh, if only I were twenty or thirty years younger again. That man is a hottie."

It took a moment for the older woman's comment to register, and when it did, Jenn stopped short and gaped at her. "What?"

Margie grinned. "Oh, honey. My husband is dead—I'm not. I can still look. Besides, it wouldn't make a difference if I were younger. That man over there hasn't been able to take his eyes off you for more than a few seconds at a time, even though he's working his ass off as much as everyone else. You know, he kind of reminds me of George. My husband was a police officer and carried himself the same way Doug and Romeo do. Lindsey too. They exude confidence and total awareness of their surroundings. It comes from their training and is hard to miss when you know what to look for."

Glancing over at Doug, Jenn found him staring at her, his gaze roaming her body as if making sure she was still unharmed. She reluctantly got her feet moving again when Margie walked toward him.

"Everything okay?" he asked as they approached.

"Yup," Margie responded. "Us girls just needed a quick bathroom break behind a tree."

Jenn's cheeks flamed. She didn't need Doug to know she'd been bare-assed a few moments ago, peeing in the woods.

"*¡Socorro! ¡Socorro!*"

They turned to see a man, in his mid to late twenties, running toward them from the other side of the village. He frantically waved at them, spoke in rapid Spanish, and pointed in the direction he'd come from. Doug looked at Jenn and Margie. "My Spanish isn't that good. I understood 'help' and 'hurry.'"

"His wife's in labor," Jenn translated. "He needs us to go to her."

"Damn it. Let me grab one of the emergency bags."

While the two women rushed toward the pleading man, Doug ducked inside the chapel and then caught up with them, carrying an oversized canvas knapsack and a handheld radio. He stuck the latter into the side thigh pocket of his cargo pants, then pulled the bag's straps over his shoulders. They followed the man down the main dirt road, past several buildings. Jenn spotted Tony and the others digging through the rubble of what had once been a large structure.

They kept going as the man repeatedly glanced over his shoulder, as if making sure they were still with him. They were almost to the other side of the village when Doug stopped suddenly and grabbed one of Margie's and Jenn's arms, bringing both to a halt. Confused, they stared at him as he released them and spun around slowly, his gaze darting around.

"What's wrong?" Jenn asked.

"The animals."

She didn't understand at first, but then realized the livestock and dogs were making a loud racket, nervously shifting back and forth on their feet. They started to run in different directions, with some barreling past the trio, who barely jumped out of the way in time. A low rumble reached her ears and grew louder. Powerful, ear-splitting cracks, like thunder, followed.

"Shit!" Doug grabbed her arm again. "Run!"

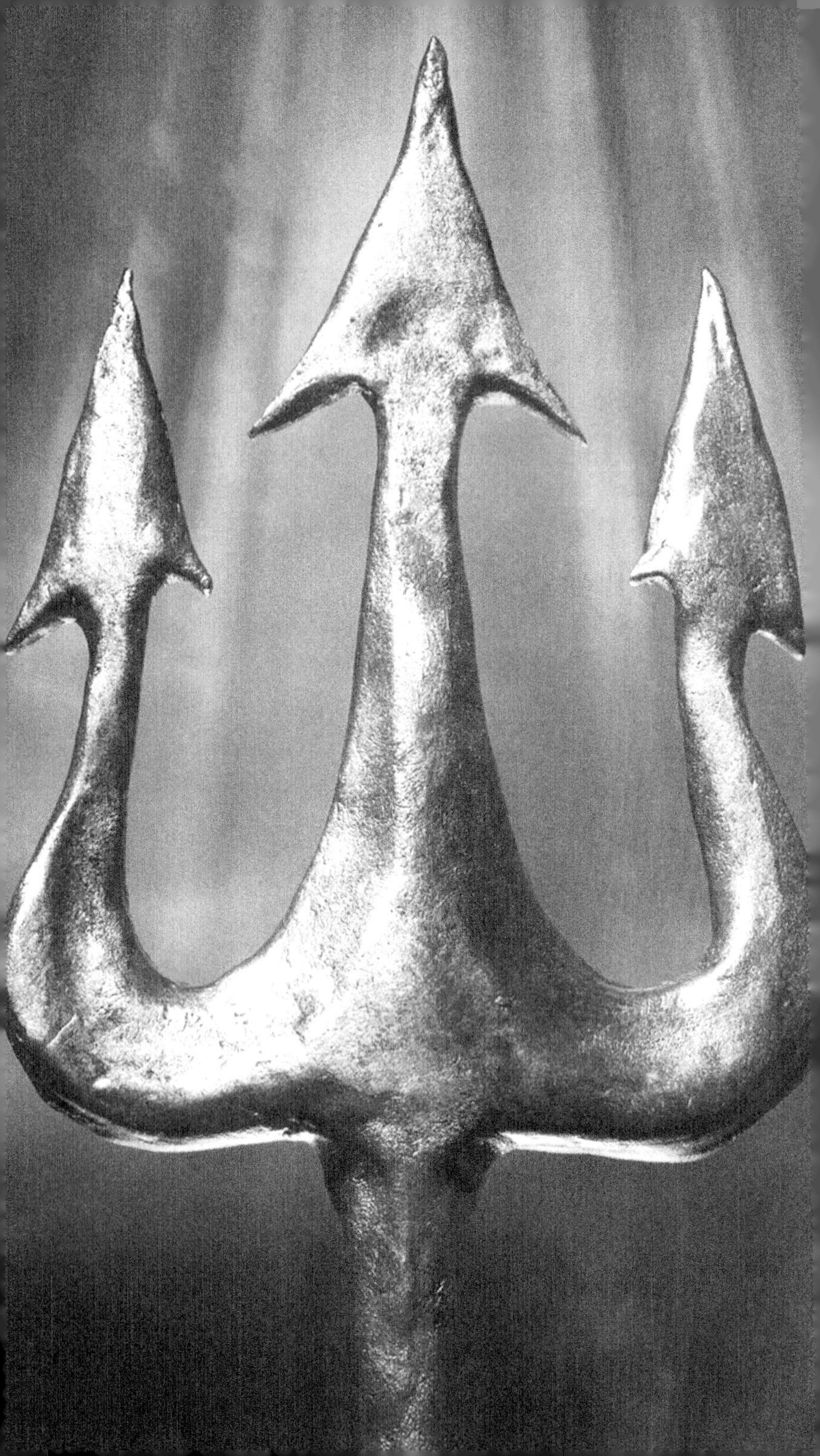

CHAPTER TEN

When he heard the rumble and splitting of wood, Doug looked upward and was horrified to see the start of a massive landslide heading toward them. Rocks, large and small, rolled downhill ahead of the earth and trees. Earlier, Rich mentioned the recent excessive rainfall. Between that and the earthquake, the mountain they were on was breaking apart, and Jenn, Doug, and Margie were right in its path.

He cursed and grasped both women by the arm again. "Run!"

"Wh-wha—" Jenn sputtered.

"A fucking landslide! Run!" He led them in the direction they'd already been going. The man who had come to them for help was in front of them, also sprinting for his life. Shouts and screams came from both ends of the village, and Doug hoped everyone would escape the new threat. He couldn't think of his teammates, the children, and all the injured victims in the chapel or those who were searching for survivors at the moment. His primary concern was getting Jenn and Margie to safety. Only then could he focus on the others.

The ground beneath their feet shook, as if there were another earthquake. He glanced to his right as rocks and dirt rolled past them. They were still in the slide's calamitous path but nearing the edge. Almost there.

They repeatedly stumbled before regaining their footing. Somehow, they managed to remain upright as they leaped over or darted around several tree limbs, shrubbery, and rocks. The pandemonium behind them was deafening, but just ahead lay stable ground—only a few more yards to go.

Margie tripped, and Doug lost his grip on her arm. He skidded to a stop but pushed Jenn forward. "Keep going! I've got her!"

She slowed, and he yelled again as he turned to help the other woman. "Go, Jenn! Run, damn it!"

Before he could move in the other direction, he saw a boulder and more shifting earth heading straight for Jenn, who was oblivious to the new danger as her attention was on Margie. Panic assailed him. Making a split-second decision, his heart raced as he ran toward her, grabbed her around the waist, and tackled her into a roll, barely getting them out of the way of the massive stone as it flew past them. It kept going, between two huts and over the edge of the cliff. A moment later, the huts disappeared into the abyss, too, as a river of loose earth pushed them over.

Dirt, tree limbs, and rocks pelted them as Doug scrambled to his feet, pulling Jenn with him, as the side of the mountain continued to move downward. On shaky legs, they reached the edge of the slide, and he pushed her a few more yards out of the way. As they tried to catch their breath, the tremors and rumbling slowed and eventually dissipated. The earth stopped moving, and everything around them stilled.

"Margie!" Jenn ran back toward the broad swath of destruction, which stretched the length of a football field or more, splitting the village in half. Everything in the middle had been swept downhill or covered.

Doug rushed after her. "Jenn! Wait!"

He knew he couldn't stop her from searching for her friend, but she needed to use caution. She could get hurt if the loose dirt and downed trees shifted again. Grasping her shoulder, he maneuvered her until she was behind him. "Let me go first. Watch your step."

"Where is she? I don't see her!"

"Easy. We'll find her. Just go slow."

"Margie!"

Doug's gaze scanned their surroundings as he carefully moved forward, trying to figure out where the older woman had been when she fell. In the distance, he heard shouts and crying, but none came from the person they were looking for.

"Margie!" Jenn yelled. "Doug, we have to find her. Where is she? Oh, God. Margie!"

After climbing over the trunk of a large tree, he turned to help her over. In his pocket, the satellite radio squawked, and he pulled it out.

"Bullseye! Sit-rep!"

He keyed the microphone as Jenn continued to call out for the other woman. "I'm here, Romeo—Jenn's with me. We're okay, but Margie's missing. We're searching for her."

"Copy that."

"Is everyone okay on your end?"

"The chapel is still standing, and the others from the commune made it back here safely. Not sure if we lost any more of the villagers, though."

"Copy." He continued to search for the missing woman, watching his step and keeping a close eye on Jenn. The dirt shifted beneath his feet, and he widened his stance until it stabilized again.

"Rich is on his sat phone, trying to get some more help up here. Will keep you posted. Stay safe."

"You too."

Jenn clambered up and over another large downed tree. "Margie! Oh, God! Doug, she's here!"

Grabbing a thick limb covered in dirt and sap, he hoisted himself up to find Margie's head, arms, and upper torso sticking out from under the tree. From the waist down, her body was crushed beneath the weight of the massive pine. Mud coated her clothes and skin. Blood seeped from her mouth and several gashes on her face and arms, but she was still alive, blinking and moaning.

Jenn sobbed and frantically dug at the dirt with her bare hands, trying to free the woman. Doug jumped down and assessed the situation. The tree had to weigh several tons, with no way to lift it off her. They didn't have access to the chainsaws or ropes. He lightly patted Margie's shoulder in reassurance he didn't feel, then moved to her other side and tried to wedge a hand into the dirt by her hip. It was packed tight and full of rocks and pebbles. Shit.

He removed the knapsack from his back and opened it, looking for anything that could be used as a shovel. While it held a first aid kit, along with some small tools and survival gear, nothing could be used to dig. Glancing around, he spotted a broken tree limb he could use. When he reached for it, the woman moaned again and grabbed his elbow.

He gently squeezed her hand. "Easy, Margie. We're going to get you out of there."

Tears rolled down her cheeks as she shook her head slightly and whispered, "No, y-you're not. Too...too much."

She coughed violently, spitting up clots of blood, and he winced at the wet rattle coming from her chest. It was the sound of impending death that he heard several times while in the military, and one that he'd never forget or mistake. Jenn took Margie's hand in hers. "Don't say that. We can get you out."

"It's my t-time." *Cough, cough.* "My George is w-waiting for m-me. It's o-okay." Her gaze veered from Jenn to the sky above. "Hi, George."

With that, her breathing ceased even though her eyes remained open. Despite the grim reaper claiming her, a hint of a smile was on her face.

"Margie?" Jenn shook the woman's shoulder. "Margie?" She shook harder. "Margie!"

Her anguished gaze met Doug's defeated one. "N-no!"

She started digging again. "Help me! We have to get her out."

"Jenn—"

"No!" She glared at him as her hands worked faster. Her nails were broken, and her fingers were smeared with blood and dirt. "Help me, damn you!"

He stood and reached for her, but she pulled away angrily. "*No*! We can still save her! We can still—we have to save her!"

When he knelt behind her and pulled her to his chest, she struggled for a few moments, then let out a wail that nearly tore his heart out. Sobbing uncontrollably, she twisted in his arms and buried her head between his shoulder and neck. Hot tears soaked through his shirt, scorching his skin. He held her tighter, wishing he could turn back time and save her from the grief of losing her friend.

"I'm sorry, sweetheart. I'm so sorry."

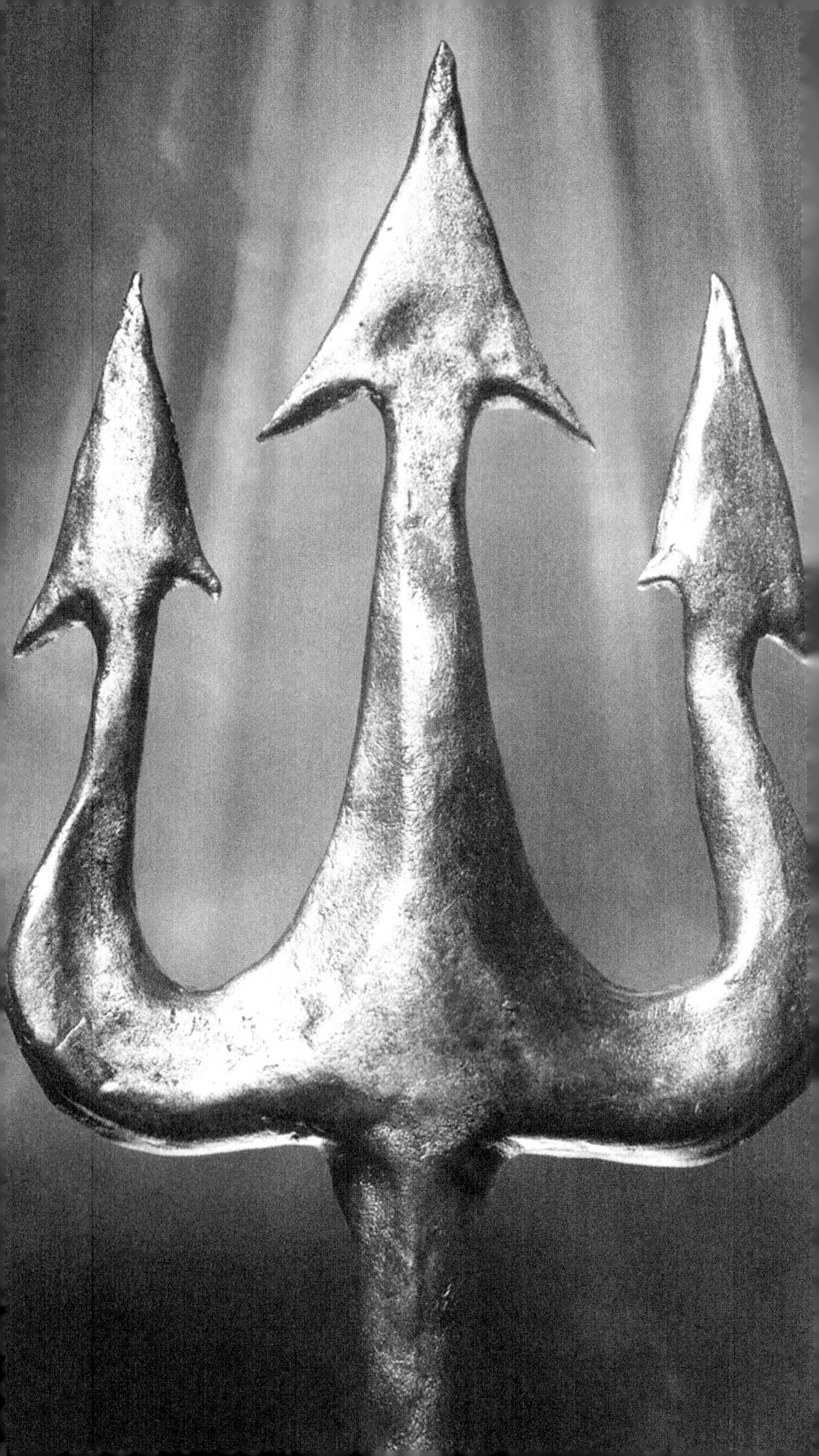

CHAPTER ELEVEN

Jenn didn't know how long they sat there in the damp dirt next to Margie's lifeless body. She cried in Doug's arms until there were no more tears. Her chest burned, and her head throbbed. If she had the option, she would climb onto a soft bed somewhere with Doug beside her, holding her tightly until she fell asleep, praying the past twelve hours were only a nightmare and Margie was still alive. That everyone in the village of Anjama was still alive.

She inhaled deeply. Despite the dirt and salty sweat coating his skin, Doug still smelled like himself. There was no hint of the cologne he occasionally wore, but she recognized his unique scent. It was all masculine—leather and musk with a hint of spice—wrapping around her, like a warm coat in the dead of winter.

The scruff of his jaw rasped against her cheek. She would give anything to be in his arms, at another time and place, filled with happiness and bliss instead of grief. She felt safe with him. Comforted. Connected. Loved.

She knew Doug didn't feel the same way about her —he'd told her that several times—but in that moment, she belonged to him. His soothing voice, his caring touch, the sound of his heart beating as her ear rested against his chest, her head rising and falling with every breath he took—all combined—felt like home to her.

"¡Por favor ayuda a mi esposa!" a man yelled. *"¡Socorro!"*

Shifting, Doug cupped Jenn's face in his hands and gently kissed her forehead. "I think that's the pregnant woman's husband. We have to help her. Let's take care of the survivors, and then we'll make sure Margie is returned home to her family."

She pulled away from him and wiped her eyes. "She didn't have any children, and her husband passed away last year. She mentioned two brothers and some nieces and nephews."

"We'll get her back to them." He stood, picked up the canvas knapsack, and held out his hand. "C'mon. They need our help."

Swallowing hard, she let him help her stand, then glanced down at Margie. Doug must have reached over at some point and closed the woman's eyes. Notwithstanding the blood and dirt, Margie looked at peace, and Jenn prayed she was. "Can we—can we cover her?"

"Yeah. I'll bring something back when we're done."

With his assistance, she climbed over the tree and then the next one, trying to keep her mind from falling back down a well of grief. Her hands and legs shook as the adrenaline seeped from her body, but she pushed onward. Injured people still needed their help, and that's who she would concentrate on. She reminded herself of the thought she had earlier—there would be plenty of time to mourn the dead later.

The sounds of the mountain forest returned to normal. Birds sang. The village's animals were still skittish but had calmed somewhat. Dogs barked, but not in alarm like they had before the landslide. A few goats and a cow called out to their herds.

The man whose wife was in labor grasped Jenn's arm and pulled her toward one of several huts that were still standing on that end of the village. *"¡Date prisa, por favor!"*

Doug caught up to them, and the three ran inside, where a heavily pregnant woman in her late teens or early twenties writhed in agony on an old metal full-size bed with only a thin mattress and a sheet under her. A scratchy-looking brown blanket covered her.

Her eyes were wide with fear and pain. Drenched in sweat, she panted as she cried out and clenched the blanket in both fists. Jenn reached out to her but quickly pulled her hands back—they were caked in blood and dirt. She looked at the woman's husband and showed him her hands. "Um. *¿Agua?*"

"*Si.*" He gestured to a pitcher and basin on a nearby metal and cracked, green linoleum table that looked like it'd been salvaged from the 1970s.

Jenn and Doug quickly washed their hands in the water, then again in sanitizer from the first aid kit in the emergency bag, before pulling on sterile gloves. Jenn glanced around. The floor was made of concrete, with a few scattered, handmade-looking woven rugs. The walls were constructed with wooden slats, and the roof was metal. Her eyes widened when a mouse ran across the floor and out the door. Thank God she wasn't afraid of them—her third-grade class had two pet mice and three gerbils. She used to love holding them whenever she got the chance.

"Have you ever delivered a baby?" she asked Doug, trying to get her mind focused on what they were about to do.

"Once. Sort of. In a village similar to this in Iraq. My medic did the actual delivery, but I helped."

"Well, then, you've got more experience than me. When all my nieces and nephews were born, I was in the waiting room. Although they did cover it in a health class I took in high school. But that was years ago and *very* basic."

"The mother-to-be will do most of the work." He pulled some supplies from the bag, including a white package labeled "OB-KIT" on the front. Hopefully, it had everything they would need. "Ready?"

"You and she are doing the hard part. I should be asking you that."

"Ready as I'll ever be. Let's do this."

They moved toward the bed, Doug at the foot and Jenn beside the woman, taking her hand. Doug set the OB kit on the mattress, grabbed the corner of the blanket, and then paused. "Again, your Spanish is more advanced than mine. I need you to translate as best you can."

"Okay."

"Ask what her name is and tell her I'm going to take a look and see if the baby is crowning."

Jenn squeezed the woman's hand. "*¿Cómo te llamas?*"

"M-Maria."

She glanced at the woman's husband as he sat by her head, on the opposite side of the bed from Jenn, holding Maria's hand and stroking her damp forehead and hair. Jenn repeated her question to him.

"Diego."

"*Hola. Mi nombre es Jenn y este es Doug. Vamos a ayudarte, ¿vale?*"

Panting, the woman glanced at Doug before her gaze returned to Jenn. *"Si."*

She explained to Maria what Doug was going to do, keeping her words simple because she couldn't think of a word that meant crowning in Spanish. Maria nodded and then yelled in pain as another contraction took hold. Doug lifted the blanket, peered between the woman's legs, and cursed. "Shit. We're doing this right now. The baby's coming."

Doug grabbed a disposable blanket from the kit and spread it out, tucking it as best he could under Maria's buttocks. There was no time to do anything else. "Tell her to push."

"Um…uh…" Fuck, what was the word for push? Jenn struggled for a moment before it popped into her head. "*Empujar! Empujar.*"

Maria bore down and shrieked, her body trembling.

"That's good," Doug said. "*Bueno. Otra vez. Empujar.*"

The woman pushed again at his order, screaming as she did so. The pain and fear in her eyes increased tenfold, and she squeezed Jenn's hand so tightly that Jenn thought she would break some bones, but she held on, encouraging Maria. If something good could come out of this disaster, with all the death and destruction, nothing would be better than the birth of a healthy child.

It took a few more contractions before Doug yelled, "That's it! That's it!" He grinned, and Jenn peered down to see the wet, slippery infant in his hands. "It's a girl!"

As he turned the baby onto her side, an exhausted Maria collapsed on the bed, completely spent and relieved. Doug used his gloved fingers to clean the remnants of the amniotic sac from the baby's tiny mouth, and suddenly, she took a deep breath and wailed. Her face was red and scrunched up as she announced her arrival into the world for everyone to hear. It was the most beautiful sound Jenn had ever heard.

"Jenn, hand me that blue suction bulb. I also need the clamps and scissors for the umbilical cord. There should be a blanket to wipe her down with and another to wrap her in."

She removed the sterile packaging from the blue bulb and handed it to him, then dug through the contents of the rest of the kit to find the other items. After he suctioned the remaining amniotic fluid from the baby's mouth, he laid her between Maria's spread knees. He then took the clamps from Jenn and applied them to two points on the umbilical cord, closer to the baby's abdomen. Using the sterile scissors, he cut the cord, making sure the clamps held and that neither end leaked any blood. A white sheet was used to clean the baby as best as possible.

As Jenn held the swaddling blanket, Doug picked the newborn up and placed her in Jenn's outstretched hands. Other than her nieces and nephews, she'd never seen such a beautiful baby before. Her heart ached at the thought of the little one growing up in an impoverished area, but a single glance at her parents made it clear that she would be loved. She already was.

Would Jenn look like that after giving birth one day? Like she'd been blessed with the most heavenly creature on Earth?

Her gaze shifted to Doug, whose eyes were locked on the baby, as if he still couldn't believe he'd played a part in bringing a tiny miracle into the world amid all the chaos. What Jenn wouldn't give to have him look at their child like that someday.

With her eyes welling up with emotion, unfulfilled dreams, and desperate wishes, she swaddled the infant in the blanket before placing her into her mother's arms. Maria and Diego stared at their child in awe, tears of happiness flowing down their cheeks.

Doug stood and gestured for Jenn to follow him as he moved over to the table again. They took off their gloves and washed their hands while giving the new family a private moment.

Because the hut was not that big, Jenn heard when Maria gave the baby her name, and she choked up a bit.

"I didn't catch what she said," Doug murmured in a low voice.

"They named her Esperanza." She swiped at the tears that threatened to leak onto her face. She didn't know how there were any left after the past hour. "It means hope."

He smiled, but it didn't reach his eyes. "Perfect name. It's just what we all need right now."

A few minutes later, two older women hurried into the hut and sighed in relief when they saw the healthy baby nursing at her mother's breast. From what Jenn gathered from their rapid-fire Spanish, they were Maria's aunts and would take over for Doug and Jenn, not that there was much left to do at that point except deliver the placenta when it was time.

As the two Americans headed for the door, Diego rushed over to them, shaking their hands. *"¡Gracias! ¡Gracias! Que Dios esté contigo."*

While Jenn was baptized as a Catholic, she'd rarely attended Mass after her parents' funeral. Stepping into a church only dredged up painful memories—the moment she was forced to accept that she would never see her mother or father again. But it was nice for Diego to wish God would bless them for helping his family.

Outside, the normal sounds of the surrounding forest were interspersed with the voices of adults and children talking or crying, dogs barking, and the roar of chainsaws in action on the other side of the mudslide.

Jenn glanced around the nearly annihilated village, her gaze settling on an approximate point of where they'd left Margie. It was difficult to tell amid all the wreckage. She shook her head, displacing the thoughts of the friend she'd lost. Nothing could be done for the older woman now. After things calmed down and it was possible, they would recover her body. "Now what?"

"Let me check in with Romeo." Doug stood beside her and pulled the radio from his pocket. "We can't risk trying to cross that mess to get to them—not yet anyway. If another slide starts, we'll go with it."

The thought chilled her to the bone. Some villagers were probably buried under the dirt and trees, while others may have been swept down the mountain and killed that way. How she and Doug had survived when others hadn't was beyond her comprehension, but she was grateful they were both still alive.

"Romeo, you there?"

A long pause was followed by a squelch and then, "Yeah, I'm here. Sit-rep."

"We helped deliver a baby—a healthy little girl, so that's good news. The bad news is we lost Margie. She was pinned under a tree, and we couldn't get her out." He eyed their surroundings. Several people comforted each other, while others gathered what supplies they could salvage. "Things are relatively quiet over here now. From what I can see, we've got a few injuries, but nothing critical yet. We'll try to locate everyone on this end and get a head count and list of injuries. We might have lost some villagers in the slide, but I don't know for sure. Unfortunately, we can't risk poking around."

"Copy that. And we've got the same issues here—not going to risk anyone digging in that mess without backup, but we still have buildings that need to be searched for survivors. Parsons got through to emergency services. They're sending a military unit up to us, but it's going to take time. The heavy equipment won't reach us until at least tomorrow morning, so you're stuck over there tonight. Do you have shelter?"

"We'll find something. Not sure about food and water, though."

"Got something you can use to make a visible target? A helicopter is en route with supplies. We'll tell them to drop what they can on both sides of the slide."

He bent over and opened the large canvas knapsack on the ground by his feet. "Roadside flares are in the emergency kit. I'll use those."

"Copy that. Stay safe, and we'll keep you posted."

"Thanks."

Doug stuck the radio back into his pocket, then pulled a wrapped silver blanket out of the emergency kit.

"What's that?" she asked.

"A survival blanket. You use it in cold weather to stay warm. We have three of them, so I thought I'd use this one for..." He gestured toward the massive pile of trees, dirt, and rocks.

Margie. He hadn't forgotten her or Jenn's request to cover her. She inhaled a sharp breath and nodded, trying to keep from breaking down again. "Thank you."

He reached out and briefly rubbed her upper arm. "I'll be right back."

"Be careful."

CHAPTER TWELVE

Doug said a small prayer for the deceased woman's soul as he covered her head and upper torso with the rescue blanket. He placed a sizable rock on each corner to keep it from blowing away.

His heart ached for Jenn. While the circumstances were vastly different from when she lost her parents, her new friend's death in such a brutal manner was understandably hard on her. He could see it in her eyes. As far as he was aware, that was the first time she had ever seen someone she knew die right in front of her, and the fact that they'd seemed close made it worse. Meanwhile, Doug had served in combat, watching his teammates die in horrific ways that he could never forget. He'd also killed many people during that time. Yes, they were the enemy, but someone must have loved them—their parents, siblings, spouses, or children. Someone mourned their deaths as Doug thanked God he hadn't been the one to fall in the kill-or-be-killed situations.

Then there was Jacob Keller, Doug's coworker at Blackhawk Security, who was shot and killed while they were protecting Jenn four years ago. The owners of Trident and Blackhawk were good friends and often shared personnel, equipment, and intel. That was how the two men from BHS ended up on Jenn's detail. It was only the third time they were partnered together. They were still in the process of learning the other's strengths, weaknesses, and personal details when Keller was killed instantly by a 9mm bullet to the head at close range.

While Doug's former boss, Chase Dixon, and his current ones, Ian, Devon, and the rest of the original Trident Security Alpha Team, told him he hadn't done anything wrong, he still wasn't convinced. Many a night, he awoke in a panic, reliving the event repeatedly in his mind. With sweat pouring off him, he'd gasp for air as if his lung was once again deflated from the bullet that tore through his chest. He'd see Keller's lifeless body, with half his face missing, and blood and brain matter splattered over the windshield and dashboard. He'd hear Jenn's desperate screams for help, knowing he couldn't do anything to save her. The kidnappers left him for dead. All he could do at the time was speed-dial Devon for help. The man passed the information to Brody before hightailing it to the scene. Yeah, it caused about a thirty-second delay in alerting 9-1-1, but Brody was able to relay more information to emergency services than Doug could before he passed out. With a computer system that some joked rivaled NASA's, Brody knew Doug's exact location and was able to give it to the dispatcher along with a description of Jenn and the probable motive behind the kidnapping.

Sighing, Doug pushed the thoughts of the dead and the past from his mind. Over the downed trees and other wreckage, his gaze found Jenn pacing back and forth outside Maria and Diego's hut. Her shoulders were slumped as she wiped her eyes and shook her head. Tension rolled over her—he could tell even from that distance. Despite her grief and being disheveled and covered in mud, she was still the most beautiful woman he'd ever met. The urge to go to her, pull her into his arms, and comfort her was too strong for him to deny.

He climbed back over the trees and strode over to her, getting in her path and forcing her to stop. Her red, swollen, watery eyes rose to meet his. The ache in his chest increased, and not where it usually hurt—under the bullet scar. No, it was his heart squeezing in reaction to seeing her so broken in her sorrow. She'd been through so much in her young life, more than anyone should in any length of time, and the past few hours heaped more anguish on her.

"C'mere." Grasping her upper arms, he drew her close and hugged her. Despite being seven inches shorter than his six-foot-three frame, they fit together like she was made for him. At first, she was stiff in his arms, tucking her own between them, but then her body melted against his, her face nestled just below his neck. A deep shuddering breath escaped her, and she wrapped her arms around his waist. Warm puffs of air caressed his skin every time she exhaled, leaving goose bumps in their wake.

They stood there silently for a minute or two, neither saying a word nor doing anything but holding on to the other. Of course, his cock didn't get the memo that nothing sexual would happen, and he cursed it in his mind and kept a sliver of distance between his pelvis and her abdomen.

Finally, Jenn squeezed him tighter for a moment before pulling away. "Thank you. I needed that."

"I did too." The huskiness in his voice caught him off guard, and he cleared his throat. Pivoting away from her, under the guise of scanning their surroundings, he furtively adjusted his semi-hard dick, willing it to behave.

Once he could do so without any discomfort, he crouched down, pulled two reusable water bottles from the knapsack, and held one out to her. "Here. Drink before you get dehydrated."

She took it and unscrewed the top before guzzling several mouthfuls of water. He had to rip his gaze from her throat. *Damn it.* Watching her swallow made him hard again, his mind drifting to how that same motion might feel if he were ever lucky enough to have her mouth wrapped around his cock.

This time, when he turned away from her and glanced around, he forced himself to focus on the survivors on that side of the village. He drank from his bottle, wishing the lukewarm water would slake his desire as much as it quenched his thirst. The bottle was nearly empty when he recapped it. "Let's...uh...let's see who else needs our help."

They worked side by side, checking on the people who were already outdoors, triaging and treating their injuries. Then, they searched each of the remaining buildings for anyone else who needed assistance. In all, Doug counted twenty-two people—nine children and thirteen adults—not including him and Jenn. More than half weren't injured with anything other than some minor scrapes and bruises. A few had broken bones, and one man suffered a compound fracture of his forearm that would require surgery. Doug did his best to splint it, keeping it immobile until the military rescue team arrived. An older woman had symptoms of a heart attack but seemed stable.

Nothing could be done beyond keeping her calm and comfortable in her home, which her family took care of. Doug passed all the information on to Romeo.

It was nearly dusk when the *thump, thump, thump* of a helicopter resounded through the air. Doug grabbed the flares from the emergency kit, lit them, and created a large triangular target in the middle of the dirt road. Soon, a UH-60 Black Hawk helicopter hovered above the tree line and slowly lowered a large bundle of supplies, wrapped in rope netting. Once it hit the ground, Doug hurried over and released the drop line's hook from the netting, which loosened from around the heap. The helicopter then flew to the other side of the landslide and dropped more supplies there.

Jenn approached him as he searched the contents of several large crates and duffel bags. "Do you need help?"

"Yeah. Help me sort what they sent while we still have some light." He used a crowbar he found attached to a duffel bag with a bungee cord to open the crates. "We've got water, what looks like the Colombian version of MREs—ready-to-eat meals—first aid supplies, lanterns, flashlights, batteries, blankets, and more."

Diego and another man came over and volunteered to assist. Between the four of them, it didn't take long to inventory everything and parcel out the supplies to those in need. While it wasn't a lot, there was enough to sustain two dozen people for at least two, maybe three days at the most, until the rescue units could safely reach them. Hopefully, it wouldn't take that long, though.

After finding a bottle of aspirin among the first aid supplies, he returned to the potential heart attack patient and gave her two pills, hoping they would prevent any clots from forming in her system. It wasn't much, but at least she and her family appeared relieved he could do something for her. As far as he could tell, her pulse and respiration rates were steady and regular. Maybe it had only been a panic attack—who could blame her after everything that happened? Either way, she was stable.

After the supplies were distributed, Diego pointed to a small cabin that belonged to his brother's family. They'd all gone to the chapel earlier, where they were hopefully still safe. Diego told Jenn and Doug they could spend the night in there. It was far enough away from the landslide for Doug to accept the offer. He'd slept in far worse places, but as long as they were protected from the elements, he didn't care—they didn't have much of a choice either.

The temperature was dropping, but Doug's go-bag, with his spare clothes, and Jenn's sweatshirt were back at the chapel, which did them no good. At least it was still warm enough that neither shivered, but that could change within half an hour.

They carried their supplies to the cabin and placed everything inside, except for two bottles of water, two green plastic bags—the MREs—and a package of unscented wet wipes. A nearly full moon rising overhead was bright enough that they didn't need a flashlight, so they decided to sit outside, on a wooden bench under a window, and eat. The light would only attract mosquitoes and gnats—it was bad enough that the scent of human sweat lured them in.

They used about a dozen wipes each to clean their faces, necks, arms, and hands as thoroughly as possible. He found a can of bug spray in the knapsack earlier, and they put a little on in an attempt to keep the flying nuisances away.

When Jenn opened her meal bag and cautiously peered inside, Doug chuckled for the first time all day. At least as far as he could remember. "Have you ever eaten an MRE?"

"Once," she replied, pulling out two white packages with labels on them. One was *tamales* while the other was *arroz atollado*, otherwise known as pork risotto. Doug pulled out the same. Other packages contained food for breakfast and lunch, along with a few additional items. "When I was a freshman in high school. One of my friends dared a bunch of us to try them. We were all military brats, so of course, no one was going to turn down a dare."

When she didn't continue, he side-eyed her as he opened his meal. "Well? What happened?"

"They had a variety of them. As I'm sure you know, it's a literal crap shoot which one you pick. And don't yell at me for saying crap." He stayed silent, and she continued. "Anyway, we put them in a bag and mixed them up, then took turns pulling one out without knowing what it was. I was lucky and got the cheese tortellini." She paused and stared out into the night. "Wow. Ten years later, I still remember which one I ate. Guess it was more memorable than I realized." She shrugged. "Anyway, it wasn't great, but it wasn't too nasty either. If I was starving and no better alternatives were available, I'd eat it again. But a few of my friends had to eat stuff that gave them...um...let's say *severe* gastrointestinal distress."

He laughed at her polite way of saying they each ended up with a bad case of diarrhea. "I'm sure they did. You learn real quick which meals are safe and which ones will leave you hurting. The chicken burrito bowl is the worst, at least from my experience."

"Yeah. I heard Cain got sick during that training mission in the Rockies. He turned green any time someone mentioned MREs—or burritos for that matter—for weeks afterward."

Cain Foster was a retired Secret Service agent who

was one of two leaders of the Trident Security Omega Team. He had his first taste of an MRE on that trip, when a routine training exercise turned into a real mission to find a missing college student in foul weather. His teammates, all of whom had served in branches of the military before being hired by the private security company, knew which meals to avoid. So the poor guy got the ones nobody else wanted and suffered for his lack of experience with them.

They ate with little talking after that, each lost in their own thoughts and meal. It had been a while since Doug ate an MRE, but surprisingly, the tamales weren't half bad. Either that or he was hungrier than he'd realized. When those were gone, he dove into the risotto, a relatively dry biscuit, and some cookies. Jenn must've been as hungry as he was since she ate the same.

Saving the breakfast and lunch packages for tomorrow, Doug gathered the leftovers and garbage, then brought them inside, stuffing them into the emergency bag and zipping it up to keep out any insects and prevent them from attracting any animals.

He turned on one of the camping lanterns that the helicopter had dropped off, lighting up the interior of the home. It was larger than Diego and Maria's, but instead of the exterior walls being constructed from wood, they were concrete, as was the floor. The non-load-bearing interior walls were made of wood, while the roof was constructed of metal. A thin full-size mattress on a wooden bed, with worn pillows and blankets, sat behind a wall and an open curtain that could be pulled to block the doorway. Two woven straw mats, with pillows and blankets, were positioned on the opposite side of the living area, which consisted of an old table, chairs, and a small kitchen area. An old potbelly stove stood in the corner—an unexpected find. A tiny bathroom was located in the back corner and consisted of only a wooden toilet and a small square table beside it, which held a pitcher of water and a bowl.

While searching the other homes earlier, he discovered the locals had a rudimentary septic system in place, and for that he was grateful. It wasn't the greatest, but at least they didn't have to go into the woods in the dark to relieve themselves as they'd both done earlier. The chapel was one of the few buildings not hooked up to the system. A nearby river and waterfall provided the village's water supply. A wood and metal chute had been built to funnel the water to the residents, but it was damaged in the quake. Diego told them earlier that the falls were close enough to carry buckets to and from until the chute could be repaired.

Jenn inspected the home's interior with her arms

wrapped around her waist. "I will never in my life take for granted what I have. These poor people. This is all they have, and then to lose half the village and possibly family members or their own lives. I just..."

She shook her head but didn't finish the sentence, nor did Doug need her to. He understood, having seen people living similarly in third-world countries during his tours in the Marines.

A noise caught their attention, and they turned to see a black and brown mid-sized mutt trot in through the open front door, its nails clicking on the concrete floor. A quick peek told Doug it was a female. Her tongue lolled from her mouth as her tail wagged, but she kept her distance from them.

He squatted and held out his hand. "Hey there, girl. Are we in your home?"

The dog whined and lowered her head but didn't come closer.

"Here. Try this." Jenn opened the emergency kit on the table, found one of the unopened MREs, and pulled out a biscuit and a package marked *"Sudado con Papas y Carne"*–stew with potatoes and meat. After giving Doug the biscuit, she opened the coated cardboard bowl that came with the stew, added a little water, and used her finger to stir the contents.

Meanwhile, Doug held out half of the biscuit to the dog. "C'mere, pup. Want something to eat?" Realizing he forgot where he was, he rolled his eyes, then repeated the question in Spanish. That and the scent of food got her attention, and she inched forward, gently taking the biscuit from his hand. At least he didn't have to worry about losing a finger since she didn't appear feral. The dog gobbled the biscuit in two bites, and Doug gave her the second half. She then scarfed down the stew when Jenn set the bowl on the floor. Once it was empty, she refilled the bowl with some water, which disappeared as quickly as the food.

With a semi-full belly, the dog was content enough to wander over to the mats on the floor. She spun around three times on top of a blanket before lying down. With a sigh, she closed her eyes.

"Guess she does live here." Jenn added more water to the bowl and placed it by the dog.

"Hopefully, she'll alert us to any danger."

Her gaze whipped to his. "Do you think we're still in danger?"

He was an idiot, scaring her like that after the day they'd had. "No, I don't. But I can't predict the future, and I don't know the area, so it's good that she's here with us. Animals sense threats before we notice anything."

"Like right before the landslide, they all started going nuts."

"Exactly."

Doug secured the front door and the wooden shutters on the home's three glassless windows. He then grabbed the rescue blankets and the wool ones they got from the military supplies and handed Jenn one of each. Since the sun went down, the temperature had dropped by at least fifteen degrees. It was probably a lot warmer back at the commune, but they were now at a much higher elevation, and the blankets were needed. While there was a small stack of wood beside the potbelly stove, Doug didn't want to risk using it. It was too dark out for him to climb onto the roof and inspect the exhaust pipe to make sure it wasn't damaged during the quake and wouldn't force carbon monoxide back into the cabin.

"You take the bed," he told her. "I'll put the other mat on the floor next to you and sleep on that." He could have left the mat where it was and slept beside the dog, but he wanted to be near Jenn in case another earthquake or landslide struck.

He nearly jumped when she touched his arm, sending shocks of desire through his body. By the grace of God, he stayed still, though. "Doug, please. I'm not letting you sleep on the floor. There's enough room on the bed."

When he started to protest, she huffed, grabbed the lantern, and walked backward toward the bedroom, staring at him like he was the most idiotic man on the planet. "Oh, for Christ's sake. We're both adults—we can sleep beside each other, *platonically*." She pivoted and turned her back to him. "I won't tell anyone. Besides, I'm too exhausted to jump your bones, and I wouldn't anyway after you've made it plain as day that you don't find me attractive."

What? She thinks I find her unattractive? What the fuck?

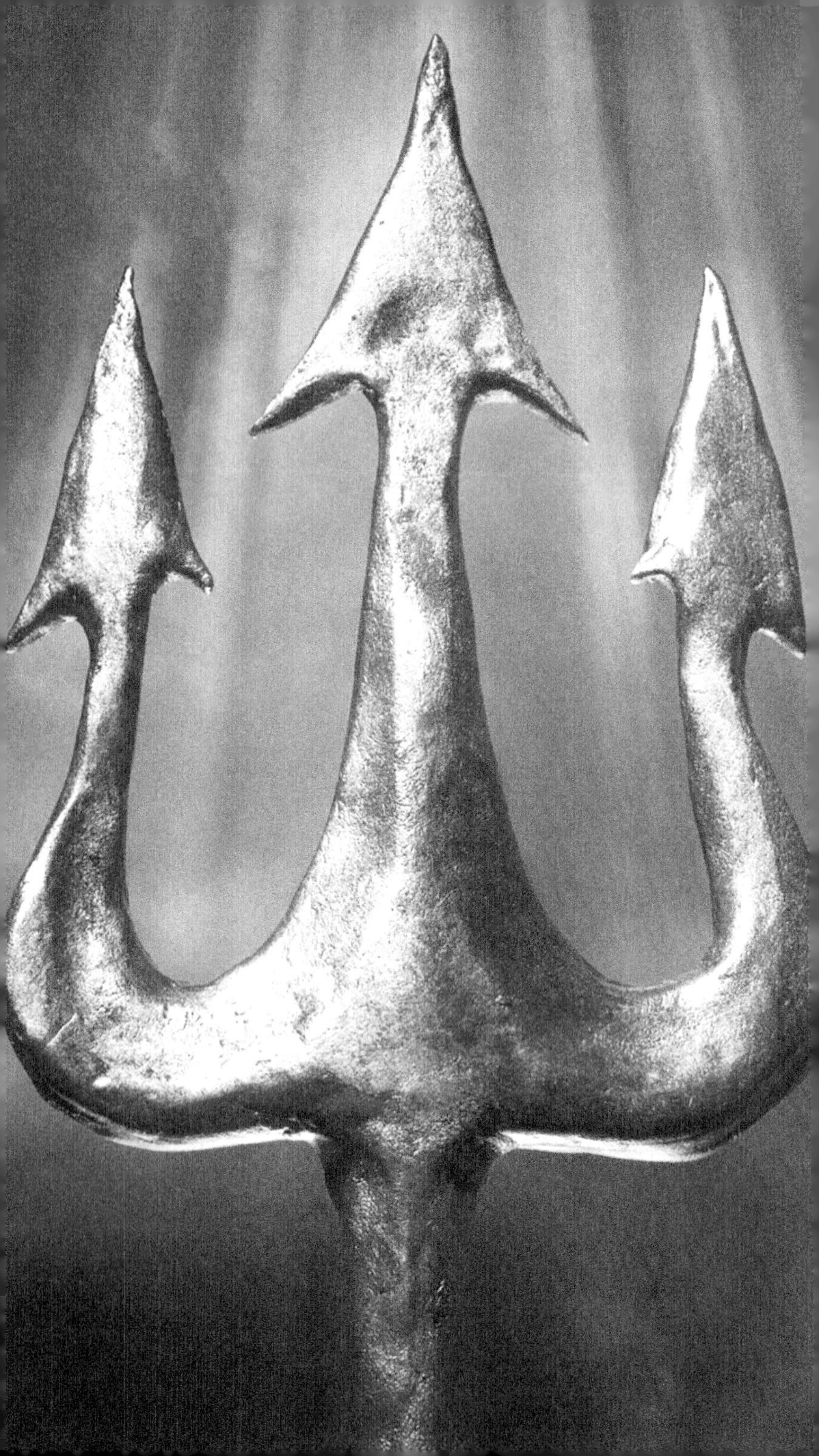

CHAPTER THIRTEEN

His past interactions with Jenn flooded Doug's mind, especially that kiss they shared. He kept his distance not because he didn't think she was beautiful—she definitely was—but she deserved someone closer to her age who didn't come with baggage like he did. He thought he'd made his reasoning for not pursuing her clear, but apparently that wasn't the case. Regardless, platonically or not, he wasn't sharing a bed with her. It wasn't that he didn't trust her. The problem was he didn't trust himself unless he managed to stay awake all night, which would be impossible—he was as exhausted as she was. The last thing he needed was to reach for her in his sleep, pull her into his arms, and wrap his body around hers the way he ached to. So the only viable option was for him to sleep on the floor.

To avoid any inadvertent unconscious cuddling during the night, he grabbed the unoccupied mat, said goodnight to the dog, and then carried everything he needed into the other room. Jenn rolled her eyes when she saw the mat but didn't say anything. While he prepared his sleeping area, she carefully inspected the mattress, blankets, and two pillows already on the bed. "No bedbugs or other creepy crawlers. That's good. One less thing to worry about."

She tossed him one of the pillows before spreading the rescue blanket over the entire bed, tucking the other pillow under it. The wool blanket went over that. After kicking off her sneakers, she turned away from him, pulled her shirt over her head, placed it on a bedside table, and started to remove her pants before he comprehended what she was doing. Doug's eyes widened at the sight of the sports bra straps over her bare back. He quickly spun around, facing the other way and staring at the wall. "What the hell are you doing, Jenn?"

"Getting comfortable. My clothes are dirty and still damp, and I have nothing else to wear, so they at least have to dry before I put them back on tomorrow."

As much as that made sense, he wasn't happy about it. His dick was, but his brain was not. "Can you at least see if there is anything you can borrow to sleep in from whoever lives here?"

"Not necessary." Squeaking and rustling sounds

came from behind him, and he realized she'd climbed onto the bed. When he just stood there, unsure of what to do, she huffed. "You can turn around now. I'm under the blanket and still have my underwear on. Who knew you were such a prude?"

His temples throbbed as he gritted his teeth. "I'm *not* a prude." Definitely not because now he tried to imagine what she looked like under the covers. Were her panties black like the bra? Did they have lace on them? *Shit!*

He furtively adjusted himself. "I was just giving you what little privacy I could in this fucked up situation."

"Well, if that's the case, then thank you."

Pivoting slowly, he was grateful and more than a bit disappointed to see the blanket covered everything but her neck and head as she lay on the opposite side of the bed, with her back to him. Her clothes were draped over a chair in the corner of the room. She glanced over her shoulder before turning away again. "Feel free to get comfortable too. I won't look."

Shaking his head, he sat on the edge of the bed and unlaced his boots to get them and his filthy socks off. No way in hell would he strip down to his skivvies in the same room as her, but he did remove his shirt and hung it to dry on a hook he spotted screwed into the wall. During his time in the military, he learned to sleep in the worst of conditions, and being in damp, dirty cargo pants didn't even come close to some of his experiences.

Jenn had set the lantern on a chest at the foot of the bed, and he moved it within reach before turning the switch until the light was almost off. It was just bright enough for them to see in case of an emergency, but it wouldn't hinder their sleep. Exhausted, he stretched out on his makeshift bed on the floor and pulled the wool blanket over him. Within minutes, they were both fast asleep.

Jenn sank onto the couch in the living room of her apartment. She was finally alone—well, except for Beau, who'd followed her from Uncle Ian's apartment and jumped up and lay down next to her. The dog always seemed to know when his humans needed him. Jenn buried her face into his furry neck and let the tears, which she had held back for hours, finally flow. She knew it was from an adrenaline crash—she'd experienced it more than once in her life—but she hadn't wanted Doug to see her cry. He already thought she was still a child, and that would have proven it to him.

Those two assholes who harassed her in the parking lot of Donovan's and then attacked Doug when he came to her defense now faced numerous charges, including assault with a deadly weapon. One was already sitting in a city jail cell, while the other was in the hospital. He needed surgery on his knee after Jenn used a collapsible baton she kept in her car to incapacitate him. Doug had taken down the other guy, then yelled at Jenn for not following his order to run inside. She couldn't leave him when it was two against one, so she did what her uncles had trained her to do in situations like that. While she was grateful he showed up when he did, it irritated her that he was still pissed she hadn't followed his orders to run away. Her uncles were annoyed about that, too, but at least they'd expressed how proud of her they were.

After Jenn called the social services department where she interned to let them know she wouldn't be back until tomorrow, Uncle Ian accompanied her and Doug to the police station, where they gave their statements. Uncle Brody also provided the police with surveillance video from Donovan's system, which he'd installed.

Once they arrived back at the TS compound and filled everyone else in, Angie invited Jenn and Doug to stay for dinner. Both declined the offer. Doug claimed he had work to finish, and Jenn thanked her aunt but said she wasn't hungry, which was the truth. She couldn't stomach anything right then. Maybe later.

At twenty-two, Jenn had already gone through plenty of emotional trauma in her life—hell, it was really only during the last five years—but today, she proved to her uncles, and herself, that the training they'd given her paid off. She just wished Doug could see she was a competent adult who could defend herself if needed.

Beside her, Beau tensed and let out a low growl. Moments later, someone knocked on her door. The dog must have sensed they weren't a threat—not that one could easily get near her apartment—because he relaxed again, his tail thumping on the couch.

Figuring it was one of her aunts or uncles checking up on her, Jenn wiped her eyes with the back of her hands, then stood and answered the door. Her heart rate sped up when she found Doug standing in the small foyer she shared with Nick and Uncle Jake, who had the apartment above her. The burning embers smoldering in her core flared at the sight of him. There was no way that what she felt for this man was a fabrication her mind had created. She just needed to convince him of that fact.

He frowned when he saw her red eyes. "You've been crying. Are you okay?"

She shrugged. It wouldn't do her any good to deny her earlier tears. "Yeah, just an adrenaline crash. I'm fine." When he remained still and silent, just staring at her, she asked, "What are you doing here?"

He suddenly seemed unsure of himself, flexing and balling his hands over and over while looking around the basic foyer like it was the most interesting place he'd ever been. His eyes darted everywhere but avoided landing on her. "I...um...I was getting ready to head home and just wanted to make sure you're okay."

"I'm fine," she repeated, doubting he believed her. "Do you want to come in?"

He glanced over her shoulder into the apartment, then shook his head. "I—um—better not."

Damn, the man frustrated her. "Why? Because we'd be alone, and you think I'm going to jump you?"

"Jenn—"

She crossed her arms and glared at him. "Don't 'Jenn' me, Doug. I get it. You think I'm too young for you, and I'll always be that way. Well, you know what? You're wrong. Look at my Uncle Devon and Aunt Kristen—she's twenty-nine and he's thirty-nine. And Jake is nine years older than Nick. And Uncle Brody is six years older than Fancy. So you being eight years older than me is not a big thing—at least, not for me or anyone else."

"They may have big age differences, but they're all a lot older than you, Jenn. And it's not just that. You've got this—this hero-complex thing when it comes to me—"

"What?" She tossed her hands into the air. The man was going to drive her absolutely and utterly insane. "Are you kidding me? Trust me, Doug. What I feel for you has nothing to do with you being my bodyguard and taking a bullet for me. Do you know how scared I was while Aunt Angie and I were being held hostage? I was scared more for you than myself—I thought you were dead or dying, and there was nothing I could do about it. If you'd died, I would've been devastated. Not only because I would have lost you, but because I would never have had the opportu-

nity to tell you I love you." Oh, shit. I did not just say that!

The stunned look on Doug's face told her she, indeed, had just confessed her love for him. Again, he shook his head. "Jenn—"

Before he could say anything else, she threw caution to the wind and wrapped her arms around his neck. Her lips met his, and Jenn almost liquefied. For years, she dreamed about what it would be like to kiss Doug Henderson, and there she was doing it.

Doug froze as she melded their lips together, then his hands grasped her hips. When he tried to push her away, she tightened her hold around his neck. If this was the only time she ever kissed him, she wanted something to remember. She wanted him to kiss her back and prove to her that it wasn't a one-sided attraction she felt between them.

Parting her lips, she slid her tongue between them and licked his mouth. His hold on her hips increased, but instead of pushing her away, he pulled her closer. Oh, God! He was hard—for her. Doug groaned, then suddenly, took control of the kiss. One hand came up and grabbed her hair. He angled her head to the side as his tongue plunged into her mouth, dueling with her own.

The kiss was better than she dreamed it would be—and she'd dreamed of it often. She ran her fingers through his silky hair and rubbed her chest against his. Her nipples pebbled and sent delicious sensations down to her clit. It throbbed, wanting more. Doug pivoted them and used his body to press her against the door jamb, and she moaned when she felt his erection thicken between them. Heaven—she was in heaven and never wanted to leave.

Without warning, Doug ripped his mouth from hers and practically leaped out from the doorway into the foyer, panting and trembling. "Shit! Jenn. That—that shouldn't have happened. I shouldn't have—"

Tears welled when she saw the horror he felt reflected in his eyes. That, more than anything, tore her heart out and threw it into the nearest garbage can. "Don't say that. I kissed you, Doug. I wanted to, and I wanted you to kiss me back. I've wanted it for so long. Don't stand there and tell me you don't feel the attraction between us. You wouldn't have kissed me like that if you didn't. You—"

"Jenn, stop." He ran a hand down his face. "I'm sorry, but it shouldn't have happened, and it won't happen again. I'm sorry."

"It will if you get over yourself and let it. Goodbye, Doug."

She was about to close the door in his face when a deafening boom accompanied the foyer wall exploding inward. She jumped back as a tsunami of mud rushed in, causing the floor to collapse under Doug's feet. Wide-eyed and panicked, Jenn screamed and reached for him as he vanished into a massive sinkhole, and the mud covered him. "Doug! Nooooooooo! Oh, my God! Doug! No! No! No! Come back!"

"Jenn! Wake up! Jenn. I'm here. Wake up!"

Her eyes flew open as she gasped for air. She was drenched in sweat as she tried to sit up, but Doug's arms prevented her from doing so. They were wrapped around her as he spoke soothingly. "It's okay, sweetheart. Just a nightmare. You're all right. I've got you."

Her chest heaved as the images of Doug dying right in front of her still swirled in her mind.

"It's okay," he repeated. "Shh. I'm right here, honey. I'm right here."

Her taut muscles began to relax as her brain finally registered that he was alive and talking to her. The last of her nightmare waned and disappeared as the room came into focus. She tried to catch her breath, but her mouth was bone dry and her throat was sore from screaming. "W-water. P-please."

"Sure. Hang on."

She instantly regretted the request because he released her and stood. He turned the knob on the lantern until it was bright enough to see better before hurrying out to the other room. Moments later, he returned with a water bottle, cracking open and removing the cap before handing it to her. "Here. Don't gulp. Take sips first."

Her stomach undulated, threatening to revolt if anything was put into it, so she did as he said, taking small sips until she was certain the water would stay down.

She was surprised when he sat beside her again,

close enough for her to feel the heat radiating off his body. It was then she noticed he only wore his pants. His muscular torso was gloriously naked, and her fingers itched to touch him and find out if the brown hair on his chest was as soft as it looked. Over his right nipple was the puckered scar from where the bullet had pierced his body, nearly killing him. She stared at it for a moment, hating the memories it conjured up. On the opposite side of his chest, over his heart, was a Celtic cross tattoo—that was new. It'd been about six months since she last saw him shirtless in the gym at the Trident compound, and he didn't have the inked image then.

"Wh—" She coughed and then cleared her throat, which still felt dry after her nightmare. "When did you get the tattoo?"

He glanced down at it. "About four months ago. My grandfather had a similar cross, and I wanted to get one in his memory."

She knew his grandfather passed away last year, but he and his wife lived in Scotland, and the funeral was only a small family gathering at the elderly man's request. Doug made the trip with his parents, his siblings, and their families. Instead of sending flowers, Ian and Devon arranged to pay for the family's after-funeral repast at a Scottish pub. It was something Doug hadn't expected, but Jenn knew he deeply appreciated the gesture.

Her gaze dropped from the tattoo to his ripped abdomen, where the hair got darker and narrower before disappearing under the waistband of his pants. She gulped the water that time, needing it to quench not only her thirst but her increasing desire.

His eyes narrowed, and he pointed at her upper arm. "Where did you get that from? The landslide?"

She glanced down at the large bruise that'd formed. It was an ugly black and blue, further along than the others she'd gotten on her legs and arms from being pelted by rocks and tripping. She had a few scraps and cuts, too, but nothing serious. "No. Tony and I were doing inventory in the clinic when the earthquake hit. I smashed my arm against the door jamb while we were trying to get outside."

Gently brushing his fingertips around the edges of the discoloration, he inspected it in silence for almost a full minute, as if reassuring himself it wasn't worse than it looked. His touch sent a shiver down her spine and sped up her heart rate. "Do you want to talk about it?"

Distracted by her body's reaction to him, she wasn't sure what he was referring to. "Hmm? The bruise?"

"No, the nightmare. What was it about?"

Another shiver coursed through her. That time, he must've noticed because he put his arm around her shoulders and pulled her closer. Unable to help herself, she sighed and cuddled against his chest, resting her head on his shoulder and placing a hand over his tattoo. Being with him like that was what she longed for every day, and she'd be crazy not to take advantage of the situation—at least until he pulled away again, which he undoubtedly would do as soon as reality hit him.

She couldn't tell him about the horrible dream except for the very last part. Talking about their one shared kiss would be too awkward. "A...um...There was another mudslide, and you got swept away in it. I-I couldn't do anything to save you."

Surprisingly, he gently squeezed her, then kissed the top of her head. She rarely saw this tender side to him and reveled in it. Usually, he always seemed to want to get as far away from her as possible. "It was just a nightmare. I'm alive and kicking. Hopefully, we'll get out of here tomorrow when the cavalry arrives. For now, we're safe."

Taking an uncalculated risk, Jenn let her fingers skate across the bare skin of his chest, and Doug froze. "Jenn..."

"Shh. Please," she whispered before leaning down and brushing her lips against the bullet scar. Doug inhaled sharply but didn't move or speak. She took that as a good sign and let her hand roam his upper torso while her tongue peeked out and licked his nipple.

"Fuck!" The curse came from his mouth as if a reverent prayer, and his hand on her upper arm tightened. A glance down told her his body reacted to her touch in a good way, if the growing erection in his pants was any indication.

Tilting her head back, she met his heavy-lidded gaze. "Kiss me, Doug. Please."

"I—"

"Please," she insisted as she sat up and straddled his hips. She crossed her arms, grabbed the bottom hem of her sports bra, and lifted it over her head, tossing it aside. Her nipples peaked in the cooler air.

Doug inhaled deeply and cursed again, his hands clutching her waist. She was unsure if it was to keep her there or to resist the urge to touch her anywhere else. Either way, she didn't care as long as he wasn't pushing her aside and running away. She leaned down, and her heavy breasts brushing against his muscular chest had them both moaning.

Her mouth hovered over his. "Don't make me beg. Just kiss me."

His gaze searched hers, and whatever he saw there had him cursing a third time before thrusting his hand into her hair and closing the distance between them. Their mouths met in a punishing yet passionate kiss that stole her breath. His other hand spread across her bare back and pulled her down until their bodies were flush together. Maddening need pooled in her core as she opened her lips and invited his tongue inside. He tightened the hold on her hair to the point of pain, but all that did was ramp up her desire. She writhed in his arms, loving the feel of his hard body against her softer one. At the apex of her legs, she felt his stiff length twitch against her throbbing clit.

Doug's mouth left hers, licking and kissing along her jaw and down her neck. "Oh, God, Jenn. Fuck, you feel so good."

He thrust his hips upward before tightening his hold on her and rolling them as one until he was on top. Lifting his head, he pushed up with his hands on either side of her ears and stared down at her. In his dark eyes, she saw the moment he considered pulling away, and she wrapped her arms around his neck, holding him there. "No. Don't you dare, Doug. I'm an adult woman who knows who and what she wants, and that's you. I've wanted you for a long time. This isn't a schoolyard crush or a fucking hero-worship thing. This is me wanting an incredibly sexy man whom I can't stop thinking about. Dreaming about. When you forget to scowl at me or avoid me, you make me laugh. You're strong, intelligent, sweet, funny, and so much more, and everything I ever hoped to find in a man. My father and uncles set a high bar. Since I was old enough to have my first crush, I knew I'd never settle for anyone they would disapprove of. That meant no jackasses who treated girls and women like they were beneath them. I want someone who will respect me like my dad respected my mom, and how my uncles respect their spouses.

"You've been a jerk to me in the past, but I know it's because you were fighting this attraction between us. You feel it—I know you do. You freaked out last year when I slipped and said I was in love with you. The only reason I regret that is because you weren't ready to hear it. But I can't deny my feelings for you. Not when they consume me. I'm not a teenager anymore and haven't been for several years. Stop fighting this, Doug. Please. Let go of all the reasons you think being with me is a bad idea because it's not."

She traced his brow with her fingers. "I came down here because I thought being away from you for a few months would help me move on and forget about you. But that didn't happen because I've been counting down the days until I could see you again, even though things would probably go back to the status quo between us. All I'm asking is for you to give us a chance."

There. She'd bared her heart and soul to him, and now the only thing she could do was wait for a response and pray it was one she wanted to hear. She didn't know what she'd do if it weren't.

He brushed a few strands of her hair off her face. "You said I thought you weren't attractive." His voice was rough, raspy, and oh, so sexy.

"Huh?"

"Earlier, you said you wouldn't jump my bones because I made it clear I didn't think you were attractive. Or something to that effect." He dropped down onto his forearms, bringing their bodies closer together but not enough for her satisfaction. "Don't you ever think I don't find you attractive, Jenn. That's so far from the truth, it isn't funny. I can't deny I have feelings for you anymore—strong feelings—but we have to consider other things."

"Like what?"

He cocked his head to the side. "Like our age difference."

"That's only been a problem for you. There are a few large age differences between my uncles and aunts—you know that. Eight years is *not* a big deal. It would be if I were thirteen and you were twenty-one, but we're both consenting adults now, so that issue is moot. What else do we need to consider?"

"I work for your godfather, who will probably torture me before dumping my sorry ass in the Gulf of Mexico if he ever finds out I touched you."

She smiled. "Uncle Ian only wants the best for me, but sometimes he forgets that I'm the one who gets to decide what that is. Or in this case, who that is." She ran her hands over his bare shoulders. "I want you, Doug. I want you to kiss me and make love to me. Hell, I just want to be with you without you frowning at me, yelling at me not to curse, or treating me like a child. I don't care what we do as long as we're together and just enjoying ourselves."

"I didn't yell when you cursed a few minutes ago."

Out of everything she'd just said, that's all he could come up with as a response? Well, it was a start, and she would take it.

Her smile widened. "That's right. You didn't. Hmm. Go figure." She slid her hands up and around his neck again before pulling him toward her. "Now, if you're done with the excuses, will you please kiss me again?"

CHAPTER FOURTEEN

Doug was digging his damn grave. It was already more than six feet deep, but he couldn't stop himself from giving in to Jenn's request, even if his life depended on it. He'd dreamed about having her naked and under him for so long that a part of him wondered if he was still asleep while his mind played tricks on him. Had his dreams become reality? Part of him hoped so. The horny part that craved her since she kissed him all those months ago. Oh, who the fuck was he kidding? He fought his attraction to her for far longer than that. And it definitely wasn't just the horny part of him that wanted her. It was his heart, mind, and soul too.

Maybe she was right. Perhaps it was time to stop battling the inevitable.

He tried to date other women over the past few

years, but being with them never felt right. He shamefully admitted to himself that he replaced some of those women with Jenn in his mind while having sex with them—a confession he would never reveal to anyone in his lifetime.

Lying atop Jenn, with them both nude from the waist up, was a fantasy come true. Her body had matured further over the past few years, and she couldn't be mistaken for a teenager anymore. But it was her expression and blue eyes that lured him in. She was no longer the naive nineteen-year-old she'd been when they first met, still grieving her parents' deaths and having her world uprooted by moving from Virginia to Florida to live with her godfather two years earlier.

Doug's assignment back then was to guard her with his own life. An assignment he failed at. Thankfully, she survived. However, she didn't look at him as if he were a failure. Nor did she gaze upon him with the hero-worship he tried to convince himself of. No, none of that was in her eyes. Instead, passion, desire, need, and God help him, love swirled in their depths. Her emotions were unmistakable, and they were for nobody but him. Was he worthy of her? He doubted it. Could he resist her? Right then, absolutely not.

He let her pull him down until their lips met, and

she parted hers for him. A surge of electric energy raced through him, and his mind and body snapped.

Gone was his control.

Gone was the catastrophic situation they'd found themselves in.

Gone was every reason why kissing her was a bad idea.

Gone was everything and everyone but her.

He gave himself over to her, yet took control in return.

Plunging his tongue into her mouth, he mapped out every part he could reach while tangling with her own tongue. She spread her legs, letting him drop onto the bed and settle between them. His cock strained against the zipper of his pants, wanting to be free to thrust inside her.

He moved from her mouth to her jawline, down to her neck, and even further to her chest, licking, nibbling, and kissing every bit of skin along the way. Despite all they'd been through, she still tasted sweet, like a combination of sunshine and the most incredible dessert he'd ever tried. He cupped her breasts, learning their weight and texture. Her skin was warm, soft, and inviting, a contradiction to the world just outside the cabin.

Shifting down the bed, he drew one of her breasts into his mouth, strumming the taut peak with his tongue. She let out an encouraging cry of pleasure and arched her back, urging him on. Her hands on his shoulders curled inward, her nails clawing him. That only turned him on even more. He didn't care if she drew blood or left marks. Nothing could stop him from devouring her right then, except a lack of consent on her part. If she got scared or decided it was a mistake or that he went too far too fast, he would stop immediately. He'd never taken what wasn't freely and consensually offered to him by a woman before, and he wouldn't start now.

He switched to her other breast, giving it the same attention as the first. She gasped and wriggled beneath him, cradling his torso with her thighs. "Doug! Oh, God! I don't want you to stop, but I want you naked. Please. I want us both naked."

Now that he was in the moment, he wanted that, too, loving the thought of having nothing between them to inhibit skin-to-skin contact.

Going up on his knees, he grasped the waistband of her black bikini underwear, pulling them down her long legs as he climbed off the end of the bed. Dropping them to the floor, he couldn't stop staring at the beautiful creature before him, spread out like a feast. As his gaze roamed her body, taking in every freckle, birthmark, and inch of perfection, his cock throbbed with need, demanding release from its confinement.

He quickly shed his pants and boxer briefs, and his

ego got a boost as her eyes widened at the sight of his thick cock standing erect, which was hard as steel and weeping with pre-cum. Circling the bed, he retrieved a condom from his wallet, setting it aside, then lowered the brightness of the lantern so it wasn't blinding, yet they could still see each other. He wanted to inspect every part of her body and watch her reactions as his fingers and tongue learned where and how she liked to be touched.

Climbing onto the mattress, he stretched out so his chest, abdomen, and pelvis were flush against her side. Desire flooded him, and his mind and body fought between needing to get inside her as fast as possible and wanting to take time to savor every moment with her. Who knew what the future would bring, after everything they'd been through—both in the last eighteen hours and over the past four years.

As his splayed hand roved her torso, he leaned down and kissed her lips, which immediately opened for him. Their tongues danced in a mating ritual as old as time. He played with her nipples, pinching and plucking them before his hand traveled south. The scent of her arousal hung in the air, and he lifted his head to inhale deeply through his nose, drawing it in.

Jenn's fingertips traced his tattoo again as she explored his chest. She gasped and her hips bucked when he brushed his fingers over her swollen clit. He gave it some attention before dipping lower to find her soaked for him. He teased her slowly, not entering her because a thought occurred to him.

"Sweetheart, have you done this before, or are you a virgin?" He really didn't *want* to know the answer if it was the former, but he *needed* to know if he had to be extra gentle because her hymen was intact.

She shook her head, and her gaze dropped to his chest as if she were embarrassed. "No, I'm not. I've only been with one other guy, though. We dated for a few months during our first year of college, but decided we were better off as friends. I haven't had sex with anyone else since."

He doubted that it was due to a lack of effort on the part of other men. Surely, she'd dated some even if she hadn't slept with them.

Tamping down his jealousy for the asshole who took her virginity—even if they remained friends, the guy was still an asshole in Doug's mind—he smiled at her before kissing her nose. "Okay. But you have to tell me if I'm going too fast or if you don't like something I do, all right?"

"Yes. I've learned a lot from my aunts and uncles about how communicating during sex is important."

A groan erupted from his throat. "Um, can we not mention them, especially your uncles, while we're naked?"

She giggled. "Noted."

Part of Jenn was apprehensive about being able to please Doug sexually. He undoubtedly had far more experience than her, and she worried she wouldn't compare to the other women he'd been with. She still couldn't believe she'd begged him to make love to her and that he'd given in. That was the most shocking part. But as she stared into his eyes, she didn't just see the desire to have sex. Raw passion and hunger swirled in their depths. What she felt was reflected there. He wasn't in bed with her to scratch an itch or out of pity for what she'd been through since yesterday morning. He wanted her. Craved her. Of that she was certain.

No man had ever looked at her like he did right then. It was how she wished he would look at her for what seemed like forever. She'd heard her aunts use the words cherished and adored when referring to how their husbands made them feel, and now she knew what they meant. This was what it was like to be the sole focus of someone you were in love with. She just hoped that in the morning, he wouldn't have any regrets.

Doug dipped his head, taking her breast into his mouth again and teasing the nipple as his fingers parted her labia and one slid inside. She was slick, making it easy for him. His touch ramped up her desire, and she licked and nibbled on his shoulder as her hands roamed across his body wherever they could reach.

She inhaled sharply, then moaned when he added a second finger to the first and bit down lightly on her nipple. Sex with Cole had never been this good, and they were just getting started. Her body was already on a trek toward utopia, climbing higher and higher, in search of the ultimate reward.

As he slowly fucked her with his fingers, his thumb brushed over her clit again and again, causing a cry of want and need to erupt from her throat. Her hips lifted and fell as she squirmed and tried to match his pace. He shifted to her other breast, laving it with his tongue. His coarse facial hair rasped against her skin, adding to the multitude of sensations racing through her body. The hand between her legs moved faster as he added a third finger, spreading her open and giving her more pleasure than she'd ever known.

Her mind spun out of control as the orgasm hovered on the edge for a heartbeat, then crashed over her like a wave, shattering her into a million fragments of utter euphoria. Her eyes slammed shut as she screamed his name, and he swiftly covered her mouth with his own. His fingers continued to thrust into her, drawing out her climax. She was in a free-fall from thousands of miles above the Earth. Her mind exploded with fireworks in myriad shades of every color of the rainbow. When he lifted his head, she gasped for air, floating back down in a cocoon of bliss. "Holy shit!"

She opened her eyes to find him grinning at her. "That good?"

"Are you...kidding?" she asked as she panted. "That wasn't just good—it was...it was...oh, God, my mind is blank! It was better than good." Her body sagged onto the mattress as the last vestiges of euphoria began to ebb. "That's all I can think of."

He laughed. "Glad to hear it. But we're not done, sweetheart. Not by a long shot."

Reaching back, he found the condom on the bedside table, but she snatched it from his hand and tore it open. "Let me."

Heat flared in his eyes, and she felt the need to tell him that she'd never done this before—put a condom on a man. "My aunts taught me how to do this using bananas and dildos."

He coughed and sputtered before shaking his head. "And that's why I try to avoid the she-shed at all costs. I once walked in on a conversation about which vibrators were the best. Granted, I hadn't knocked because I was in a hurry to check on something for Ian, but yeah, I knock now."

Laughter spilled from them, but then Jenn got serious again. She pushed on his shoulder until he was flat on his back, then ran her hand down his sculpted torso to the prize jutting proudly from his groin. When she wrapped her hand around his thick cock, he hissed and bucked his hips. "Damn, woman. I'm going to come from just your touch before you even get that thing on me."

His words thrilled her. To know he was already on the edge gave her confidence. She set the condom on the tip of his shaft, then gripped him tightly as she rolled it on. He moaned, but as soon as she finished, he grabbed her waist and flipped her over before draping his body on top of hers. From chest to toe, they fit perfectly together. He brushed a few strands of her hair back, staring into her eyes. "You're so beautiful, sweetheart. So damn beautiful. How I stayed away from you for as long as I did..." Not finishing the sentence, he shook his head. "I was an ass, and I'm so sorry. But that's in the past. This is now."

Her heart filled with more love for him, which she hadn't thought possible.

Brushing his lips against hers, he whispered, "Let me know if I need to slow down or if I'm hurting you."

"You won't."

He narrowed his brow. "That wasn't the answer I wanted. I'll try my best not to hurt you, but you have to tell me if I do. That's not a request, Jenn."

Holy hell. Neither was in the lifestyle—she had no desire to be and thought he felt the same—but whether he was aware of it or not, he was a Dominant. She'd been around enough of them to recognize one in a heartbeat. She didn't like him being bossy outside the bedroom—like when he reprimanded her as if she were a twelve-year-old whenever she cursed—but it kinda turned her on right then.

"I promise, I'll say something."

"Good girl."

Shit. Those two words got her engine revving even faster.

Lifting her head, she kissed him. "I want you inside me. Now. Please."

He brought one hand down between them and prodded her entrance. She was still wet and ready. A moment later, he replaced his fingers with the tip of his cock. Jenn lifted her legs and wrapped them around his hips. "Please!"

As he eased into her, she reveled in the sensations that bombarded her. As he retreated and pushed forward again, a little farther each time, her body willingly yielded to the sensual invasion. She rocked her hips in time with his. The orgasm she already felt building threatened to be stronger than the first one. She slid her arms around his neck and held on for dear life.

They both moaned when he was fully seated, filling her to perfection, and he peered down at her. "Shit, you're so tight. Are you okay?"

"More than." She tilted her pelvis and gasped when his cock hit her G-spot. "Oh! Please, fuck me! Please!"

Instead of chastising her for the vulgar demand, he gave her a hungry grin. "With pleasure, sweetheart."

Leaning on his forearms, he took possession of her mouth, plunging his tongue inside while thrusting his cock in and out. His pace was slow at first—infuriatingly so—but when she dug her heels into his ass, urging him on, he fucked her faster. Perspiration coated their skin. The only sounds were heavy breathing, gasps, moans, murmured words of endearment, the crinkling of the rescue blanket beneath them, and the slapping of flesh against flesh.

He made her body sing, a chorus of passion and all that was beautiful in the world. Reaching down, he maneuvered his hand between them and found her clit, rubbing it with enough pressure to send her hurtling toward the edge of another orgasm. "Come for me, Jenn. Let me feel you shatter around me."

That was all she needed to let go. "Oh, God! Yes! Yes!"

Her mind and body detonated, and after a few more thrusts, Doug shouted, too, while his muscles stiffened and jerked as he came.

They collapsed in an exhausted heap, and Doug turned them onto their sides. Their limbs entwined as their lungs struggled for air. He wrapped his arms around her, pulling her close, as he kissed her forehead.

Despite everything else that'd happened in the last day, Jenn had never felt something so right, so perfect, as what she just experienced. She just hoped that when the sun arose, Doug wouldn't take a step back instead of forward. This couldn't be the only night she spent making love to him. If it were, it would destroy her.

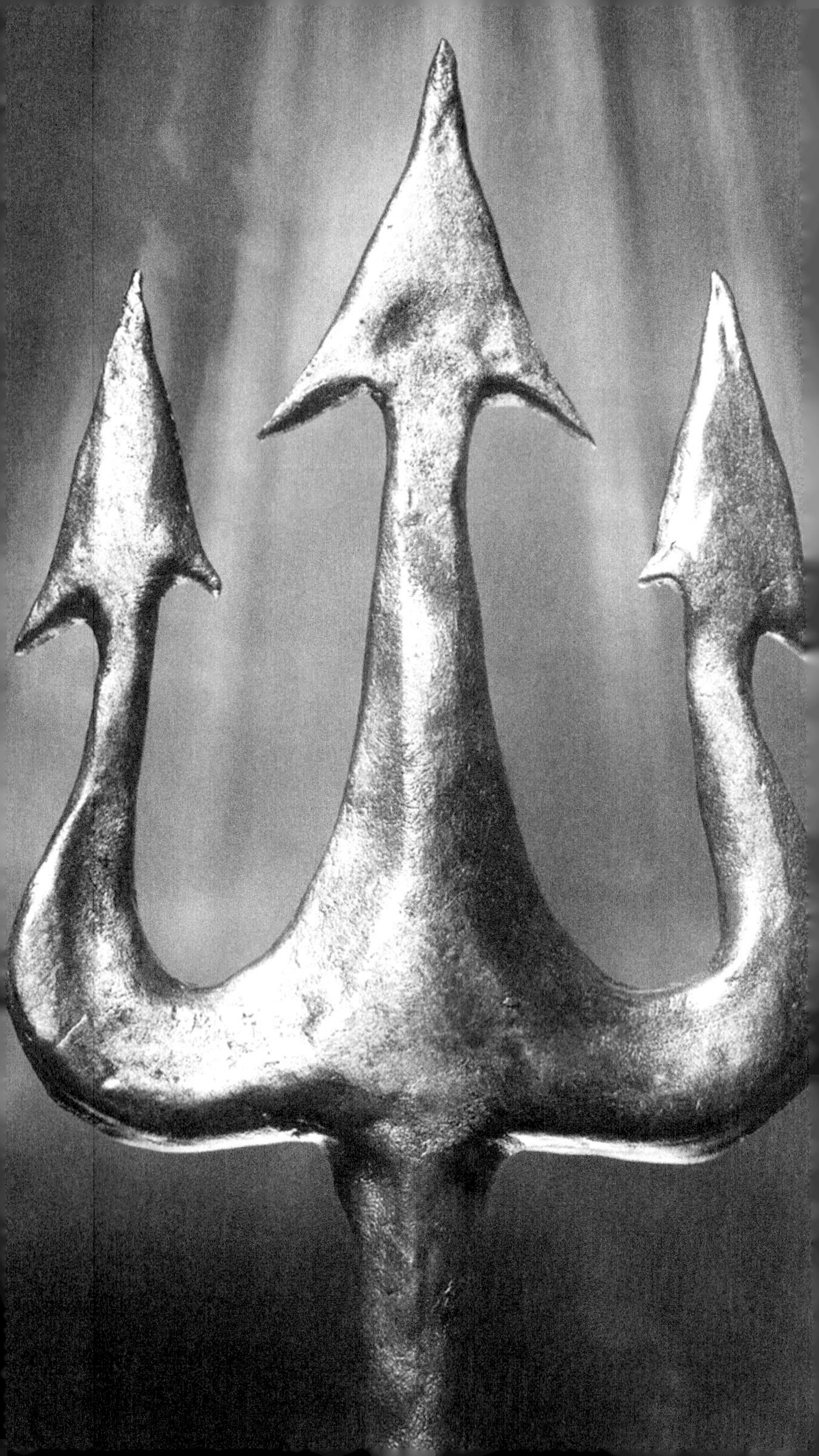

CHAPTER FIFTEEN

Jenn snuggled against Doug's side, her head resting on his shoulder. She woke up a few minutes ago as the early morning light filtered through the cracks of the bedroom window's shutters, but he was still asleep. Hell, he'd barely woken up when a few minor aftershocks hit during the night. They were strong enough to rattle things in the cabin, but not cause any damage.

She stretched her legs, reveling in how her body ached in the most glorious way. Sex with her first and only other lover had been nice—she even had a few orgasms after a while, once she relaxed and banished her nervousness about being intimate with Cole. Nothing earth-shattering, but enjoyable. She'd also masturbated since then and used a few toys to pleasure herself. However, none of that came even close to having sex with Doug.

Holy shit, the man made her body soar, and she finally realized what all her aunts and their friends meant when they discussed the big-O. Doug had made love to her a second time and given her another orgasm before she passed out from exhaustion, her nightmare long gone. It'd been mind-blowing, and she couldn't wait to do it again.

Torn between wanting to wake him and letting him get some more well-deserved sleep, Jenn turned her head to kiss his throat while her fingers lightly caressed his bare chest, alternating between the bullet scar and his tattoo. It wasn't long before he stirred, his legs stretching under the blanket as he arched his back. The arm around her tightened, and his eyes blinked several times before remaining open.

Jenn tilted her head back until their gazes met. "If you say one word about regretting last night, I'll plan the ultimate revenge on you. I don't know what that is yet, but I'll come up with something."

He chuckled and pulled her until she was draped over his body. "No regrets, other than I know I'll get my ass kicked by your godfather the minute he finds out about us. I could've lost you in that landslide yesterday, sweetheart. Or even during the earthquake. That scared me more than anything and made me realize fighting my attraction to you was useless. The age thing still bothers me a bit, but you're much more mature than other women your age. I'll get over it because now that I've had you, now that I've made love to you, I don't think I can live another day without holding you in my arms."

She smiled, his words warming her heart and vanquishing any doubts she had. "When did you become such a romantic?"

"After you stole my heart last night."

Brushing her hair back over her shoulders, he gently urged her head down until their lips met. Jenn melted against him as he plundered her mouth. The kiss was so incredible and distracting that she didn't even think about the fact that she had morning breath and was in desperate need of a shower. Doug's hands roamed her back and ass, and he lifted until his stiff cock slipped between her legs. When it hit her clit, she hissed and winced.

Ending the kiss, Doug nuzzled the spot where her ear and neck met. "Sore?"

"Yeah. Sorry."

"There's nothing to be sorry about. I'm the one who should apologize."

"For what? Making me come so hard three times that I thought there was another earthquake?"

Boisterous laughter erupted from his chest, causing Jenn to jiggle on top of him. As she studied his handsome face and chest, she decided that if she was too tender to have sex, that didn't mean she couldn't take care of her man. And yes, he was now all hers, in every way. Well, maybe not *every* way. While she'd told him several times that she loved him, he hadn't said the words back to her. Part of her was worried that he didn't feel the same way, despite his earlier comment about her stealing his heart. But the other half knew Doug still had to come to terms with everything that happened between them, while she'd known for a long time that he was the only man she'd ever been *in love* with. Hopefully, he didn't make her wait too long before getting completely on the same page as her.

In the meantime, she wanted to pleasure him and began kissing his chest as she maneuvered her body down his, her target pressed hard against her abdomen.

"Jenn, you don't have to." His words were his only attempt to stop her while his hands caressed her shoulders and back. Clearly, he wouldn't argue if she continued.

She gave him a wicked grin. "What if I want to?"

His breath caught. "Jesus, woman. You're going to be the death of me."

"Not too soon, I hope."

While not very experienced with blowjobs, she was determined to do her best. She kissed and licked his stiff shaft before opening her mouth, taking his length inside, and closing her lips around it. Doug moaned and gripped a handful of her hair. As she sucked and bobbed her head, getting used to his taste and the feeling of her mouth stretched around him, she lifted her gaze to meet his. His eyes were half-lidded and filled with desire. His nostrils flared as she flattened her tongue against the underside of his cock and licked it like an ice cream cone before releasing him. "Am I doing it right?"

"Oh, sweetheart, trust me when I say nothing you're doing to me is wrong." His voice was deep, gravelly, and incredibly sexy.

She blushed. "Tell me how you like it."

"Wrap your hand around the base of my cock, then take me into your mouth—as far back as you can without choking—and suck hard."

She loved how explicit he was, so she didn't have to fumble her way through trying to please him. Following his instructions, she inhaled him and went a little too far because her gag reflex kicked in. Using his grip on her hair, he yanked her off him and caressed her cheek as she coughed and her eyes watered. "Easy, sweetheart. Take it slow. There's no rush and no right or wrong way of doing this. Eventually, you'll relax enough to take me all the way into your mouth and swallow around the tip. But it won't happen right away. I don't expect it to. Just do what feels natural and comfortable. Okay?"

Nodding, she tightened her hold on his cock and

tried again. Instead of attempting to take all of him at once, she did as he suggested and figured out how far she could go down on his length without it being uncomfortable. Closing her eyes, she used her tongue and mouth to pleasure him. Pre-cum flowed from his slit, tantalizing her taste buds. She never thought she'd enjoy giving a blowjob as much as she did in that moment, but as her aunts had told her many times, sex with someone you loved more than life itself put it on a whole other level.

When her teeth lightly scraped his cock, he hissed and then groaned, thrusting his hips but not to the point he hit the back of her throat. "So good, Jenn. Damn, you feel so good. I'm not going to last long. Cup my balls gently."

Leaving her one hand around his cock, which helped prevent her from going too far down on him, she raked her fingernails over his thigh before sliding her hand under his balls and fondling them. Doug's hand in her hair tightened, as his hips lifted and fell a scant inch or two. He writhed under her ministrations, empowering her. His other hand fisted the blanket to the point his fingers turned white. "I'm close, sweetheart. If you don't want me to come in your mouth, now's the time—oh, shit!"

Yeah, no way would she release him before he came. Instead, she sucked hard, hollowing her cheeks. She doubted she could swallow everything when he climaxed, but would try her damnedest. As she increased the suction of her mouth and the pressure of her hand wrapped around his cock, she studied his face. His lips were parted, and his eyes were barely open, but she knew he still watched her. He panted and moaned as his legs twitched and shifted on either side of her body.

"Oh, fuck! Jenn, I'm—arrrghhhhhhh!"

Warm, salty cum erupted from him, and she swallowed as fast as possible, but there was too much of it. Some oozed from her lips, as more spurts hit the roof of her mouth. When the tension eased from his body, and he melted into the mattress, she released him and smugly grinned like the Cheshire cat. She licked her lips, wiped her chin, and crawled up his torso, hoping he wouldn't mind tasting himself when she kissed him because she desperately wanted to right then. She didn't have to worry about it, though, because he cupped her cheeks and drew her down until their mouths met. His tongue swept between her lips and tangled with hers.

After a few moments, he slowed the kiss and rolled them until they were side by side on the bed. Brushing her hair back from her face, he grazed his lips over her closed eyelids. "That was amazing, sweetheart. Thank you."

She smiled and cuddled against him. "It was my

pleasure. I'm glad you enjoyed it because I certainly did."

As much as she wanted to stay there all day, wrapped up in his arms, reality crashed in when his satellite radio squawked. "Bullseye, you there?"

Sighing, he rolled over and reached for the radio, which was on the floor next to the mat and lantern that were no longer needed. Jenn admired his bare ass until he flopped onto his back again and keyed the microphone. "Yeah, Romeo, what's up?"

"Military units are about ten minutes out. As soon as they figure out the best way to get everyone on your side to ours, I'll let you know."

"Copy."

Jenn was disappointed when Doug sat up, but then he leaned over and gave her a sweet but all-too-brief kiss. "We've got to get up and moving. We can eat our MREs while checking on the newborn and the heart patient. No matter what the rescue units decide, it won't be easy or quick to transfer everyone to the other side of the village—especially the people who are elderly or injured."

When he turned to climb out of bed, she placed a hand on his shoulder, and he glanced back at her with his eyebrows raised in question. Jenn swallowed a lump that had suddenly taken up residence in her throat. "What happens after we're rescued? I mean, you and me and this." She gestured between them and then to the messy bed.

Doug smiled and reached out to cup her jaw. "This doesn't end here, sweetheart. Let's get out of here first, then I'll figure out how to tell Ian that we're a couple in a way that won't result in my death."

Relief coursed through her. "Can we wait a bit before telling anyone?" When his eyes widened, she quickly added, "I just know everyone is going to have an opinion about us, and while we can tell them eventually, for now, I just want to enjoy being with you without anyone else's comments or interference. I'm not ashamed of what happened, Doug. I want to be with you, but I just know my uncles will go berserk when they find out. My aunts will be happy for me—they all like you—but I know my uncles will haze you."

"I was kidding about Ian killing me—he won't be thrilled but won't resort to murder. At least I don't think he will. Anyway, I can handle your uncles, sweetheart, but if you want to wait a bit, we will."

"Thank you." She gave him a sheepish grin. "And thank you for calling me sweetheart and not baby. Don't think I didn't notice that. Unless you don't like baby as a term of endearment."

"I never gave it any thought until you. I know you're sensitive about your nickname, and I'll do my best to avoid it." He gave her an evil grin before nuzzling her neck with his mouth, chin, and nose. "But

I can't guarantee I won't slip in the throes of passion at some point."

She rubbed her cheek against his. "If that happens, I'm sure I'll find a way to forgive you."

The satellite phone on the bed beside him rang, signaling a call instead of the walkie-talkie feature. Doug glanced at the screen, then handed the device to her. "It's your godfather. Probably wants to make sure we haven't gotten you killed."

After taking a deep breath and letting it out, she pulled the blankets over her naked body while Doug quietly climbed out of bed and began to dress in his still dirty clothes. Jenn would have to do the same after she reassured her uncle she was safe. The last contact with him that she knew about was when Romeo called him shortly after they'd arrived at the village. After hitting the button to connect the call, she put it on speaker. "I'm alive, Uncle Ian, and not hurt. Doug, Romeo, and Lindsey are fine too."

"Thank God." His relief was palpable even with thousands of miles separating them. "What about everyone else?"

Her eyes filled with tears as yesterday's horrific events raced through her mind, and she stared at the blanket over her lap. "We came to help out at this village in the mountains. Some people were killed and others injured during the earthquake and more in a landslide. We lost one of our volunteers—Margie is...*was* a retired school principal. She was such a nice lady, Uncle Ian."

"I'm sorry for your loss, Baby-girl."

She cringed at her nickname but didn't say anything about it. Once she returned home, she'd have to sit her uncles down and ask them to use her given name from now on. If she didn't put her foot down, she'd be in her fifties, and they would still call her Baby-girl.

"I know it's a lot to ask, but can you arrange for her...her body to be transported home to New Mexico, just outside of Albuquerque? If it's too much trouble, I'm sure the volunteer organization will—"

"It's no trouble at all, Jenn. I'd rope the moon for you." She knew he would, but sometimes she felt like she asked too much of him. While many people called him a sarcastic son of a bitch, Ian Sawyer had a heart of gold when it came to those he loved and respected. Thankfully, Jenn was one of them. "I'll have Colleen find out what we have to do to make the arrangements —I'm sure there's paperwork that has to be filed to transport a deceased American out of Colombia. When you can, get her emergency contact information from Ramona. She'll probably want to make the notification to the woman's family, but then I'll talk to them and take care of everything else."

"Thank you."

"Anything for you."

Doug left the room and returned seconds later with their MREs and two bottles of water. She smiled at him as he opened one of the bottles and handed it to her.

"Can I convince you to fly home with the others when you're done at that village?" Ian asked. "This is not me ordering you to come home—it's me asking you to. I'm worried about you. I know you're doing good work down there, but that doesn't mean I'm not scared shitless that something will happen to you. This isn't anything new—it's just gotten worse since the earthquake. And now, knowing there was a landslide and the death of your friend..." A long pause filled the air. "You're family, Jenn. My daughter, in almost every way. I have the right to worry about you and want you to be safe."

Jenn's eyes watered at the tangible concern in his voice. Her gaze met Doug's understanding one as he sat on the foot of the bed, facing her. "I-I don't know. I want to stay to help, but so much has happened since yesterday. Let me think about it. There's still a lot to do here. I'll call you later. Hopefully, we'll be back at the commune by tonight."

Another pause was followed by a loud sigh. "Okay. Just stay safe and keep me updated. I love you, Baby-girl."

"I love you, too, Uncle Ian. Give Peyton a kiss from me."

"You've got it."

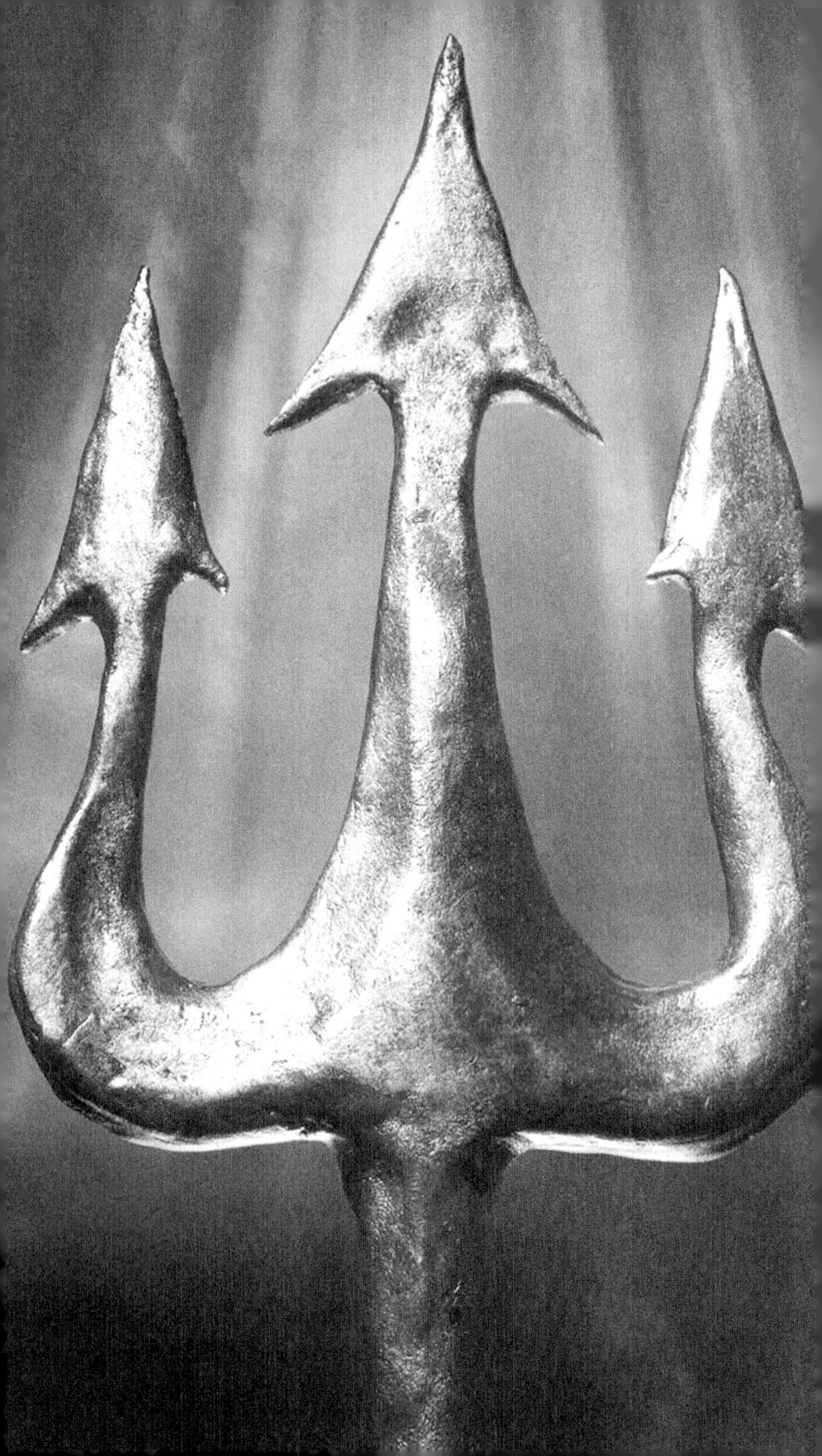

CHAPTER SIXTEEN

After checking on Maria, Diego, and their newborn baby, the elderly cardiac patient, who appeared more stable than the day before, and the other injured individuals, Doug received an update from Romeo. Across the massive pile of rocks, mud, and downed trees, he could see multiple military vehicles and dozens of uniformed soldiers had finally arrived at the entrance to the village. It took about twenty minutes for them to decide on the best strategy for a rescue. They planned to rig up a traverse highline, which involved stretching rope horizontally over the area impacted by the landslide. A trolley or pulley system would then safely transport a person across it, either in a sling or on a stretcher.

A team of soldiers began to scale the mountain to circumvent the area where the landslide had started and bring equipment to help those cut off from the others. Once the high-line was set up, they would transport those in need of medical care first. Then, Jenn, Doug, and the rest of the villagers would be transferred over to the other side. It would take the soldiers about an hour to reach them and then a few more hours to rescue everyone. It was impossible for a helicopter to descend into the area, which lacked a sufficient landing zone, and high winds prevented them from lifting people to safety. So, the only other option, aside from the traverse high-line, was to climb out, reversing the same route the rescue team had used. However, most of those in need of extrication were in no condition to make the arduous journey, especially when another landslide could occur.

While waiting for the team of soldiers, Doug and Jenn spent their time triaging the villagers and explaining the rescue to them. Understandably, some were frightened, but Jenn was able to reassure them that they would be safe. He was proud of how calm she was and how well she handled the situation. She was even able to make some of them laugh, despite their circumstances.

The dog that'd slept in the cabin last night followed them around—probably because they shared part of their breakfast with her—while a few others kept their distance. Doug made a mental note to ask the army if they could somehow supply food and water for the domesticated animals stuck on that side of the village or lead them over to the other side. He would hate it if they had to be left behind to fend for themselves.

Two more minor aftershocks occurred, but like the three they'd experienced overnight, they hadn't caused any further damage or injuries. While a few rocks had tumbled down the remains of yesterday's landslide, the earth and trees didn't follow.

After the triage was completed and everyone was hydrated, they took some latex gloves from the medical supplies and inflated them, making improvised balloons for the few children awaiting rescue. Doug found a marker in one of the bags and drew happy faces on them, which the kids loved.

When the soldiers finally arrived, Doug was grateful the officer in charge spoke English, so he didn't have to keep asking Jenn to translate the words he was unfamiliar with. Several of the men were medics, and Jenn brought them to the victims who needed to be rescued first while Doug helped set up the traverse high-line. From the other side of the village, a throw-line launcher was fired, sending the initial rope and then another over the debris field. The soldiers determined the best anchor point was a massive tree about thirty yards from the edge of the landslide. The ropes were also attached to another anchor point on the far side. It took over an hour for the rigging to be completely set up, tested, and deemed safe for transportation.

It took a bit of persuasion for Esperanza's parents to allow a medic to take their newborn on the stretcher, with her strapped to his chest, and carry her to safety. Diego wanted to do it, but the soldier had extensive experience in that type of rescue and wouldn't panic if the basket swayed or dipped without warning. Finally, after a few minutes of assurance that the infant would be in good hands, they tearfully watched as she and the medic were secured into the Stokes rescue stretcher and slowly pulled across the debris field. Jenn put her arm around Maria to comfort the distraught woman, who cried with relief when the stretcher and its precious cargo reached the other side safely.

One by one, the injured were brought to safety, where they immediately received further medical care, with some being loaded into one of the army's ambulances for transportation to the hospital.

Once the last of the victims who needed the stretcher had been rescued, the crew switched it out for a harness, similar to what is used for zip-line adventures. That way, people could sit during the transfer, which gave them a better sense of control and stability during the rescue, rather than staring helplessly up at the trees and sky. It also went a bit faster.

The children went first, and each was attached to one of the soldiers as they were moved to the safe zone.

When there were only a few villagers left to transfer, Jenn whispered to Doug, "I have to pee so bad. I'll be back in a few minutes."

She gestured to the cabin they'd slept in, and Doug checked his watch, then nodded. It was a little after three p.m. Rescuing everyone had been long and tedious, and at the rate they were going, it was doubtful they would get back to the commune before dark. "Okay. We have at least twenty or thirty minutes before it's your turn, then mine."

They'd decided to go last, allowing the frightened villagers to join their loved ones first. After that, the few remaining soldiers would trek up the mountain again with their equipment and supplies.

Hurrying over to the rustic home, Jenn disappeared through the door. Doug watched until she was no longer in sight, then returned his attention to the rescue in progress. It was a few minutes before the middle-aged man in the harness reached the other side. He was in the process of being unhooked from the pulley system when the ground began to shake violently. The aftershock was more substantial than the previous ones, and Doug spun around and raced toward the cabin, stumbling and trying to stay on his feet, desperate to get Jenn out of there in case it collapsed. He ignored the shouts and yelps behind him, focusing only on one person—Jenn.

As he neared the cabin, he glanced up the mountain, relieved that the quake hadn't triggered another landslide—at least not yet. The tremors eased, but then his heart nearly stopped when he heard Jenn scream. He rushed inside, finding her on the ground with part of the roof collapsed on top of her. He quickly pushed aside a metal sheet to reach her. "Jenn! Are you okay?"

She was covered in dust, dirt, and fragments of building material, but alive and conscious. Her eyes were filled with a combination of pain and relief at seeing him. "Help! I'm stuck!"

It was then he noticed her lower left arm was pinned under a support beam that had fallen. With massive doses of adrenaline coursing through his veins, he lifted the beam off her just as two soldiers appeared in the doorway. One was the officer in charge, the other was a medic. As the quake ceased, they helped clear the area around Jenn as Doug gently assessed her arm, which was at an odd angle just above her wrist—definitely broken.

"Can you wiggle your fingers?" he asked.

She moved them just enough to reassure him, but winced and cried out in pain. "Ow! Yeah, but it hurts like hell." Panting, she glanced at her arm. "It's broken, right?"

"Yeah, but the good thing is the bones didn't break the skin, so it's not a compound fracture."

"Damn it! If Uncle Ian says, 'I told you so,' I'm going to smack him silly. I tried to run outside when it started, but I tripped, and then the blasted roof came crashing down. Is anyone else hurt?"

He didn't know and, honestly, didn't care at the moment. She was his main priority. Thankfully, the officer responded, "Everyone else is okay, senorita. Let's put your arm in a splint and then get you out of here."

They worked quickly but carefully, applying an inflatable splint to immobilize her arm, wrist, and hand. Doug cringed every time she moaned or gasped in pain. The medic had given her a shot of morphine before doing anything else, but it didn't kick in until they were ready to move her. Then her eyes glazed over, and she began to giggle. Lord, the woman was cute when she was stoned out of her mind, and it helped ease Doug's mind just a bit. He'd feel much better when they could get her somewhere more civilized with an X-ray machine and people with M.D. after their names.

The three men helped her stand and held on until she was steady on her feet. Doug moved to her right side, wrapping his arm around her waist in support. "Lean on me. I've got you."

She gave him a lopsided smile as she swayed into

him. "You most certainly do." Another giggle escaped her. "Wow, that stuff packs a punch!"

"I know."

"When did you have some?" Her eyes widened in horror. "Oh, that's right! After you were shot!"

He took a step toward the door, and when she followed, he continued forward. "Yeah, after the surgery, though. I was unconscious by the time they got me to the hospital." Why were they talking about the day both of them almost died? He tried to change the subject to something less morbid. "How's the pain?"

"Sss-all right." Another giggle. "Oh. Em. Gee. I sound drunk. Drunk as a skunk. Although I don't think skunks get drunk. But I am. Sort of."

"Yes, you are. It's cute." He couldn't help the smile that crossed his face. She was adorable in her current state, despite her broken arm and being covered in dirt and grime.

"Really?"

"Really."

They gradually made their way to the staging area, where an empty harness awaited them. After a few minutes of discussion between Doug and the commanding officer, a second harness was added to the traverse high-line. Doug was strapped in first, and then the soldiers gently lifted Jenn until she sat on his lap, facing him, and wrapped her legs around him. Her injured arm rested on his shoulder while her other hand latched onto the back of his neck. He held her snugly against him while their harnesses were attached to each other. While they could've brought the Stokes back over for her, he hadn't wanted her to be alone when she was high as a kite.

"I like this," she said against his ear. "Well, not exactly. I could do without the broken arm and the audience, but I like being this close to you."

"Me too."

Once they were ready, Doug kept one hand around Jenn's waist and grabbed the harness strap above his head to try to reduce the swaying while they were in motion. The pulley system was then activated, and they were towed across the debris field, about eight feet off the ground. Mindful of Jenn's injury and the duo's positioning, the soldiers kept the pace slower than the others transported in the harness had experienced.

When they passed over the tree that Margie's body was pinned under, he was grateful the rescue blanket was still in place, covering her. Worried Jenn would be upset if she saw it, he glanced at her face and noticed her eyes were closed. Good.

What felt like an hour was in reality only about ten minutes before they reached the other side and were disconnected. Romeo, Lindsey, and Tony were there to help Jenn to the ground before Doug dropped down beside her. Parsons was nearby with his Chevy Suburban ready and waiting.

As Doug helped her into the back seat of the vehicle, she suddenly stopped, swayed, and grabbed onto the door frame. "Wait. Margie. We need to—we can't leave her here." Her gaze darted over his shoulder. "Tony—"

Her friend stepped forward and gently took her uninjured hand in his. "I'm staying here with Roland and one of the guards. We'll bring her back to the commune once it's safe for her body to be recovered. I promise."

"Thank you." Tears filled her drug-glazed eyes.

"Let them get you back to Ramona, and I'll talk to you soon."

Doug ground his back molars together to keep from shoving the other man away from Jenn and publicly claiming her as his. But he promised that he'd keep their relationship a secret for now, and therefore, Romeo and Lindsey couldn't find out yet. That didn't mean he had to like it, though.

"Okay." She solemnly nodded and let Doug settle her in the middle of the seat. He climbed in next to her, and Lindsey got in on the other side. Parsons was behind the wheel while Romeo took the front passenger seat. He glanced over his shoulder and looked at Doug. "Your go-bag is in the back with ours. Anything left behind that you need them to recover?"

He thought for a few moments before shaking his head. "Just the commune's medical bag we had with us when the landslide hit. It's on the porch of a cabin—can't miss it—but we used a lot of stuff, so there's not much left in it."

"No worries," Parsons said as he steered around a dip in the dirt road. He was driving slower than he had the day before, probably because of Jenn's injury. "We have more that were donated at the commune."

Between the effects of the morphine and the rocking motion of the vehicle, it wasn't long before Jenn fell asleep. He didn't miss Lindsey's curious expression when he put his arm around Jenn's shoulders, tucking her close to his side to keep her from pitching forward as Parsons drove them down the mountain.

When they finally reached the commune, just before sunset, he woke Jenn up. Dr. Sanchez was already waiting for them to exit the vehicle. They brought Jenn into the clinic, where the splint was removed so the doctor could assess her arm. "Well, definitely broken, but the capillary refill in your fingers is normal, so that's good. Any numbness?"

She shook her head. "Nope. It hurts, but the drugs are still working, so it's not that bad."

Dr. Sanchez reapplied the splint and inflated it again. "I don't want to cast it here without an X-ray first, and the hospitals are overloaded with earthquake victims. I hate to say it, Jenn, but I think the best thing for you to do is return to the States and see an orthopedist as soon as possible."

"But you need help—"

"And we have it," Dr. Sanchez cut her off. "You'll be no good with a busted arm that needs to be cast. I spoke to your uncle a little while ago, before and after I called Margie's brother to notify him of her death. Ian told me he'll arrange to transport her body after it's recovered. That was nice of you to ask him to do that. You've been a wonderful help here these past few weeks, and we'll all miss you, especially the children. I hope you'll come back again, maybe next year, but for now, it's time for you to go home, get that arm taken care of, and then rest."

Crestfallen, Jenn stared at the older woman for a few moments before nodding. "I guess you're right. I would love to come back next year, though."

Dr. Sanchez smiled. "I'll look forward to seeing you then. Now, why don't Lindsey and I help you pack your bags? I'll make sure Margie's things get back to her family. Our residents are already talking about planting a tree or some flowers in her memory after things calm down. She was well loved here, as are all our volunteers, including you."

Hoping off the examination table, Jenn hugged the doctor with her good arm. "I'm going to miss everyone."

"We'll miss you too."

After Jenn's belongings were packed and loaded, it took much longer than expected to leave for Bogotá since she had to say lengthy goodbyes to everyone in the commune, at least twice, especially the children. Hugs and tears were aplenty. She left notes for Tony and Roland because they wouldn't be back until she was most likely already on the private jet, and it grated on Doug's nerves. He wanted to see what she wrote to the two men, but short of ripping them out of her or Ramona's hands, he didn't have an opportunity.

She tried to stay strong and smile while talking to the children, but completely lost it in the back seat of the Suburban about a mile down the road, sobbing into Doug's chest as he held her tightly. Once again, he ignored Lindsey's curious look. It would be a long and exasperating flight if he couldn't pull Jenn onto his lap and comfort her the way he craved.

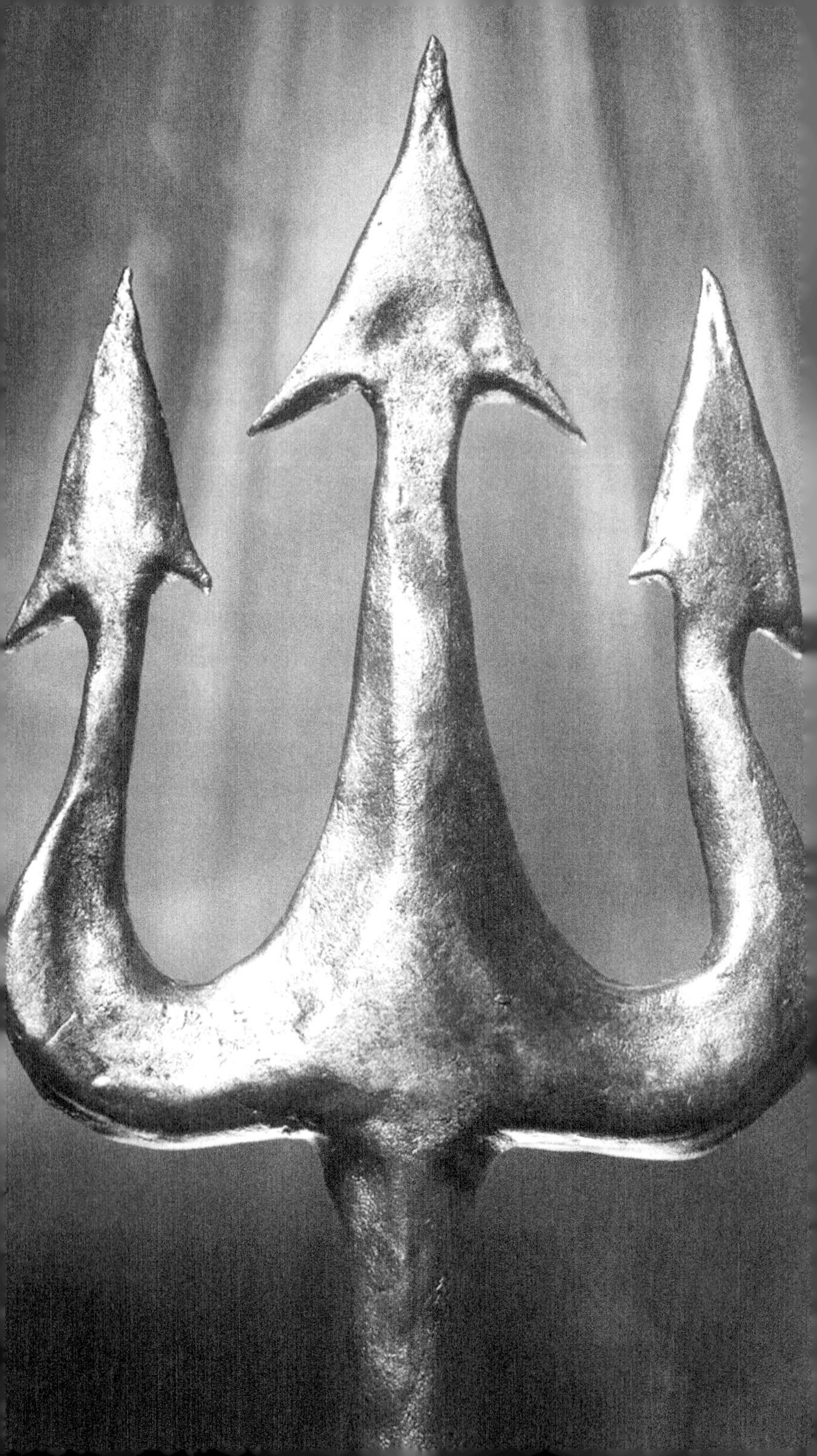

CHAPTER SEVENTEEN

"Do you want to take one of the pain pills Ramona sent?" Doug asked Jenn, squatting beside her as she lay on one of the jet's couches, trying to get comfortable and warm under a fleece blanket.

They'd finally taken off about forty-five minutes ago, after another minor quake temporarily halted traffic at the small airport for almost an hour while the buildings and single runway were inspected for damage. Once the private jet reached cruising altitude, the four passengers got comfortable for the long trip. Doug sat on a recliner beside Jenn, while Romeo and Lindsey were stretched out and already sound asleep on first-class-style seats near the front of the jet on either side of the aisle.

Jenn took a moment to assess her level of pain. The morphine was nearly out of her system, and her arm throbbed more than it had earlier. When she tried to wiggle her fingers or adjust her position, it felt like someone stabbed her with a knife. "Yes, please. The pain is getting worse again, so I'd better take one now before it becomes unbearable."

He stood and strode to the back of the jet, where the small kitchenette was always stocked with assorted beverages and snacks, before returning with a bottle of ginger ale, a Percocet pill, and a granola bar. The doctor had given her a two-day supply to manage the discomfort until she could see an orthopedist and warned her not to take the pills on an empty stomach.

Since she was basically useless while Lindsey and Dr. Sanchez packed her things, she'd called Ian to let him know she would fly home with the others. Thankfully, he didn't say, "I told you so," when she explained about her broken arm. He was just grateful it wasn't worse and would make an appointment for the following day with the orthopedic surgeon who had treated several Trident employees in the past. According to Ian, Dr. Bardot was the best in Tampa and always made room in her schedule for them, ever since the Alpha Team rescued her brother years ago after he was kidnapped for ransom in Mexico. Her godfather and his good friend, Chase, the owner of Blackhawk Security, had connections in various professional fields, and it seemed many owed one or both of the men favors that they could cash in whenever necessary. Jenn knew she should be used to it, but sometimes it still amazed her that there were people willing to drop everything to help out anyone from either company. It was a testament to the good work both Trident and Blackhawk did, some of which was classified.

Jenn sat up, took the medication from Doug, popped it into her mouth, and then washed it down with the soda before eating the granola bar. She wasn't overly hungry since the commune's kitchen staff had given them lunch to eat on the road, but that was about two or three hours ago. "Thanks."

"You're welcome." He sat beside her, set her pillow on his lap, and patted it. "Lie back down." When she glanced toward the front of the aircraft, he added, "Don't worry. They're both out for at least a few hours. It's been a long three days."

As much as she wanted to put her head down and let him care for her, she hesitated. "You should get some sleep too."

"I will. Later." He took the ginger ale bottle from her and placed it on a small side table. "For now, I just need to make sure you're comfortable and in as little pain as possible."

She snorted while lying back down on her right side, facing away from him, and settling her head and injured hand on the pillow.

"What's so funny?" he asked as he unraveled the

now-bunched-up blanket, draped it over her body, and tucked it around her shoulder.

"You."

"Me? Why?"

She shifted just enough so she could see his beautiful eyes. "Are you sure you don't have any interest in the lifestyle? I mean, have you ever gone to the club when it's open or taken any of the classes they offer?"

When they were hired, all Trident's employees had to sign contracts that included ironclad nondisclosure agreements for both the security company and the BDSM club on the property. They also had access to The Covenant if desired. Classes were mandatory for those interested in playing there. Some employees were members, while others weren't, which was fine. Either way, they couldn't talk about what happened there or who the members were with anyone.

Doug's eyes narrowed as he stared down at her. "What are you talking about? I don't go in there unless I have to for some reason—and that's usually when it's closed. That's not my thing, Jenn. I don't think there's anything wrong with it, but it's just not for me." His brow shot up. "Wait a minute. Are you saying you're interested in it?"

"No!" Realizing she protested too loudly, she lowered her voice, hoping Romeo and Lindsey hadn't heard her. "No, I'm not. I just know more about Doms and submissives than the average person, since I'm surrounded by them. What I laughed about was you being all Dom-like, wanting to comfort and care for me, even though you should be resting too." She shrugged and settled back onto the pillow, hoping that the pain pill would start to take effect soon. "It's like you're a Dom-unaware."

"A *Dom-unaware*? What does that mean? Is that even a lifestyle term?"

"Probably not, but it should be. I should tell Kristen to put that in one of her books. Anyway, you're all alpha and dominant, like my uncles, without realizing it. You don't need to be into the kink to be a Dom. According to my aunts and Nick, it's an innate behavior—Doms are natural caregivers and nurturers who feel compelled to keep their loved ones safe at all costs. While some people might say that makes them overbearing, true submissives crave it and want to please their Doms in response. I have to admit my uncles sometimes drive me crazy with their dominant natures, but there are moments when I like that they care enough to want to keep me safe. I also like it when you get all Dom-unaware—not all the time because you can be irritatingly bossy—but knowing you care about my safety makes me feel special."

He caressed her shoulder. "You are special, and I'm more than happy to do anything to always make you feel that way. Just do me a favor?"

Her eyelids felt heavy as the medication began to

combine with her exhaustion and drag her toward slumber, and she closed them. "Anything. What is it?"

"Just don't call me that within earshot of any of your uncles, okay?"

She smiled as the fuzzy edges of sleep began to overtake her mind. "'Kay."

Doug sat with Jenn's head in his lap for about half an hour, gently stroking her silky blonde hair as she slept. It was still a little damp but would be completely dry soon. While waiting for the airport to reopen, they'd all taken advantage of the jet's private shower to wash the dirt and grime from their bodies as fast as possible and leave enough water for the next person. If Doug and Jenn were alone, he would've stripped them both, taken her into the stall, and scrubbed her body from head to toe and back again. However, in keeping his promise to her, he had to pretend like he hadn't already seen her gloriously naked. Instead, Lindsey helped Jenn shower and wash her hair before swapping places and then getting them both dressed in clean clothes.

He knew he had to get up soon and move back to the recliner before he fell asleep where he was, in case Lindsey or Romeo woke up and needed the bathroom or something from the kitchen. It was doubtful either would question Jenn sleeping on his lap or say anything to her uncles, but he couldn't risk word getting around about how close they'd gotten before Jenn was ready to tell anyone.

Now that he'd made love to her, he was amazed he'd stayed away from her for so long. His attraction to her had been there since way before she kissed him all those months ago, but he'd been fighting a losing battle. The war was over. She'd won his heart. It was hers for the keeping. The age difference issue had lessened for him over the past two days, mainly because he finally realized she was much more mature than most women her age. She lived through the aftermath of her parents' murders when she was seventeen, a kidnapping by drug dealers at nineteen, and being accosted by two gang-bangers outside Donovan's Pub. Doug was grateful he'd been there and able to intervene before she got hurt. But Jenn had proven she was no shrinking violet. His biggest regret was that he freaked out when she kissed him, and he ran away like a goddamn idiot. Not only did he hurt her emotionally, but they lost all that time they could've had together if he'd taken his head out of his ass and really looked at the amazing woman she'd become.

Well, his eyes were open now, and there was no way he could turn back time, even if he wanted to, which he didn't. After having her in his bed for just one night, he never wanted to sleep without her again. Yes, he knew their budding relationship would have consequences when her uncles found out about it, but he was determined to do whatever it took to have Jenn in his life, in every way possible.

A smile crossed his face. His family would love her when he introduced them, especially his mother, grandmother, and sisters. Maybe now they would stop bugging him about finding "a nice woman to settle down with."

Was he ready to settle down with Jenn? He didn't know but was willing to find out. She fascinated him like no other woman, but it had taken him a while—okay, a *long* while—to admit that to himself. He just hoped to God that he didn't hurt her somewhere down the line. That was the very last thing he'd ever want to do. He'd been in relationships before, but while they were fun at the time, he hadn't been able to see himself with any of those women long-term, like for decades. But with Jenn, he could imagine them having children and grandchildren and growing old together.

His heart hammered away at the thoughts bombarding him. *Holy shit.* He was in love with her. When it happened, he wasn't sure, but deep in his gut, he knew it wasn't a new feeling, just an undiscovered one. It made him nervous as hell, and the age gap thing smacked him in the face again. At twenty-three, she had many years and new experiences ahead of her. What if she reached thirty and realized that what she thought was love for him had really been just a crush? What if she left him to be with someone else? That would destroy him.

Movement from the front of the jet disrupted his grim thoughts, and he noticed Romeo stretch his arms over his head. Thankfully, the man settled back into the reclined seat a moment later. Gently cradling Jenn's head with the pillow, Doug eased out from under her and stood. He made sure the blanket was tucked around her before moving to the back of the jet to use the bathroom.

When he returned from relieving himself, he was surprised to discover Jenn's eyes open and staring at him. He squatted down and brushed a few strands of hair behind her ear. "Are you okay?"

"Uh-huh. Just woke up, and you were gone. I figured you were in the back since the only other option was that you parachuted out of the plane."

He chuckled. "I could've been up front with Clinton."

"Okay, so there was a third option." She reached out with her good hand, grabbed his shirt, and pulled him down for a quick kiss—too fast for his liking. Apparently, she felt the same way. "If we were alone, I would've kissed you until we both needed the oxygen masks to drop from the ceiling, but that will have to satisfy us both until later. For now, you need to get some sleep."

"We both do." He brushed his lips across her forehead. "Sleep well."

"You too."

Once her eyes closed again and her breathing evened out, he sat in the recliner beside her and used the handle to extend the footrest. Within minutes, he was out like a light.

CHAPTER EIGHTEEN

"Thanks for taking me," Jenn said, using her good hand to buckle the seat belt over her sling while settling into the passenger seat of Angie's Audi Q3. "Uncle Ian would've driven Dr. Bardot, her staff, and me crazy with his glaring, non-stop questions and demands."

The older woman laughed and put the vehicle in drive. "Dr. Bardot is used to it and ignores him. However, most of her staff hide whenever he visits her office for one reason or another. I pray Peyton never breaks a bone or needs stitches. He'll have doctors and nurses pissing in their pants, yelling that they're treating her wrong and he can do it better. As if he suddenly has a medical license." She snorted, then glanced at Jenn. "And it was no trouble to take you. It was my pleasure. Peyton is teething and slobbering all over the place. Ian can get his shirt sopping wet for a change."

That mental image made Jenn laugh for the first time all morning. As suspected, her radius and ulna were both broken above the left wrist. After inspecting the X-rays, the orthopedist declared the breaks were clean and didn't require surgery, which was a huge relief. It was bad enough she had to wear a cast for the next six weeks, so she was thankful that pins and screws weren't necessary to help the bones heal.

When they landed at the private airport near Tampa, where the TS jet was kept yesterday, Uncle Ian and Uncle Jake were waiting for her. Since the pilot and the rest of the passengers had all driven their own vehicles there several days earlier, she had no choice but to give Doug the same grateful yet platonic hug of thanks she gave the others. No kiss goodbye. No longing looks of desire. No secretive winks or smiles. No invites to sleep over each other's apartments. Nothing.

She hated every minute of it and the hour that followed. Once back at the TS compound, she was surrounded by a bunch of mother hens and father roosters. One would think she was made of glass and could shatter at any moment by the way all her uncles and their spouses fussed over her. She had to pretend she hadn't slept well during the four-hour flight and faked yawning until they finally filed out of her apartment, telling her to call any of them if she needed something. Unfortunately, she couldn't say that the only thing—or rather person—she needed was Doug.

Once alone, she got comfortable in her bed with Beau by her side. Evidently, he'd missed her as much as she missed him. She'd debated between texting and calling Doug, but before she could make up her mind, her phone rang and his name appeared on the screen. While he initially said he only wanted to check on her quickly before she went to sleep, they ended up talking for an hour after switching over to a video call. Any drowsiness she'd experienced dissipated as soon as she heard his voice and then saw his face. How she wished it was him in bed with her all night instead of her favorite fur-baby. It was only when the Percocet she took kicked in that they said goodnight. Thankfully, she didn't have any nightmares while she slept.

Doug promised he would bring her lunch today after she got home from the doctor's office. However, they'd have to pretend that they were just friends because at least a few people might drop by unannounced to check on her. It was the only downside to living at the TS compound, with everyone coming and going at all hours of the day. Back in college, she developed the habit of sticking Post-it notes on her door, warning not to disturb her unless it was an emergency, whenever she was studying for an exam or working on a term paper. Unfortunately, that probably wouldn't work anymore since she'd graduated, which meant she couldn't sneak Doug into her apartment for some sexy alone time.

Why had she insisted on keeping their new romance a secret again? Oh, yeah, because her uncles would flip out when they discovered she was dating their employee, who was eight years her senior. None of that made a difference to her, but she wanted to enjoy the peace and quiet for a while.

It was a hot, sunny day, so maybe they'd sit in the yard under an umbrella, with the water misters on to make it a little cooler and more bearable. That wouldn't appear suspicious to anyone, although there was a good chance more than one person would decide to join them. Many of the TS employees and the compound's residents enjoyed taking advantage of the beautiful yard during their downtime.

"So," Angie started. "Are you going to spill the tea about what's going on with you and your McDreamy?"

Jenn's head whipped to the left so fast, she nearly gave herself whiplash. "Wh-what do you mean? My McDreamy? Who's that?" Well, she knew who the original McDreamy was—Dr. Derek Shepherd from *Grey's Anatomy*, but who was Angie talking about? Did she know about Doug?

"Oh, don't play dumb, Jenn. You graduated magna cum laude and want to get your Master's degree in social work. Dumb doesn't become you. Before you left for Colombia, the sexual tension between you and Doug was off the charts—it has been for a long time. The way you two bickered and couldn't keep your eyes off each other had a bunch of us making bets on when that man would finally cave. Did he?"

Her eyes grew wider with every sentence that came from Angie's mouth, until they almost burst from their sockets. "Wh-what? Oh, God. Don't tell me my uncles know."

"Ha! Those idiots?" She pointed a finger at Jenn. "Don't tell them that I called them idiots, but they are. For men who are trained observers and can smell danger coming from a mile away, they're oblivious to whatever's going on between you and Doug. Nick doesn't know either, as far as I can tell. Just us women were making bets. Now, spill, because last night, it looked like all he wanted to do was shove everyone out of your apartment, sweep you up into his arms, and carry you into the bedroom to ravish you."

Well, at least her new relationship was still under wraps as far as her uncles were concerned. She was kind of glad her aunts knew because she needed someone to talk to. Keeping a secret was difficult when you were so ecstatic about it.

She checked the time on the dashboard. It was almost eleven a.m., and Doug said he'd get them lunch at noon, so she still had an hour. "We're almost home. Can we talk in the she-shed with Kristen?"

Angie smiled. "Of course. If you don't mind Shelby being there. The boys are at summer camp for the day, and she's helping Kristen with some social media posts for her upcoming indie book."

She loved and trusted Shelby as much as she did her aunts and had no problem talking about Doug in front of her. The woman had the bubbliest personality and had her friends' backs no matter what. She wouldn't betray Jenn's confidence. "Kristen isn't going through her publisher for her next release?"

"Nope. This is the new paranormal romance series she started writing last year in between her books for Red Rose. They wanted her to make too many changes to the first story that she disagreed with, so she decided to release the series herself instead."

It wasn't as if the now-famous author hadn't self-published before. She'd done that with her first few books before Red Rose Publishing took a chance on her debut BDSM romance novel, which readers went crazy for. That was how she met Devon. She needed to do research for the second book in the series, and Shelby was one of her original beta readers. At the time, they only knew each other online. Since Shelby was a member of The Covenant, she offered to speak to the owners to find out if Kristen could tour the place when it was closed and ask some questions. Devon showed up during her meeting with Mitch, and the rest, as they say, is history.

"Oh, cool. I didn't know that. And it's perfectly fine if Shelby is there."

"Good. And you know, whatever you tell us in the she-shed stays in the she-shed."

Ten minutes later, the four women relaxed in the eight-hundred-square-foot cottage's comfortable seating area. The setup included two matching loveseats and three cozy, oversized reading chairs arranged around an oval wooden coffee table, which had a protective rubber bumper in case a toddler tumbled into it. Ian still had Peyton in his office, and little JD was down for a nap in a playpen in the children's area. Both Kristen and Angie had their own workspaces, and a kitchenette and a full bathroom completed the floor plan.

"Before you get started, Jenn," Shelby said, "I have to tell you something. Now, don't get upset..." Jenn was about to do just that because of the woman's words, but then Shelby grinned. "But Franco has a girlfriend."

"Awwww. But what about me?" Everyone laughed. Shelby's eight-year-old son had a crush on

Jenn ever since he and his best friend, Victor, were adopted into her huge extended family. She babysat them occasionally, and Franco always said he wanted to marry her someday. Victor, however, had a crush on Shelby's friend, Cassandra Myers, who was engaged to a TS employee, Stefan Lundquist.

Placing her hand on her chest, Jenn bowed her head. "I'm heartbroken. What's the little trollop's name?"

Shelby giggled. "Olivia, and she's smart and cute as a button. I'm not surprised he's smitten with her."

"Oh, well." She sighed dramatically and wiped away a non-existent tear. "I guess it's for the best."

"Absolutely," Kristen agreed. "Because now you have Doug. I mean, you do have him, right? Angie and I weren't imagining things last night?"

"Dish, girl," Shelby added. "Now!"

She rolled her eyes, then shifted to sit cross-legged on her chair. "Okay. So, I've been in love with Doug for a few years now."

"Obvious to us but not to your uncles," Kristen said with a nod before taking a sip from her glass of flavored seltzer that each of them had.

"Thank God for that. Anyway, he told me that he didn't want to admit his attraction to me for three reasons. One, the age gap."

"What? Eight years? So, big deal. Devon is ten years older than me."

Jenn nodded. "That's what I said. And Uncle Jake is nine years older than Nick."

"Okay, so what was reason number two?" Angie asked before sipping from her water tumbler.

"He thought I had hero-worship feelings toward him because he got shot when I was kidnapped with you."

"Ah. Okay, I can see his point about that. It could've happened. Hey, Kristen, didn't you write a hero-worship trope in one of your books?"

"Uh-huh." She sheepishly glanced at Jenn. "I got the idea from you and Doug. I thought that's what was going on with you, but in my defense, it was only a few months after the whole kidnapping thing."

Jenn's jaw dropped, and it took a moment to find her voice again. "Oh, my God! I'm Crystal in *Denim & Diamonds*?"

"Yup." She popped the P. "And Doug is Master Gideon."

"How did I not figure that out before now? Well, at least Crystal didn't have to wait four years for Gideon to get his head out of his ass."

"That's true. So, I take it Doug finally got *his* head out of his ass?"

She spent the next twenty minutes or so explaining everything, from when she kissed Doug last year and he ran away, to the earthquake, and how he, Lindsey, and Romeo showed up. Then she filled them in about everyone going to the mountain village, followed by the landslide, and her and Doug being trapped on one side. She told them about Margie dying, how she and Doug helped deliver the baby, and how they had to spend the night together in a borrowed cabin. Finally, she reached the part where she had the nightmare, and how Doug's comforting her turned into something more. Something surprising and wonderful.

The women were silent for a few moments when she stopped talking, then Shelby sighed loudly. "Kristen, if you don't write all of that into your next book, I'll bug the shit out of you until you do."

"Don't worry. I'm already plotting it in my head."

Satisfied with that response, Shelby turned back to Jenn. "Okay, so what am I missing? You sound happy that you and Doug are together, yet something is bothering you. Wait, didn't you say there were three reasons why he was reluctant to be with you? What's the third?"

"The Sexy Six-Pack," Kristen proclaimed. She had secretly dubbed Jenn's uncles that when she saw them at Donovan's pub before actually meeting them and getting involved with Devon. The fun moniker had stuck with the women—well, all except Jenn, who couldn't call her uncles sexy. *Ew*. "Am I right? The six annoying grown-ass men who still think of you as the little girl they've protected all your life, and not as an adult who can make your own decisions. A woman with wants, needs, and desires who finally has the man she's been dreaming about for years. Damn, I should be writing this down." She jumped up. "Let me get a pad and pen, but keep talking."

Jenn nodded to the other women. "Yes, it's my uncles, and the fact that he works for them. He thinks Uncle Ian is going to kill him and dump his body in the gulf."

Reaching over, Angie patted her uninjured arm. "Don't worry. I'll make sure that doesn't happen."

"Oh, *I'll* make sure it doesn't happen. I love my uncles, and not just the Six-Pack, but all the SEALs who worked with my dad and were there for me whenever I needed them. But it's time for them to realize I'm a grown woman, and if I have to stand up to them to be with Doug, then that's what I'll do." She glanced nervously at each of her confidants as Kristen retook her seat with a pad and pen in her hands. "Just not yet. I think Doug still needs a little time to get used to us. I don't want to lose him after everything we've been through. He fought his feelings for me for so long, and I want us to grow more comfortable with each other without any outside interference. And you know damn well my uncles will interfere as soon as they find out. So, for now, will you please keep it quiet for me?"

"Of course. Mum's the word," Shelby said. "Right, ladies?"

"Right!" Kristen and Angie agreed.

Shelby lifted her glass of seltzer and held it aloft, encouraging the others to do the same. "To Jenn, for finally claiming her man."

She laughed as the other women chorused, "To Jenn!"

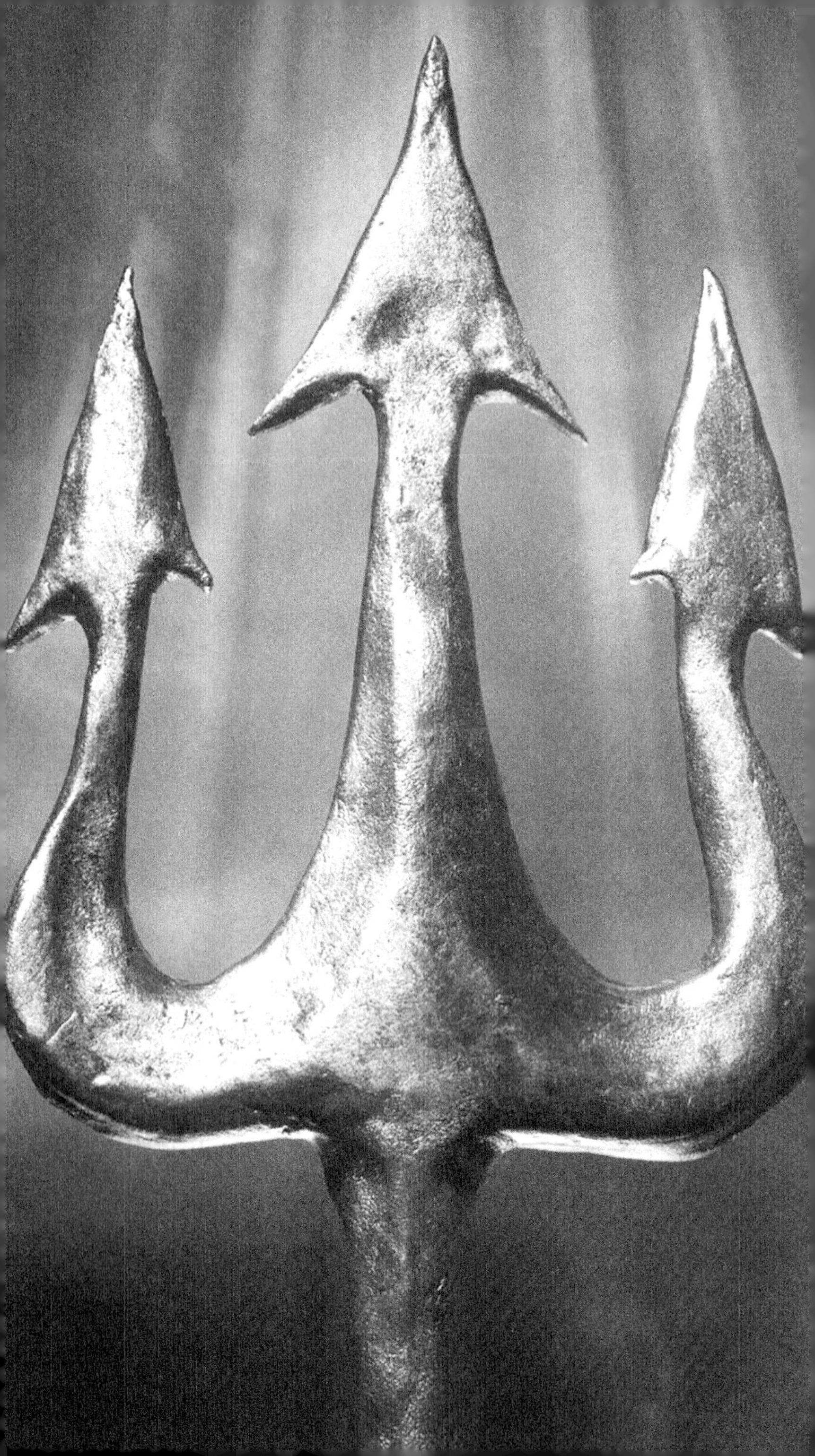

CHAPTER NINETEEN

As Doug stood with his back to her, lowering the anchor, Jenn stripped down to her royal blue bikini on the deck of his boat—*A Salt Weapon*. He'd cringed when she said the name was cute due to his profession and time in the military, which made her laugh. Men could be as sensitive about their toys as they were about getting their dicks injured or insulted, not that Doug had anything that could be insulted, even though she only had one other man to compare him to.

It was a beautiful Sunday afternoon, perfect for a few hours on the gulf's calm waters, away from everyone else. While Doug mostly used his boat for fishing excursions during his downtime, it had a kitchenette, a bathroom, and a table and couch that converted into a bed below deck. They could stay there all day and night as long as no storms were predicted.

They'd been home from Colombia for almost three weeks now, still keeping their relationship undercover. It hadn't been easy. Meeting up at places for dates during the day or evening, such as lunch, dinner, or the movies, was fine. They just avoided anywhere they might run into her uncles or people the men knew.

The problem was not being able to stay together overnight and waking up to each other every morning. Her place was out because everyone, meaning her uncles, would notice and question it if Doug's truck was at the compound in the middle of the night when it wasn't work-related. The same thing would happen if her car *wasn't* there. Since she shared a foyer with Jake and Nick, it was possible Doug could run into them too.

If all that didn't already make things difficult enough, the twenty-four-hour guard at the front gate was another issue. So was the fact that a text message would alert the on-duty guard, the Sawyer brothers, and Jake if any of the compound's other perimeter fence gates were opened, whether by a hand being scanned or a breach. That included the doors leading to a tunnel connecting the gym's panic room to an exit beyond the fence line, opening into the forest to the west. No, that hadn't been the retired Navy SEALs' idea, but she wouldn't be surprised if it were. The secure room and tunnel were discovered during the warehouse's renovations years ago after Ian and Devon purchased the property. They kept the panic room, updating it and reinforcing the door at the far end of the tunnel, which was concealed by landscaping. Even though the exit was outside the fence line, the brothers owned that land, too, and used the wooded area for training exercises.

They'd never needed to use the panic room, but it was fully equipped just in case. While she understood their business required various extreme safety measures, they made it nearly impossible for Jenn and Doug to spend the night together. A few times, she'd stretched the truth and told them she was sleeping over at a friend's house, but she couldn't do that every night and had to be satisfied with leaving his bed at a reasonable hour to go home. It was frustrating for both, but Doug didn't complain beyond asking her to stay for a little longer so they could cuddle.

While she felt guilty sneaking around, she couldn't bring herself to announce to everyone that they were a couple yet. Other than her aunts and Shelby, the only people who knew were her friends Daniella and Yardley. Oh, and Tony, of course—they'd stayed in touch.

It was inevitable her uncles would find out—it was

a miracle they hadn't already. She needed to tell them soon, but then the blessed silence would be broken. They would go apeshit, without a doubt.

She hoped her aunts' and Shelby's Dom husbands wouldn't take her secret out on their backsides—she needed to ensure that didn't happen. But for today, she put the thoughts of her overprotective uncles out of her mind so she could enjoy the day with her sexy man.

Strong arms wrapped around her bare waist from behind as she sorted through her tote bag to find the sunscreen she'd brought. Doug nuzzled her neck, and she felt his erection rub against her ass. "Damn, woman. You drive me crazy in these bikinis."

She smiled as she reached back and clutched his hips, holding him in place. "Why do you think I buy them?"

A deep growl emanated from his chest. "You've been wearing them for years, sunbathing in the yard."

"I repeat, why do you think I buy them? It sure wasn't to drive my uncles nuts. However, that was a bonus. You would think men who own a BDSM club wouldn't be so prudish."

"That's because they never changed diapers on the women in the club." He froze, then groaned. "Shit, maybe they have. That's one of those kinks I have no desire to hear about."

"Ew. Me either." She turned in his arms, then gave

him a sultry look while holding out the bottle of sunscreen to him. "Put this on me, please?" She could apply it to most parts of her body, but the cast made it impossible for her to reach the rest. Besides, she would take any excuse to have his hands caress her skin.

He shifted his hips and adjusted his cock before taking the bottle. "That cast is torturing me."

"You? Do you have any idea how much my arm itches under this thing? Now that's torture." The day after the cast was put on, she ordered a flexible plastic "cast scratcher" and had it shipped overnight. It came with sanitizer and was designed to prevent damage to her skin while providing her with much-needed relief.

As he rubbed the lotion into her back and shoulders, another boat passed by with three men in their early to mid-twenties aboard, who whistled and catcalled at Jenn. She rolled her eyes as Doug glared at them. She hated the immaturity and offensive sexual behavior some men exhibited toward women, as if they thought the women would be flattered by the attention. No matter what the male population thought, most females despised it. Maybe that was another reason she'd been so attracted to Doug over the past few years. She never heard him say anything derogatory toward women. Whether it was natural or nurtured, he respected the opposite sex and didn't seem intimidated by them in any way. She watched him get his butt kicked by Lindsey in the sparring ring a few times, and he gave her full credit for defeating him. Many men would've said they'd taken it easy on the female sniper, but not him. The Alpha and Omega Team members responded the same way if Lindsey won a sparring match against them. However, a few of the bodyguards were unhappy about losing to a woman, although they didn't vocalize it, as Doug and Ian wouldn't tolerate such behavior from their employees. In Jenn's opinion, it was nobody's problem but their own if they got their asses handed to them.

"Assholes," Doug muttered with a growl.

He lifted his hand, most likely to give them the finger, but she stopped him, not wanting said assholes to turn around and harass them. "Nope. Ignore them, please, and finish putting the sunscreen on me. Then, catch our dinner since I can't with this stupid cast." She was bummed about that. Being out on the water brought back fond memories of her father. She enjoyed fishing ever since her dad and Uncle Ian first took her on a charter boat at the age of seven, and she caught a flounder big enough to keep. Of course, her dad helped reel it in, but he let her do most of the work while both men coached and encouraged her. From that day on, she was hooked on fishing—pun not intended.

After Doug spent an extraordinary amount of time applying the suntan lotion to every inch of her exposed skin, she returned the favor before lying down on a bench seat with a book while he fished. He tried to convince her to go below deck for some sexy time, but she insisted he catch their dinner first. She even offered to clean and cook it if he caught a keeper, but he turned her down, saying it would be too difficult with the cast. At least he agreed to try to reel in a fish they could eat.

Even though the book was by one of her favorite authors, a friend of Kristen's, Jenn didn't get much reading done. Between her and Doug's conversation on several subjects and his coming over to kiss her multiple times, she didn't care about the book, which she could dive into later. Growing their connection to each other was more important—and a lot of fun. She loved discovering new things about him, and he seemed just as interested in her.

It was over an hour and three too-small-to-keep fish later before he caught one he didn't have to throw back into the water. The twenty-inch red snapper was on the menu for dinner that night. After she took a picture of him holding his prize, he tossed it into the cooler with ice before going below to use the head.

While waiting for him to come back, she texted the picture to Daniella and Yardley, wishing she could post it in the family's Facebook group, but that would bring up far too many questions she didn't want to answer. Sighing, she admitted to herself it was time to tell her uncles. She could do it at Peyton's first birthday party next week. With the number of people Angie and Ian invited, maybe they wouldn't make a scene. Oh, who was she kidding? They might not make a scene, but instead, would quietly drag Doug outside and lock him up somewhere until after everyone else left. She would have to discuss the best way to approach the subject with her aunts.

"Hey, Jenn. Come down here for a minute," he called from below.

Narrowing her eyes, she stood, not realizing how long he'd been down there. Holding onto the railing and ducking her head, she descended the stairs and stopped short when she saw him. The sneaky little bastard had converted the table and booths into a bed, stripped off his clothes, and gotten himself comfortable. His gaze met hers as he slowly stroked his stiff cock.

Deciding to tease him, she crossed her arms and leaned against the closed bathroom door to keep steady from the gentle rocking motion of the boat. "Whatcha doin'?"

His eyebrows shot up. "If you need to ask, sweetheart, we have a problem. I caught dinner, so now I get my reward. C'mere."

So much for teasing him. His husky voice and intense stare made her wet and needy in an instant. They sparked an inferno inside her that only burned for him.

After a few tugs on the strings of her bikini, she was naked and crawling up his body. His hands gripped her waist and pulled her up, settling her over his mouth. She cried out when his tongue speared into her, driving her wild. Within minutes, he sent her over the edge.

She straddled his hips and slowly lowered herself down onto his cock. It was a good thing she was now on the pill and they'd ditched using condoms after they both got a clean bill of health, because taking any precautions was the furthest thing from her mind. With his help, she rode him hard until they both came with shouts of ecstasy.

Still inside her, he pulled her down for a sweet and gentle kiss, then cupped her jaw. "Look at me." When she met his gaze, he brushed his thumb across her cheek. "I love you, Jenn. I know I should've said it before now, but that's the first time I've said those words to a woman who wasn't family. I love you, and I'm so grateful you waited for me to come to my senses."

Her heart pounded, and her breath caught as a sense of euphoria came over her. *He loves me!*

Bending down, she kissed him on the nose. "I'm so glad I waited for you too. I love you, Doug, and it's time to let everyone know that. I'm going to tell my uncles about us at Peyton's birthday party next week."

He smirked. "So there will be too many witnesses for them to kill me?"

A laugh erupted from her. "Something like that." She wriggled her hips and felt his cock respond. "Make love to me again."

He rolled them over until he was on top, still inside her. "With pleasure, sweetheart."

CHAPTER TWENTY

Two days later...

Doug's eyes narrowed at the text message on his phone as he turned off the treadmill and wiped the sweat from his brow with a towel. He'd been running for over half an hour and still had ten minutes left on his routine run, but apparently, it would have to be cut short today.

> **IAN**
> Conference room. Now!

Something big must've happened. But Doug was the only person the text was sent to. It wasn't posted in one of the multiple group chats he was in. That was strange, and he wondered what was up. A flash of worry shot through him. Had Ian found out about

Doug and Jenn? God, he hoped not. She wanted to tell everyone on Sunday at Peyton's birthday party, and even though he wasn't thrilled with keeping their relationship a secret any longer, he agreed to wait until then.

Maybe something had happened with one of the bodyguards under Doug's command. *Shit.* He hoped everyone was okay. Well, whatever was going on, he'd find out soon enough.

He ran the towel over his bare chest, abs, and under his arms before picking up the T-shirt he'd tossed aside earlier. The gym's air conditioning was on the fritz, not dropping the temperature below seventy-eight, and the HVAC company hadn't gotten there yet, so it was too warm to run in anything more than a pair of shorts. He pulled the shirt on, strode outside, and entered the warehouse next door, where the AC was cranked up, sending goose bumps skittering across his still-damp skin.

Surprisingly, Colleen wasn't at her desk, and the offices were quiet except for some low murmurs coming from behind the conference room door. Even the phones weren't ringing. It was all very odd for ten a.m. on a Tuesday.

As he approached the conference room, the door opened, and Nick stepped out, a massive grin lighting up his face when he spotted Doug. He left the door only slightly ajar and clapped Doug on the shoulder as they passed each other in the hall. "Hey, man. It was nice knowing ya. I'll be sure to send flowers to your funeral."

His heart rate sped up as Doug stopped short and stared at the younger man. "Shit. Ian found out—"

"About you and Jenn?" Nick walked backward toward the reception area. "Yup. *All* her uncles know. I'm supposed to get the shovels and a tarp. Sorry." Laughing, he shrugged, turned around, and jogged toward the front door.

Sighing, Doug hung his head for a moment. He knew Nick was kidding about the shovels and tarp—at least he hoped so—but it was time to face the music.

"Henderson, get your fucking ass in here!" Ian bellowed from the conference room.

Taking a deep breath, he exhaled forcefully, pushed open the door, and entered. *Crap.* Ian, Devon, Brody, Jake, Marco, and Boomer all stood on the opposite side of the table, with their arms crossed and fury in their eyes. To top it off, standing at attention beside Boomer were BDS&M—two Belgian Malinois and two German shepherds Ian had dubbed Bravo, Delta, Sierra, and Mike because he was a sarcastic son of a bitch. Boomer's wife, Kat, had trained the protection dogs, so he often worked with them. With a simple German command, Doug would become their target, their sharp teeth tearing into his flesh. It was a good thing he also knew their commands so that he could stop them in their tracks—hopefully. They would just think it was a new game, and he preferred to keep his limbs intact, thank you very much.

Shit. He was so screwed. At least they hadn't called in Carter, who worked for a covert US agency and probably knew over a hundred ways to torture a man, or more of Jenn's surrogate uncles from her father's SEAL team for reinforcements. Over thirty hardened military men from across the country had called her their Baby-girl since the day she was born. And every single one of them would kill or die for her.

As Doug shut the door behind him, Ian leaned forward and set his hands on the table, pushing down so hard that his fingers turned white. His expression was fierce and murderous. Well, Doug had led a relatively good life, but it looked like that was over now.

"Give me one good reason," Ian demanded, "one *damn* good reason why I shouldn't take my K-bar and rip you to fucking shreds before feeding your sorry ass to the dogs."

Trying not to show fear that they might take turns beating the crap out of him before dumping his body somewhere, Doug leaned against the wall beside the door as sweat beaded at his temples. At least he had an escape route, although he suspected he'd never reach the parking lot before someone or the dogs tackled him.

"It's not a fling."

"Let me just kill him," Devon said, taking a few steps toward the end of the table to circumvent it.

His older brother growled. "Not yet."

Ian had been the commanding officer of the other five men on SEAL Team Four, so it was natural that they always deferred to him or heeded his advice, both in the security business and in the BDSM club, and sometimes in their personal lives.

Doug fought the urge to roll his eyes. That wouldn't go over well in a roomful of Doms, even though he wasn't submissive or in the lifestyle. "Look. I know you all would kill and die for Jenn. I would too. This…this thing between us is something I've fought for a long time. Our feelings for each other didn't just happen overnight. Am I in love with her?" He paused before nodding. "Yeah, I am. She's the most incredible woman I've ever met. I want to wrap her up and keep her in a safe room where no harm would ever come to her. She wouldn't allow it—you all know that. Whether you like it or not, she's no longer a little girl. She's a beautiful, intelligent, amazing woman who, for some stupid reason, wants me. I'm humbled that she does."

"You're eight fucking years older than her!"

"Yeah, Boss-man, I am. And Devon is ten years older than Kristen. Jake is nine years older than Nick. Trust me when I say the age gap was one of my arguments while fighting my attraction to her, but she threw those numbers in my face and said she didn't care about our ages. Another reason I tried to avoid her was that I thought she had some hero-worship thing for me or something. But after spending time with her and talking, I realized that wasn't the case."

He ran a hand down his face and stepped forward. "Guys, look. I can't predict the future and say that every day will be smiles and roses between Jenn and me. Just like you can't with your spouses. But what I can say is I will protect her and treat her with the respect she deserves. I love her. And the only way I'll walk away from her is if she tells me to. No one else gets a say in that—not even you."

"How long have you two been together?" Jake asked.

"Only a few weeks. Since Colombia. But the attraction's been there for a while now. I was just fighting it until Jenn won me over."

His gaze flittered from one man to the next. The only two who still looked like they wanted to bury him under an ant hill were the Sawyer brothers. The others weren't happy, but they no longer appeared homicidal.

Ian stalked around the table and got in Doug's face, glaring at him. "Did you take her virginity?"

Rage flooded Doug's system, and his jaw tightened. He clenched his fists and stepped closer to his boss, until their chests bumped. They were the same height, so neither had that advantage. Although he knew Ian could take him in a fight, Doug would go down giving as good as he got. He dropped his voice to a low and threatening tone. "Watch it. You may be her godfather, but that's none of your fucking business. It's *nobody's* business but Jenn's."

Silence permeated the room as the two men stared daggers at each other. After a few moments, Ian nodded, and some of the tension eased from his body. "Good answer. But you're still not allowed to date her."

"What?"

Ian stepped backward and leaned against the conference table, crossing his arms again. "You heard me. Either break it off with her today, or you're fired and won't be able to find a job in Florida that doesn't pay more than minimum wage."

"You're not serious." Doug's gaze darted from his boss's face to that of every other man in the room.

"As serious as a heart attack," Devon said.

As Doug gaped at them, unsure of how to respond, Devon moved to the door and yanked it open. One by one, the men filed out, with Marco and Boomer giving him aggressive shoulder bumps as they passed. When Doug was the only one left in the room, except the dogs, he dropped into one of the chairs and shook his head in disbelief. After a few moments, he muttered a command in German, and BDS&M hurried over, sat by his feet, and stared at him. One of the Malinois, Delta, let out a sharp bark and tilted her head at him. Her expression was a bit goofy, almost as if she were laughing at him. She barked again, like she wanted to tell him something. Too bad he didn't understand canine. Maybe he should ask Kat to teach them how to use those dog talk buttons he occasionally saw in social media videos.

When Delta barked a third time, almost insistently, an idea popped into his head, and the corners of his mouth pulled up into a slow grin. Leaning forward, he scratched the top of the dog's head. "Thanks for the pep talk, D. I know just what to do."

CHAPTER TWENTY-ONE

Jenn stormed into Ian's office and slammed the door behind her. "How—"

She was seething, tension and rage rolling off her body in waves, but she cut off her rant when she noticed he was on the phone. His eyebrows lifted as he studied her from the executive chair behind his heavy mahogany desk. "Chase, I'll call you back. I think my goddaughter wants to kill me."

When he hung up the landline, she marched across the room and stood in front of the desk. "How dare you?" she shouted as her hands curled into tight fists.

Leaning back, he set one ankle upon the opposite knee, like he didn't have a care in the world or any idea what she was talking about. It only pissed her off even more. She usually found his arrogance and sarcasm amusing, but not when it was directed at her.

"How dare I what, Baby-girl?"

"No." She shook her head and crossed her arms. "No more 'Baby-girl.' I'm an adult, Uncle Ian. You don't get to treat me like a child anymore. And you sure as hell don't get to threaten the man I love."

"Is that what Doug told you? I threatened him?"

"Didn't you?"

He shrugged nonchalantly. "I guess it could've been interpreted that way. I'm surprised he mentioned it."

"Don't you always say that honesty is important in a relationship? That keeping secrets only causes problems down the road? Well, Doug was honest with me about your meeting with him yesterday. I mean, really? All six of you had to confront him? And with BDS&M there too?"

"Are you going to read the rest of them the riot act, or just me?"

"All of them are on my shit list right now—well, not the dogs. But the rest will get an earful, too, in a few minutes. I just started with you since I'm sure you were the ringleader. In the conference room, now!" Without waiting for a response, she turned on her heel, stalked out of the room, past Colleen's empty desk, and entered the conference room, where her backup awaited. Angie, Kristen, Kat, Harper, and Fancy stood at the head of the table with beguiled vengeance in their eyes—the vengeance was on her behalf.

After Doug relayed to her what had happened the day before, she told him she would take care of it, as if he had known she would. Her man wasn't stupid, and she was glad he let her be the one to stand up to her uncles. It was time the six of them had a come-to-Jesus moment together. Of course, she brought her tribe of trusted women to get her point across to the thick-skulled men. While there to support her, they promised not to intervene unless necessary. Jenn needed to stand up to her uncles and make them see she was no longer a child.

Nick wasn't invited to join either group since she was mad at him for being part of yesterday's antics, even though he hadn't been in the room when the others accosted Doug. She already yelled at him, and his punishment was to babysit Mara, Luca, JD, Zane, and Peyton in the she-shed while their mothers were with Jenn. Nick could handle one or two of the kids at a time, but she wouldn't be surprised to find him pulling his hair out after minding the five little ones by himself.

She joined the others at the far end of the room as Boomer, Marco, and Brody entered, their expressions quizzical. At her request, before Colleen went out to lunch, she sent a group text to Jenn's uncles, demanding their presence in the conference room.

Jenn pointed to the chairs at the other end of the table. "Sit and don't say one fucking word."

Their respective eyebrows shot up, and she wasn't sure if it was because of her tone, the command, or the fact that she'd cursed at them, something she rarely did. Whatever the reason, they did as they were told.

Ian strode in next, and when he spotted her posse, he stopped short and rolled his eyes. "Are you kid—"

"No! You sit with them with your mouth shut until I've had my say." When he glared at her, she stabbed her finger toward the chair closest to him. "Now, Uncle Ian."

With a frown, he pulled out the chair and sat. Jake and Devon were the last two to walk in, and after quickly reading the room, neither needed to be told what to do. They took seats next to the other troublemakers.

"Baby-girl—"

She gave Ian a dirty look, cutting him off with a low growl. Sighing, he held up one placating hand. "Go ahead. Say your peace."

After a glance at her support team leaning against the wall behind her, who all gave her nods of encouragement, she took a step forward, straightened her back, crossed her arms, and glared at her uncles. "Number one—Doug and I are a couple. We're not breaking up because you don't want us to date, so get over it. I've been in love with him for a long time, and I had to deal with him fighting his attraction to me ever since. Now that we've gotten over a bunch of hurdles, we're both committed to each other, and it's going to stay that way unless we—*he and I*—agree to go our separate ways with no input from you. When y'all met these amazing women behind me, and Uncle Jake got together with Nick, you eventually reached the point you knew they were your soulmates, the partners you wanted to spend the rest of your lives with. That's how I feel about Doug. He means the world to me, and I'll fight anyone who tries to come between us—even the six of you.

Before anyone could say a word, she continued. "Number two—how dare you confront him like that, as if he's an enemy or a traitor or something. And threatening to fire him over me?" She snapped her pointer finger through the air. "Yeah, that's not happening. If you had a problem with his performance at work, which I know for a fact you don't, it would be a different matter. But firing him because of our relationship? You do that, and I'll move out of the compound so fast it'll make your heads spin, and I'll never speak to you again."

Pivoting, she paced back and forth several times, trying to get her anger and imminent tears under control. She didn't want to cry in front of them and look like the child they seemed to think she still was.

However, the betrayal she felt got the best of her, and a few drops fell. She angrily swiped them away.

"Jenn—"

"No! I'm not done, Uncle Jake."

Chastised, he let out a heavy breath. "Okay."

She stopped pacing and resumed her earlier stance. "Look, I love y'all more than I can ever express. You've been there for me my whole life and took me in after my parents' deaths, and I could never repay you for everything you've done for me. Not that you'd let me, I know. But it's time you accept that I'm an adult now. You can't keep me in bubble wrap, and you sure as hell can't keep me isolated from the rest of the world. You have to let me live my life the way I want to and make my own decisions, whether you agree with them or not. I deserve to have someone love me in a way nobody else can—the way Doug loves me. Will I always look to you for guidance and support? Yes. That's a given. But in the end, I will make the final decisions that affect me. You also have to accept that I've fallen in love with the most wonderful man I've ever known, other than the six of you and my dad. He's smart, funny, protective, gentle, caring, giving, and so much more, and I would think..." She fought her quivering chin and swallowed a thick lump developing in her throat. "I would *hope* that's the kind of man you'd want to love me in return."

When she paused, her godfather started, "Baby-girl—"

"Nope! No!" She threw up her hands in frustration. "*Arrrghhhh.* Please, no more Baby-girl. It's time to stop calling me that."

His expression softened. "*Jenn*, please sit for a minute."

Since it was a polite request, and her earlier adrenaline was slowly seeping from her body, she sat in the closest chair. She was still pissed, but her mind was now a jumble of thoughts and emotions, and she forgot the rest of her practiced rant to them.

Ian leaned forward and rested his arms on the table. "First, I'll try to curb the use of your nickname and encourage the rest of these twats to do the same, but you'll always be my Baby-girl, so I may slip at times."

A pang of guilt squeezed her heart. "I know, Uncle Ian. I honestly never minded it before, but now that I'm twenty-three and in love, it feels childish. It's time to pass the nickname on to Peyton or Mara."

His smile didn't reach his eyes, which were full of understanding with a touch of sadness. "Nope. They may get their own nicknames someday, but there's only one Baby-girl in this family. However, now that I know your feelings about it, I'll do my best to use your given name."

"Thank you."

"Now, the second thing—me and your uncles confronting Doug." He shook his head. "Did you honestly think we'd let it slide after you both hid your relationship from us? It took balls for him not to come to us—or at the very least me—and say, 'Hey, I'd like permission to date your niece.'"

Her ire rose again, and she smacked the conference table with her uninjured hand, the loud *slap* echoing off the walls. "We're both adults. He doesn't *need* your permission, and neither do I."

"Fair enough. But hiding it from us wasn't very adult-like, was it?"

Okay, he did have a point there. "Maybe not, but that was my decision, not his. We were going to tell you at Peyton's birthday party—

"Where we couldn't kill him because there would be too many witnesses," Brody interrupted.

His words were almost exactly what Doug had said on the boat, and she grimaced. "Something like that. Look, I just...I didn't want y'all putting us under a microscope and waiting for us to...I don't know. For us to screw up or have a fight." She glared at the men. "Or for you to do something insane like threaten to fire him or kill him."

"I'm not saying any of us were thrilled to find out you and he are...are dating." Ian ran a hand down his face. "As far as I'm concerned, *dating* is the only word we'll use to describe whatever you two are doing. I don't want to know any details, and I'll die on a hill thinking you're still a virgin. And don't give me shit about that because it's the same hill I'll die on when Peyton grows up."

"Seriously, Ian?" Angie retorted. "Were you still a virgin at twenty-three?" She didn't give him a chance to say a single syllable. "I know for a fact you weren't unless you lied to me. Even if you were, it wouldn't be anybody's business but yours once you hit eighteen. And you're one to talk about not keeping secrets, especially after everything that happened with Jace."

He winced—his wife would never let him live that down—but it had nothing to do with the current situation, so he didn't respond to Angie's accusation. Instead, he studied the five women standing behind Jenn, his eyes narrowing. "Why are you all here?"

Jenn jumped in before any of them could answer the question. "Because I asked them to be here. They're my tribe."

Marco cocked his head. "Tribe?"

"Yes, Uncle Marco, *my tribe*. The women who will support me no matter what, even if that means going up against their big, bad Doms. And if I hear that any of them were punished for being here today, there will be more hell to pay with me."

If she wasn't mistaken, she saw surprise and respect in her uncles' gazes as they stared at her—she hadn't expected the latter but liked how it made her feel. Maybe they were finally getting it through their thick skulls that she was no longer a kid. Regardless, she got to her feet. "Now, this conversation is over. You *will* leave Doug alone. You *won't* fire or harass him. You *won't* punish your wives either. You *will* stay out of my love life unless I come to you for advice, which I probably won't do because—ick." At least that brought a smile to the men's faces and a chuckle from a few.

She pointed at them. "I'm still pissed at all of you, and it's going to take some time for me to forgive you for what you did. But I do know that you did it because you love me. And in some weird way, I love that you cared enough to try to intervene, but that doesn't mean I'm happy about it." She paused when a thought occurred to her. "By the way, how did you find out about Doug and me?"

"Nope," Boomer immediately blurted. "I'm invoking the man-code and not throwing anyone under the bus."

Brody shook his head. "Same."

She studied the rest of them, and only Jake wouldn't look her in the eye. "Uncle Jake?"

"It wasn't me, Jenn." He still wouldn't meet her gaze.

Her eyes narrowed. "It was Nick, wasn't it?" When no one answered, she knew she had her culprit. Technically, Nick wasn't a snitch. If she figured out he knew before he told anyone and asked him not to say anything, he would've kept quiet, but the man could spill the tea more than the women behind her combined. It looked like his current punishment wouldn't be enough. She'd have to think of another way to get back at him. "How did he find out?"

Jake sighed. "He was at the marina the other day on a case and saw you and Doug get off his boat and kiss."

"And of course, he couldn't keep his mouth shut or come to me first. Even though I love him like a brother, he's the worst gossip I know." She shrugged. "Making him babysit all the kids in the she-shed right now isn't enough punishment for him."

Marco's, Brody's, and Devon's eyes widened before they jumped up, cursing, and ran from the room. With confusion on his face, Boomer looked at Jake and Ian. "What's wrong with that?"

"He's probably teaching them to give the middle finger and feeding them all something with lots of sugar," Ian responded, getting to his feet. "So they'll be bouncing off the walls soon."

Boomer barked out a laugh while Jake grinned and rolled his eyes.

Turning to the women she considered both aunts and friends, Jenn gestured toward the door with her cast. "Ladies, it's time for our spa appointments. I need a massage, a facial, and a strong mimosa, and not necessarily in that order."

She strode toward the door where Ian stood. The sadness at the loss of his "Baby-girl" was written all over his face, making her stomach drop. But she had to be firm and stand her ground. "I'm sorry that I don't want the nickname anymore, Uncle Ian, but it's time for me to be the woman you and my parents raised me to be."

His stormy blue eyes brightened, and he nodded. "I know. And I couldn't be prouder."

CHAPTER TWENTY-TWO

Doug sighed as he stared at the text message.

IAN
My office now!

"Here we go again," he muttered under his breath before he tapped Stefan on the shoulder. "Boss-man wants me. You got this?"

He'd been helping Stefan with a class of police officers. Trident offered training sessions to teach them tricks of the trade that the military and black ops teams used. Many small-town police departments lacked SWAT or HRT teams and often had to wait for backup from larger agencies, which could sometimes arrive too late to save everyone during high-risk incidents. The training the officers received at Trident could give them the chance to reduce the number of victims, even with limited resources. Stefan was offered and accepted the position to oversee the new TS program after he was forced to retire from the Coast Guard for medical reasons.

Not taking his eyes off the cop shooting targets in the Hogan's Alley setup on the vast property, Stefan nodded. "Yeah. All good."

Doug jogged back to the main office. After leaving the conference room yesterday, he'd taken the rest of the day off and gone to talk to Jenn. His schedule was already free of any appointments and meetings, so he left a message on Colleen's desk, instructing her to call him if an emergency arose. His team would contact him on his cell phone if they needed anything. Despite his bosses' threat of dismissal, he still considered himself employed until he heard otherwise, so he'd arrived on time that morning, prepared to work.

Leaving Jenn to confront her uncles as she requested, he avoided going into the office and joined Stefan's training session at the south end of the compound instead. She'd already called him on her way to the spa to let him know she thought things had gone well with her uncles, but Doug might want to give them time to chill out after the dressing down she gave them. With a smile on his face, he agreed, but damn, he wished he'd been a fly on the wall of the conference room when she went off on them. It had taken a lot of convincing yesterday to keep her from reacting and going after her uncles immediately. He hadn't wanted her to say anything to them that she might regret. Sleeping on it gave her a chance to calm down, regain control of her emotions, and consider how she wanted to approach them. Thankfully, she'd heeded his advice before spending the night at his condo, letting him make sweet love to her.

When he strode into the reception area, wiping the sweat from his forehead, Colleen was at her desk. She glanced up, grinned at him, and gestured toward Ian's office. "He said to send you in as soon as you got here. By the way, I'm happy for you and Jenn. I always hoped you'd end up together. You're good for each other."

"Thanks. Too bad her uncles don't see it that way."

"Mmm. I wouldn't worry. They'll come around soon."

Doug wasn't sure of that but hoped she was right.

He knocked on the closed door and opened it after Ian barked, "Get your ass in here!"

Surprisingly, the man was alone in his office. Doug half-expected the rest of Jenn's uncles to be there too.

From behind his desk, Ian glared at him. "Sit down, tinsel-twat."

Suppressing a grin, he sat in one of the guest chairs across from his boss. It appeared Ian had given Doug a nickname off his infamous twat-roster, which likely meant death or loss of employment weren't imminent.

Rumor had it that you were only blessed with an insulting moniker if the man cared for you and you screwed up, or if you required a swift kick in the ass. Doug figured, in his case, it was a little of both.

"You need Jenn fighting your battles for you?"

Doug shook his head. "Nope. But it was never my battle. It was hers. You and the rest of them needed to hear from her that she's an adult and can make her own decisions. I could've talked until I was blue in the face, and it wouldn't have made a difference to any of you. But hearing it from her seems to have gotten the result *she* needed. I love her, Boss-man. That's not going to change because of an order or threat from you."

Leaning back in his chair, Ian nodded. "Understood. And I wasn't really going to fire you—thought about it, but you could've successfully sued us, so..." He shrugged. "I also wouldn't have fed you to the dogs—you'd give them indigestion, and Kat would have my head. Those damn dogs eat better than I do. Anyway, at least I don't have to worry about Jenn falling for some piece of shit I hate or someone from my club."

Doug smirked. "Nope. That's your thing. Neither Jenn nor I have any desire to participate in the lifestyle."

"Thank fuck for that. It's bad enough to know you're sleeping together. I don't need thoughts of you two involved in any form of kink play bombarding my brain."

He had to fuck with the man. Just *had* to. "Well, we're not into a lot of the stuff that goes on at the club, but a little spank—"

Ian slammed his hand down onto his desk so hard that it had to hurt. "No! I will fucking shoot you in the balls if you say one word about what happens between you and her behind closed doors, and I won't think twice about it."

Chuckling, Doug held up his hands in surrender. "Message received."

"All right. This is the part where I say, if you hurt her, they'll never find your body." When Doug just grinned, Ian gave him the finger and then changed the subject, handing him a blue folder. "Fair warning, the rest of her uncles and I will grumble about this for a while, but as long as Jenn is happy, we'll back off...for the most part.

Doug took that as a win and kept his mouth shut.

"Now, moving on. We have a new client in need of a bodyguard. Lainey Hall is a twenty-six-year-old," Ian paused and glanced at a piece of paper on his desk, "*social media influencer*, whatever the fuck that is, with a stalker. The police took a report but told her, since there were no threats or laws broken, there wasn't much they could do. So, she wants twenty-four-hour protection until the guy is stupid enough to do something and get arrested or smart enough to leave her alone."

While Doug knew what an influencer was, as did most people under sixty-five, Ian didn't have a single social media app on his phone or computer. He also resisted anyone's attempt to educate him on the current trends. His response was always that he paid his employees well to scour various sites or apps for intel on a target or client when needed, so he couldn't care less about not knowing anything about them.

Opening the file, Doug scanned the intake form, which contained the client's basic information that Colleen had collected during an initial phone call. A few pages from Brody were under that. He'd tracked down the stalker's name, date of birth, home address, driver's license, vehicle information, and place of employment just from the guy's TikTok handle, @4evrLaineys. For TS's head hacker, it was probably child's play to get all that.

Their new client resided in nearby Palm Harbor, while her stalker lived in East Tampa—too close for comfort. Usually, that type of creep was across the country or even on the other side of the world from their victim, and just harassed them online. But so far, according to the intake form, he'd only made contact with Ms. Hall through direct messages on her social media accounts. "Okay. This works out perfectly. Madsen, Spade, and Jacobson finished up their last detail on Saturday, so I'll put them on it. I'll grab Spade now and head over to the client's house for the interview, if she's available, then set up the schedule."

"Good. Now get out of my sight, tinsel-twat. And yes, I've penciled you in on my twat-roster. If you don't piss me off anymore, I may change it to ink in a year or two."

Doug's jaw clenched. He'd been the bodyguard for some brats and elitists before, but few compared to Lainey Hall, "Social Media Influencer, Extraordinaire." Her words, not his. He was surprised she knew any fourteen-letter words. Most of her sentences included many of the current slang and buzzwords, as if she were filming a video to upload to the internet later. She kept flirting with him and Nolan Spade, who would be her lead guard, while trying to impress them with her self-proclaimed celebrity status.

Through Trident, Doug knew several famous people—some well-known actors, a director, two record producers, a few professional athletes, and an internationally adored country music star—and this chick didn't even come close to being in their league.

A glance at Spade said the man was no more impressed than Doug was, which was nil. Granted, the woman was physically attractive, but she thought way too highly of herself, which was a huge turnoff—not that Doug was interested in her in any way, shape, or form. She was dressed in a baby-pink cotton crop top, which showed off her tan abdomen and belly piercing, and a matching pair of shorts that were so skimpy, they were almost indecent. Combined with her flirting, he was a little uncomfortable and kept biting his tongue to avoid telling her to go put on something more appropriate. She had no situational awareness and appeared oblivious to the fact that she was alone while scantily dressed, with two strange men she'd only met a few minutes ago. Doug had no doubt she would be a source of annoyance to the guards protecting her.

She seemed to think everyone in the world knew who she was, given that she had over a million followers on TikTok. Doug didn't want to burst her bubble—only because she was a paying client—and tell her that left about eight *billion* people in the world who didn't know or follow her. Neither Doug nor Spade had heard of her before looking up her social media accounts prior to the meeting at her home. Her videos primarily focused on fashion, makeup, and local clubs and restaurants in and around Tampa. He wouldn't be surprised if she were one of those influencers who demanded free stuff to promote a brand.

"So," Doug interrupted her bragging about how

many views her latest video had gotten. "Tell us more about this guy who is allegedly stalking you." He glanced at the first page in her folder that he'd brought with him. "His TikTok handle is @4evrLaineys, and he's been messaging you?"

"Yes! And it's not *allegedly*—he's stalking me. And that's not his only profile. He's creepy A.F."

Doug nearly snorted when she used the initials for "as fuck" in her dialogue. God, she was three years older than Jenn, and yet he thought Jenn was far more mature than her. In the past, he wouldn't have hesitated at dating a twenty-six-year-old, only five years his junior. But now, after talking with Ms. Hall for all of ten minutes, the age gap between him and Jenn seemed smaller than ever.

Removing a picture from the folder, he showed it to his new client. "Have you seen this guy before?"

She flipped her hair over one shoulder before leaning forward to study the photo. With her arms crossed under her breasts, it pushed them up and together. If she was trying to seduce either of them, it wasn't working because both men averted their gazes.

"Damn, he's hot!"

Gritting his teeth, Doug fought the urge to tell her off before walking out. "That wasn't my question. Have you seen him before?"

"No, I definitely would've remembered him. So, that's the guy who's stalking me?"

"We believe so. His name is Evan Jenkins. Sound familiar?"

She shook her head. "Never heard of him. Why doesn't he have photos of himself on his profiles? If he wasn't so creepy, I might've agreed to go out with him. I keep blocking him on all my accounts, but he just makes more profiles with similar names. Since you know who he is now, can't you go threaten him or something and force him to stop contacting me?"

As Spade bit his bottom lip to keep from either laughing or saying something rude, Doug took a deep, calming breath and released it. "Um, that's not how this works. We can pass on his information to the police and ask them to speak to him, but we don't go around threatening people. The police can't force him to stop either, unless things escalate. My guards will protect you while we gather evidence of the stalking, and when we have enough, we'll file for an order of protection on your behalf. Then, if he shows up anywhere you are, we can detain him and have him arrested."

"So, until something happens, you two will be my bodyguards wherever I go? Cool. At least you're both seriously hot." Before either man could stop her, she spun around on the couch and used her phone to take a selfie with them in the background.

Doug stood, snatched the phone from her hand,

and quickly deleted the photo before she had a chance to post it anywhere.

"Hey! What did you do that for?"

"No photos of your guards. It defeats the purpose of them trying to blend in so they can catch this guy doing something he can be arrested for. We don't want him to know who's guarding you or that you're even being guarded, so keep that information off social media. Now, I won't be on your detail, but Nolan will start today, then he'll rotate in eight-hour shifts with two other guards. I'll need a detailed account of your agenda for the next few days, but I'd prefer it if you stayed home for the most part. We need to know in advance whenever you'll be leaving here, so we can plan accordingly to ensure your safety. If need be, a second guard will be assigned if you're going anywhere crowded."

She sighed dramatically. "I can't stay home all the time. I need to see my friends and go places to make videos and take pictures. I have to post at least five times a day to keep all my followers and collaborators happy. The more views and clicks I have, the more money I make with my sponsors and affiliates."

"I'm sure you can figure out some videos that can be made here, but if you do need to go out, it has to be scheduled with the guards first. And no announcing where you are or where you're going on social media."

"But—"

He held up a hand. "No buts, Ms. Hall. Posting about where you're going will just invite this guy to show up. We still don't know what his plans are, but from his messages to you, he appears to be delusional enough to think he has a relationship with you. People like that can escalate to violence if they think they've been rejected or if someone like a guard stands between them and you. So, I repeat—no announcing where you are or where you're going. Take your pictures and record your videos, then wait until you're home or somewhere else before posting them. Nothing live."

"Fine. Whatever. This sucks." She stood and stalked toward her kitchen, leaving the two men alone.

Spade, a retired Marine Doug had served with, leaned toward him and lowered his voice. "You fucking owe me for this one, Bullseye."

"Yeah, I know. Your next detail will be an easy one."

"It better be."

CHAPTER TWENTY-THREE

When Doug strode into Jenn's apartment, she was busy in the kitchen preparing a salad. Now that her family and friends knew about their relationship, she had asked Brody to allow Doug's handprint to unlock both the inside and outside doors to her apartment, using the scanners on the walls beside them. Of course, Brody teased her about it, at first refusing to comply. But then she threatened to ask Fancy to cut off the supply line of sinfully delicious pastries, cookies, pies, and cakes that she sent to the TS offices every few days, which caused him to cave immediately. Fancy owned a bakery and pampered him with sugary confections whenever he wanted. Where he put it all was beyond everyone's comprehension because the man barely had an ounce of fat on him, despite the goodies and sitting in his war-room most days, monitoring the computer system in there and gathering intel. While Fancy wouldn't deny her Dom/husband the treats, a mutiny would occur at the TS offices if the rest of them had to suffer the loss, and Doug would lead the charge. Fancy's creations were worth the extra time he needed to spend at the gym.

"How was your day, dear?" Jenn asked in an overly sweet tone as he shut the door, dropped a duffel bag on the floor, and kicked off his shoes.

"Perfect, now that I get to see your pretty face." He meant it. She was the balm that soothed him at the end of a hectic day.

They met each other halfway across the open floor plan of the apartment's living, dining, and kitchen areas. Ignoring his sweaty TS polo shirt, Jenn wrapped her arms around his neck as he cupped her ass with both hands and squeezed. He leaned down and kissed her soundly on the mouth before tucking his face where her neck met her shoulder and nibbling on her skin. "I missed you. It's been a long day."

"Everything okay?" She pulled back and stared at him, her eyes narrowing. "My uncles didn't do or say anything to you after I left, did they?"

He shook his head. "Nope. In fact, Ian added me to his twat-roster."

A smile spread across her face before she burst out laughing. "Of course he did. So, what's your nickname?"

"Tinsel-twat," he replied, followed by a snort.

"What? Oh, my God. Where does he come up with some of these?"

"I have no clue, but I'm sure it could've been worse."

"I'm sure too. One of these days, I'm going to search his office for the list. I want to see what other potential names are on it." She gestured to his duffel bag. "Do you want to take a quick shower? Dinner's almost ready. I have chicken and dumplings cooking with another ten minutes or so left on the timer."

"A shower is definitely needed." He'd already taken two that day, one in the morning and another before he met with Lainey Hall, but with the temperature reaching a humid ninety-six earlier, just stepping outside had him drenched in sweat again. The apartment's air conditioning skated over his damp skin, making him shiver. "Want to join me?"

She ran a seductive finger down his arm, and her touch was like a direct line to his cock, which twitched. "As much as I want to say yes, I think once we're both naked, we'd go over the ten-minute mark. Honestly, I'm starving. Raincheck?"

He kissed her cheek. "You've got it. I'll be out in a few minutes."

After washing away the sweat and grime from his body, he put on a pair of gray sweatpants and a faded blue T-shirt. Their only plans for the evening were dinner and binge-watching a few episodes of *Grey's Anatomy*. While Jenn had been a fan of the show for years, Doug never watched it until she got him into it. Now, they were on the third season, and he was hooked.

He liked the domesticity of their time together. She still had another few weeks before she started her job in Tampa's Department of Social Services. While they did go out occasionally for dinner, a movie, or something else fun, staying in and relaxing was what they enjoyed most. Because their relationship had been a secret until yesterday, they'd spent their alone time at his place, but now he looked forward to nights at Jenn's. He'd only been in it a few times before. His condo was sparsely decorated, featuring only the bare necessities. The only things he'd splurged on were his recliner, TV, and bed. The rest of the furniture was chosen for its practicality, rather than comfort. However, Jenn's place felt more like a home. It was warm and inviting. While Ian and Devon had hired professional interior decorators to furnish their homes before they met their wives, Jenn had designed her own, personally choosing every item in it that wasn't a gift from someone else. A few decorative or functional pieces had belonged to her parents, like some of the artwork, knick-knacks, and kitchenware, and she cherished them.

He'd never realized it before, but Jenn was what

his mother would call an extroverted introvert. If she was out with friends or family, she enjoyed herself and chatted with everyone. However, she preferred to be a homebody more often than not, staying in and reading, watching TV, or doing stuff on her computer. With his wild oats days behind him, Doug was more than happy to spend quiet time at home with her. While the sex was amazing and he was always up for it, he also liked just being with her, even if they each had a book in hand, not saying anything while they cuddled on the couch and quietly read.

Jenn had just put the food on the dining table when he strode into the great room. "Mmm. Smells delicious."

She beamed at him as they both took a seat and filled their plates. "Thanks. It's my mom's recipe. Actually, it was her mother's, but my grandmother passed away before I was born. Mom made it a lot because it was one of my dad's favorites. I used to watch her sometimes, but never really paid attention to every little thing she did. After they died, it was a few years before I tried to make it." She shrugged. "It's a part of her that I really missed. I thought that if I could make it, it would bring back a lot of good memories, which it did, even though it took several tries before I finally got the dumplings right. Now, I cook it about once a month. It's comfort food, which with this cast making me itch like crazy and dealing with my insane uncles today, I could really use."

"It's also delicious," he said after swallowing a piece of chicken. "I'm glad you'll always have those memories of your mom. And someday, you'll pass the recipe down to your children."

Her hand holding a fork froze in midair. "Um. Wow. That's not something we've talked about yet. I love my nieces and nephews and hope to have kids of my own someday. Is that what you want too?"

He nodded and gave her a reassuring smile. "Yeah, it is. I love kids, but I was never sure I'd meet someone I would want to marry someday and have them with."

"And now?"

Putting down his fork, he crossed his arms on the table and gazed into her beautiful blue eyes. "I don't want to jump the gun yet, but yeah, I think I finally found that someone. I love you, Jenn. But I also don't want to rush things. We still have so much to learn about each other. We've known each other for years, but there's still so much about you that I don't know."

She reached across the table and laid a hand on his arm. "I love you, too, and you're right—we still have a lot to learn about each other. But I almost lost you once, and then I waited for what seemed like forever for you to come around and finally admit you had feelings for me. I don't want to pressure you, but I've known for a long time that you're the man I want to build a life with. Having said that, I can wait for you to catch up, even if it takes months or years. As long as I'm with you, I'm happy. Just know that, if and when you're ready to commit to a forever with me, my answer will be an immediate and emphatic yes."

Releasing his arm, she stabbed her fork into her salad. "Now, let's move on to a lighter subject. I stopped in the office earlier, and Colleen said you went to interview a new client. Is it classified, or can you talk about it?"

If he weren't already in love with her, he would've fallen right then. He didn't feel like she was demanding a formal commitment with the promise of a ring, a big wedding, a house with a picket fence, and enough kids to make their own baseball team. She just wanted him to know that she considered him to be her soulmate. Even though he wasn't ready to voice it, he felt the same. Someday, he'd get down on one knee and propose, of that he was certain now. But until then, he wanted to become an expert in everything that made Jenn the woman she was. Once again, he wanted to kick his own ass for fighting the attraction between them for as long as he had. So much time lost that he could've spent in her loving arms, in just her presence. He'd been a fool, but those days were gone, and he planned to spend the rest of his life making it up to her.

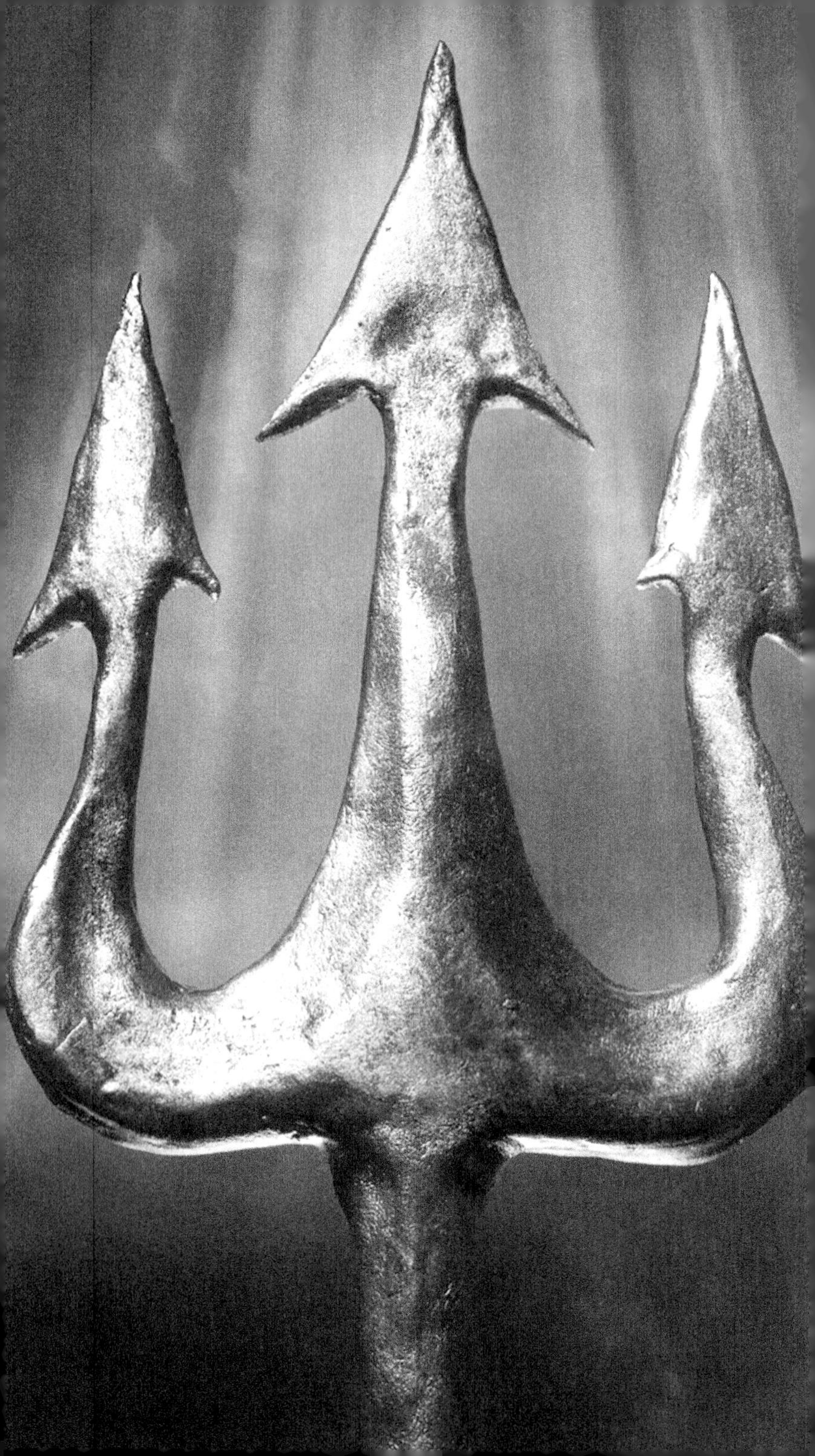

CHAPTER TWENTY-FOUR

Jenn's shoulders were stiff, her stomach in knots, and she hoped Doug didn't notice her distress. Since high school, the only other time she'd met a boyfriend's parents was when she and Cole were dating, and his folks visited the University of Tampa's campus for a family day. They were nice, but that was the first and last time she'd seen them since they lived outside of Chicago. Now, she was in the passenger seat of Doug's truck on their way to his parents' house for Sunday dinner. His grandmother, his sisters and their spouses, and his nieces and nephews would also be there. Insecurities flooded her mind. What if they didn't like her? What if they thought she was too young for Doug? Had she dressed okay? Was her outfit not formal enough for dinner?

She brushed a piece of lint off the cute navy-blue

capris she'd paired with a conservative but fashionable baby-blue top and red espadrille wedges. Some understated makeup and jewelry completed the look. Her top's right sleeve covered most of the still noticeable and ugly bruise on her upper arm, which had turned yellow and green as it healed. All her other cuts and bruises were gone, and her cast was due to be removed the following week.

Somehow, after Doug was shot protecting her, she hadn't run into any of his family when she visited him twice in the hospital before he was released. Now, she wished she had so they wouldn't be complete strangers to her. She knew Doug was close to his family, seeing them often and having lunch with his grandmother at least once a week at her assisted living facility. Would the older woman approve of Jenn? What if she didn't?

Maybe I should've worn that white and brown dress instead of capris. Ugh.

As she tried to rid her mind of all the negativity, she let out an exasperated sigh. Doug reached over and linked their pinkie fingers together. With her cast in place, he couldn't hold her hand. "What's wrong?"

"I'm nervous," she confessed.

He smiled at her before returning his attention to the road. "There's nothing to be nervous about. I told my mom all about you, our age difference, how I was an idiot for not seeing what was right in front of me, how I'm head over heels in love with you, and everything. She can't wait to meet you. The same goes for my sisters and grandma. My dad and brothers-in-law are all laid-back and not as nosy, so you have nothing to worry about with them. Listen, I know it'll be a little overwhelming at first—I'm sure they'll ask you dozens of questions—but trust me when I say your extended family is far worse."

A wry laugh escaped her. "Nobody is as bad as my family. Did I tell you that Uncle Marco and Uncle Brody wanted to sit you down and ask you about your *intentions*? Yes, that's the word they used—as if this were the 1950s. They also threatened a shotgun wedding even though I'm not pregnant. I shut that stuff down quickly and told them that if they did either of those things, I wouldn't babysit for them anymore. Not that I would go through with it because I love when Zane, Mara, and Luca come to visit, but they didn't need to know that. Anyway, they backed off."

"They mentioned the shotgun to me too. I think they just like busting our chops. They all still give me shit whenever I mention you, but it's no big deal. It just proves they love and care about you. They'll get over it sooner or later."

"Hopefully, sooner. Oh, I forgot to tell you." She turned a bit in her seat to look at him. "The charity that organizes Dr. Sanchez's volunteers sent me an email. Next month, since the funeral was private, Margie's family is holding a memorial for her in Albuquerque, and they've invited the volunteers who worked with her at the commune. It's on a Saturday. I told Uncle Ian that I wanted to attend, and he said Clinton could fly me out there if the jet wasn't needed for anything. If it is, I'll get a plane ticket. I'd like you to go with me, if you want."

He gently squeezed her pinkie. "I'd be honored to go with you. It's nice that her family wants you all there. Just give me the date so I can add it to the schedule. If we can, we'll make it a long weekend and go sightseeing or something."

"That would be awesome. I've never been to New Mexico."

"Neither have I."

She settled back in her seat. "Oh, and Tony called to check up on me. He said he got the email, too, and plans to be there if he can get the day before it off." Doug growled, causing Jenn to giggle. "What's wrong with Tony? He's a nice guy."

"Who wanted to get into your pants!"

"What?" She playfully slapped his bicep with her free hand. "You idiot. Tony's gay."

His gaze whipped to hers. "Huh?"

"Yes, my sweet, jealous boyfriend. God, I love calling you that—the boyfriend part." He liked hearing it. "But yes, Tony is gay. If anything, he wanted to get into your pants or Romeo's, not mine. He's heading home next week because the school year opens soon, and I hope he finds someone special. His last partner dumped him by email while we were in Colombia after they were together for two years."

"What a douche. His partner, not him...Tony. It sucks that happened to him."

She smirked because apparently, he now agreed that Tony was nice since he wasn't interested in the female sex, especially Jenn. "Exactly. I told him good riddance."

Their conversation had a calming effect on her, but when Doug pulled up to a house in Tarpoon Springs and parked beside the curb, her gut twisted again. "Oh, God. We're here."

After turning off the engine, Doug leaned over and kissed her gently. "You'll be fine. I promise. Just be yourself, and they'll love you."

She wished she felt as confident as he did. "Right. Well, here goes nothing."

Shaking his head and smiling, he opened the driver's door, climbed out, and rushed around to open her door. Her heart fluttered when he held out his hand to help her down from the elevated truck seat. Yup, he was still a Dom-unaware. Her parents would've loved him and all his gentlemanly gestures toward her. He opened doors, pulled out chairs for her to sit, walked between her and the street whenever they were on a sidewalk, and did many other things that showed how much he loved and cherished her. Over the years, she'd watched her uncles perform similar acts with their partners, and she knew the man she gave her heart to would have to be cut from the same cloth.

In return, Jenn treated Doug as if he'd hung the moon. She loved cooking and doing special things to show him how much she adored him. They might not live the BDSM lifestyle, but the mutual respect and care they showed each other could rival any couple who did.

After shutting the passenger door, Doug opened the one behind it and handed Jenn a bakery box while he carried another. They'd picked up desserts at Fancy's on their way to meet his family. Cupping Jenn's elbow, Doug led her up the walkway to the front door, which opened before they reached it. An older couple stood there, beaming at them, and Jenn gulped. They had to be his parents. She hoped her attempt to put on a sunny expression belied her anxiety.

"It's about time you got here," Doug's mother said as she stepped out onto the small porch and opened her arms.

Doug released Jenn's elbow and gave his mother a hug and a kiss on the cheek. "Hi, Mom. Hey, Dad." He stepped aside and pivoted to face her, giving her an encouraging smile. "This is Jennifer Mullins, the incredible woman I've been telling you about. Jenn, these are my folks, Eleanor and Owen Henderson."

Before Jenn could get a word out, his mother stepped forward and embraced her. "It's so nice to meet you finally, Jennifer." She leaned back to look her in the face. "Please, call me Ellie."

She grinned, thinking her own mother would've greeted Doug in the same way. "It's nice to finally meet you, too, Ellie. And you can call me Jenn. Everyone does."

"Nice to meet you, Jenn. Let me take that from you." Owen opened the door further to let her in, took the bakery box, and offered his elbow to her. "Let's get you inside and introduce you to the rest of the family before they burst. They've been waiting a long time for Doug to finally bring home a woman he's dating."

Her eyes widened as she placed her hand in the crook of the older man's elbow and glanced over her shoulder at Doug, who shrugged apologetically. He'd never brought someone home to meet his family? How did she not know that?

Great. Now, the knots in her stomach became flying bats, which seemed to be creating their own little tornado.

She was led into a large living room filled with three couples and one elderly, slender woman. Except for the latter, they all stood. The men smiled warmly at her, but it was the women who caught her attention. Their expressions were filled with a combination of glee and curiosity. Owen patted her hand and then released it. "Everyone, this is Jenn Mullins. Give her a few minutes to get used to us before you start bombarding her with questions." He leaned toward Jenn, gave her a wink, and stage whispered, "They can be a loud and nosy bunch, but they don't bite."

She smiled at his attempt to put her at ease, as he gestured toward the older woman. "Jenn, this is Doug's Nana, my mother, Janice Henderson."

With a twinkle in her eye, the woman smiled at Jenn and held out her hand. "It's a pleasure to meet you, dear."

She stepped closer and gently shook the wrinkled but surprisingly strong hand. "It's a pleasure to meet you, too, Mrs. Henderson. Doug has told me so much about you."

"All good, I hope."

"Oh, yes. I promise it was all good."

The woman nodded her approval before her son cupped her elbow and cocked his head toward the three couples.

"Jenn, these are my daughters and their husbands." Owen pointed at each person as he introduced them. "Grace and Julian Stoll, Lila and Christopher Yearwood, and Rowan and Wesley Gannon. The grandkids are playing in the backyard—all six of them. We'll introduce them to you later after they've burned off some of their rambunctious energy."

Doug's sisters and brothers-in-law exchanged greetings with her before Julian took the bakery box from Owen. "I'll put this in the kitchen, Pops. Have a seat, Jenn. Can I get you something to drink?"

Glancing around, she noticed all the women, except a heavily pregnant Rowan, had glasses of wine, while the men held bottles of beer. "Um. If there's more white wine, I'd love a glass, please." It would help settle her nerves.

"You've got it." He glanced over her shoulder. "Hey, Doug. Let me take that box from you too. I'll grab you a beer."

"Thanks, Jules," Doug responded, moving to stand beside Jenn. After his mother joined them, he gestured for Jenn to sit on a loveseat, then perched beside her as his family settled onto a long couch and several chairs around the large, but comfortable, room.

"So, Jenn," Lila started. "Tell us how you finally got my little brother to commit to the point he brought you to meet us. He's *never* done that before—not even in high school. I was starting to think he was in the closet or he'd be a hopeless bachelor for life—not that there is anything wrong with either of those."

She tittered nervously and blushed. "Would you believe me if I said it took a few years to break down his walls?"

"I can *absolutely* believe that. He can be a stubborn schmuck at times."

"Hey!" Doug cried. "No picking on me. You did that enough when we were kids."

"That's what big sisters are for!"

"Well, all I can say is it's about time," Ellie chimed in. "And from what Doug told me about you, Jenn, I think he found a winner. I couldn't believe it when he explained what happened to you in South America during that earthquake. I would've hopped on the next plane out of there, but you insisted on staying. You're a brave woman."

"What happened?" Jules asked as he returned, handing Jenn and Doug their drinks. "I only heard you were both in Colombia when the earthquake hit, but didn't someone mention something about a landslide too?"

Jenn nodded. "Yes. And neither of those things were on my bingo card for that trip or even in my lifetime."

Everyone laughed, then asked for details, which she and Doug supplied while keeping the private, intimate moments to themselves. After an hour of chatting, appetizers, drinks, and football on the TV in the den, Ellie announced that dinner was ready. By then, Jenn felt much more at ease with Doug's family. They'd briefly stepped outside to the fenced-in backyard so she could meet his nieces and nephews, ages four through thirteen. The adults took turns checking on them every five or ten minutes, while Lila's oldest girl, Emma, kept an eye on them until it was time to come inside.

The meal was delicious, and Ellie beamed when Jenn asked for the recipe for the pot roast she'd made. Everyone, especially Nana and the children, enjoyed the treats from Fancy's bakery, and Rowan commented she would love to check out the cakes there when it was time for her baby's christening. Jenn wrote down the business's name and address for her. "Just tell Fancy I sent you. She's married to one of my uncles and is one of the sweetest women I know. Her cake designs are amazing. I'm always in awe of her talent."

Earlier, she told Doug's family that her parents died—omitting that they were murdered—when she was seventeen, how her godfather had taken her in, and how her "uncles" were men who'd served closely with her dad. The group had been sympathetic and, thankfully, hadn't asked too many invasive questions. When Lila asked how her folks died, before Jenn could answer, Doug simply said it was an accident and subtly steered the conversation in another direction. Under the table, he'd squeezed Jenn's thigh, silently telling her that he knew she was reluctant to talk about it, and she was grateful he'd read her body language correctly. Since the first night they'd made love, they seemed to grow more in tune with each other as the days and weeks passed. Someday, she might fill his family in on the morbid details, but for now, they seemed content with what they knew.

Everyone but his parents and Nana was surprised to learn that Jenn was the asset Doug had been protecting when he got shot. Though the revelation sparked more questions, it was Ellie who shifted the subject, offering Jenn a knowing look that showed she understood the younger woman wasn't ready to talk about the painful incident. His mother probably also didn't want to relive the horror of almost losing her only son.

By the time the sun went down, they were all stuffed and exhausted. When it was time to say goodbye, his sisters invited Jenn to join them for lunch one day soon, and Nana told Doug to bring Jenn the next time he visited her at the assisted living facility. Ellie said she expected Jenn to attend the family's next Sunday dinner in two weeks. No one had questioned the age gap between her and Doug, nor did they give any indication they weren't happy for the couple. Everyone had been pleasant, making her feel welcome and accepted.

Relief that all had gone well warmed over Jenn as she climbed up onto the passenger seat of Doug's truck. After shutting her door, he circled the vehicle and got in. Before starting the engine, he leaned over and kissed her softly on the lips. "They loved you."

"Really?"

"Mmm-hmm. My sisters don't invite just anyone to join their lunch dates. My dad and brothers-in-law all said I was a lucky man. And my mom and my grandma both pulled me aside a little while ago and told me to hold onto you with both hands."

She sagged into the seat. "Oh, thank God."

He chuckled and started the engine. "I told you there was nothing to worry about today. Now, when it's time for your family to meet mine—*yyyyeah*, that's when we should both start to worry."

"Why?"

"Um...have you met your uncles?"

She stared at him, wide-eyed. "Oh, shit. You're right."

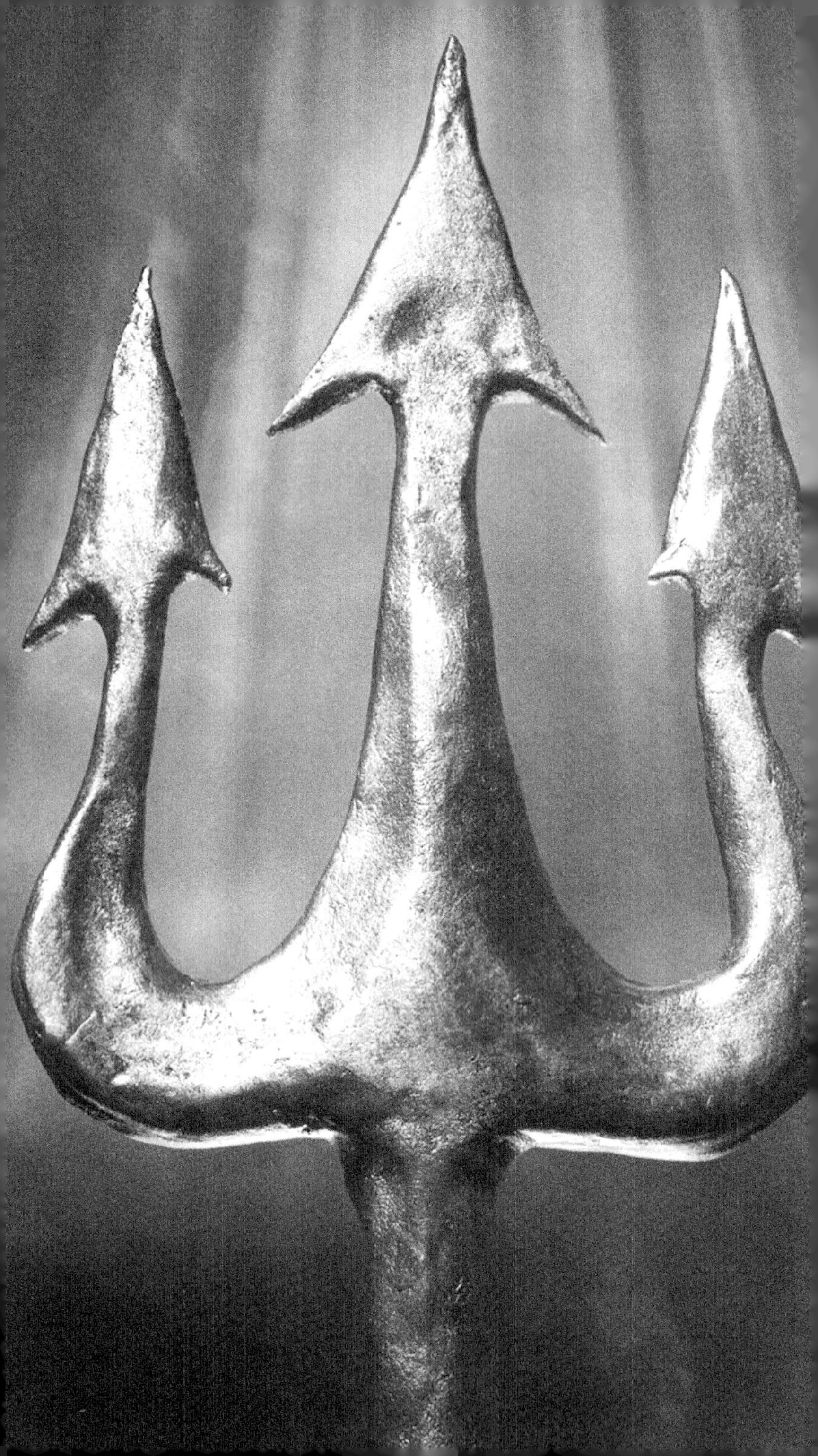

CHAPTER TWENTY-FIVE

Irritation coursed through Doug's veins. The last thing he wanted to do was babysit Lainey Hall, but there he was, standing in a dance club she insisted on going to with her obnoxious friends as they sat in the VIP section. The music was so loud, to the point that the bass reverberated through every cell in his body, and he wondered how anyone could hear themselves think, much less talk to anyone else. He hadn't been able to talk her out of going because other social media influencers were there, and she refused to be left out. God forbid they were at a popular event while she stayed home, safe from her stalker.

Other than constantly creating new profiles and messaging Lainey, Evan Jenkins hadn't done anything else that they knew about. None of his DMs threatened her—they were just of the "Oh, you're so sexy" and "We should go out sometime" variety. Doug was beginning to wonder if they were wasting their time protecting Lainey, but as long as she paid Trident's fees, they would stay on her detail.

While she hadn't posted any of her guards' faces in her online photos and videos, they hadn't been able to stop her from talking about the stalker and the fact that she now had bodyguards. Despite their repeated warnings that doing so was counterproductive to reducing any threat against her, she continued to post, mentioning one or both at least once a day. She'd tried to snap a photo of herself with Peter Jacobson in the background the other night, but the TS employee noticed it right away and demanded she delete it. She reluctantly did that, complaining that she'd only taken the photo because her followers kept asking if her bodyguards were hot and wanted her to post pictures of them.

On the other side of the roped-off VIP section, Nolan Spade had his head on swivel as he kept an eye out for any threats. Doug was only stuck with the assignment because every other bodyguard in the Personal Protection Division was either already on a detail, recovering from long shifts, or out sick. Over the past few days, a stomach bug had affected about a quarter of the TS staff. Anyone with even the slightest symptoms was ordered to stay home in an attempt to prevent it from spreading further.

A waiter appeared, carrying another full tray of drinks. Scowling, Doug unhooked the gold velvet rope blocking anyone not invited from entering the area. He lost count of how many drinks had been delivered to the party of eight—five women and three men, who were well on their way to being drunk off their asses. Doug had demanded all their car keys two rounds ago. While his asset was Lainey, he couldn't in full conscience allow any of the others to drive drunk and possibly kill themselves or anyone else. After giving him shit, they finally handed over their keys when he threatened to call a few friends on Tampa PD to wait in the parking lot and nail each of them for DUI.

"Wahooo!" Lainey shouted before downing half her drink. She spilled the rest of it on the table when she tried to put the glass down, which didn't seem to bother her at all. "Let's go dance."

Doug met Spade's gaze as the other man shook his head and rolled his eyes before watching the crowd again. It was the fourth time Lainey had tried to leave the VIP section, but Doug refused to allow her out on the dance floor, which was too crowded for the men to protect her.

He grabbed her arm as she tried to pass and pulled her out of the way of her friends, who were free to go wherever they pleased. Dressed in a silver, metallic dress that stopped mid-thigh and matching high-heeled shoes that he had no idea how she walked in, Lainey pouted and stomped her foot like a petulant five-year-old. "I wanna go dance! Let me go!"

Leaning forward so she could hear him, he repeated the same thing he'd told her the three previous times. "Either obey our rules or hire another company." Ian had permitted him to tell her that after learning how difficult she could be. If a client refused to follow the rules for basic protection, Boss-man was more than happy to drop them rather than putting his employees at risk. "We can't protect you on the dance floor. It's bad enough that there are far too many people in this place. Unless you have to use the restroom, you're staying right here."

She ran her hand up his arm to his shoulder in a provocative caress. "You're a party-pooper, you know that?"

"Yup, I do." He tried to shrug off her wandering hands, now that the other one had joined the first. "Either stay in this section, or we're taking you home. If that happens, then tomorrow you can find new bodyguards to put up with you."

Stepping closer, too close for his comfort, she wrapped her arms around his neck and rubbed her body against his. He put his hands on her hips and tried to push her away, but she stumbled back into him, her face pressed up against his neck. After being with Jenn, having another woman who was intimately close to him felt wrong and unwanted on so many levels.

"Come on, Doug! Don't you wanna have some fun? Let's go somewhere private."

"Ms. Hall." He made an effort to back her up again but held on to her waist to keep her from falling when she swayed. He had no desire to take her to the ER if she injured herself. Unfortunately, she leaned forward, wrapped her arms around his neck again, and tried to kiss him. He dodged left to avoid her lips. When she dropped one of her arms and made a grab for his crotch, he was done. Enraged, he snatched her wrist and twisted it away from his family jewels. "Lainey! Knock it off!"

"Yeah, *Lainey*. Knock it the fuck off!"

Doug froze as his gaze found a livid Jenn standing on the other side of the VIP rope. *Oh, fuck.*

Her arms were crossed over her chest as she glared at them. Beside her was Yardley Adams and two other women he recognized as her friends. He'd known Jenn had made plans to go out with them since he was stuck working, but he didn't realize they would be at the club. Then again, Jenn hadn't known he would be there since he didn't specify which client he'd be protecting and where she wanted to go.

"Who the fuck are you?" Lainey asked Jenn as she staggered away from Doug and leaned against a round support pillar.

"Doug's girlfriend who's going to bitch slap you if you don't leave him alone. He's made it perfectly clear he doesn't want you to touch him. And don't try to tell me otherwise. I saw the whole thing."

Oh, thank God. Hopefully that means she's not pissed at me!

He glanced at Spade, who seemed to have one eye on the disaster unfolding and another on the crowd. The man knew Doug could handle the situation he found himself in and continued to do his job. Until a TS supervisor indicated that the detail was over, the bodyguards remained alert for any potential danger.

Lainey looked Jenn up and down with a sneer as if his gorgeous blonde bombshell were a piece of trash. "Oh, please. He must have better taste than you."

Infuriated, Doug was about to say something beyond rude, but stopped when Spade yelled, "Hey!" and jumped over the short wall between the VIP section and the dance floor, diving onto some guy and taking him down. A few people around them screamed and scrambled backward, uncertain of what was happening. Doug spotted several security guards headed their way. He hopped over the rope and told Jenn and her friends to stay back. Once he was sure they were out of the way, he helped Spade restrain the man.

"Get the fuck off me!" the guy bellowed as he

thrashed about, but Spade had him secured. "I'll fucking kill you! Get off me!"

With one of his arms pulled behind his back and up, Spade and Doug hauled him onto his feet, where he continued to throw out demands and threats at them. Doug finally got a good look at the guy's face and realized it was Evan Jenkins, Lainey's stalker. He must have seen the woman's posts on social media—the ones Doug and Spade had told her not to upload. *Damn it.*

Doug was surprised when someone punched him in the back, not hard enough to hurt him. Spinning around, ready to deck the person, he faced Lainey who feebly thumped his chest with her fist and yelled in his face, "Leave him alone, you assholes!"

"What?" He stared at her in shock. "Why? This is the guy who's been harassing you!"

Jenkins stopped trying to get away. "Harassing her? What the fuck are you talking about? We've known each other for years. Those DMs? She told me to make a bunch of profiles and send them to her so she could go viral for having a stalker! She said not to make any threats because then the cops wouldn't do anything if they even bothered to track me down. She paid me to do it!"

"Shut the fuck up! I did not!" Lainey stumbled into one of the burly security guards, who managed to catch her.

Doug's gaze went back and forth between the two. Within seconds, he was ninety-five percent certain that Jenkins was being truthful. "You've got to be kidding me."

"Hey!" the guard holding Lainey up shouted over the music. "Can we take this outside?"

"Yeah. Good idea."

Spade and Doug led Jenkins out to the parking lot, while the security guards escorted Lainey. A decent-sized crowd followed them, including Jenn and her friends, with many recording the incident on their phones. As long as they stayed back and weren't in any danger, Doug was okay with that. He had to deal with Lainey and Jenkins first.

Two Tampa PD patrol cars pulled up, lights flashing but sirens off. Four officers got out and strode toward them. They didn't hurry, as it was apparent that things were somewhat under control.

"Look, I can prove it to you," Jenkins said when Spade released him and pushed him against the club's exterior wall.

"Shut up, you idiot! You can't prove shit!" Lainey yelled at him.

Jenkins reached into his back pocket, but Doug grabbed his arm, earning him a glare. "What? It's just my phone."

"Pull it out slowly," Doug ordered, letting him go.

It was probably a phone, but he was ready for a weapon just in case.

When Jenkins showed him the latest iPhone, Doug relaxed a bit. The guy entered his password, then opened his text app. "See?"

Lainey screeched and lunged for the phone, but one of the security guards caught her around the waist and held her back. Doug took the phone and scrolled through the messages. The contact's name was Lainey, and the phone number matched hers.

"Son of a bitch," he muttered before stepping forward and getting in her face. "You made this whole fucking thing up for social media views? It was all a hoax? What the hell? You're nothing but an egotistical fake!"

"I'm not a fake!" she screamed and tried to slap him across the face, but the guard yanked her backward and dropped her on her ass, clearly without remorse. With her hair and makeup now a mess, Lainey continued her drunken rant and tried and failed to get to her feet several times, much to the amusement of the bystanders.

Doug turned to the police officers and recognized one of them, Lynette Johnson. He'd gone on a few dates with her last year while trying to avoid Jenn. Lynette had been with him when Jenn was accosted by the gang members in the parking lot of Donovan's

Pub. Thankfully, the two women became friendly with each other after the incident and Doug was no longer dating the pretty officer. "Hey, Lynette. I'm pressing assault charges. She hit me inside the club—twice. Not that she did any damage, but she still assaulted me. And she also filed several false police reports about a stalker and hired us to protect her. It was all a ploy to get social media views." He handed her Jenkins' phone. "Here's the proof."

The female officer smirked. "She's also drunk and disorderly. We'll add that." She glanced over his shoulder. "Hey, Jenn."

Jenn and Yardley stepped forward. It was then Doug noticed the latter was filming everything on her phone, although she kept it pointed at the train wreck named Lainey. Jenn smiled. "Hi, Lynette. We have the entire incident recorded. You can add sexual assault to the charges too. Yardley has her on video trying to grope Doug without his consent."

The female officer arched her eyebrows at him. "Did she now?"

He rolled his eyes and sighed. While he was a little embarrassed about it, he knew Jenn would feel better if the charge was filed. "Yeah, you can add that too."

Lainey screamed her head off as two of the other officers helped her stand, then placed her in handcuffs. She racked up more charges when she tried to kick them and spit on one's shirt. They ended up using a hobble restraint, a device that wrapped around her ankles and was connected to the handcuffs behind her back, limiting her movements even more, before placing her into the rear of a patrol car.

Since Yardley's video was live, she emailed the link to a Tampa PD address that Lynette had given her for evidence. The club's security guards dispersed the crowd, and two officers took statements from Jenkins and several witnesses. As they did that, Doug walked with Lynette and her male partner to their vehicle, providing them with a few more details about what had led up to the night's events. "I'm not sure if there's anything you can charge Jenkins with. I mean, it's not a crime to send texts to someone who asked for them and paid you."

Lynette agreed with him. "She's an idiot, but at least she knew that if she made the profiles and sent the DMs to herself, you guys would've figured that out right away."

"I wish she did. I'll have Colleen charge her credit card first thing in the morning for the remaining hours we logged this week, before she gets bailed out. If she tries to back-charge it, we'll sic the lawyers on her."

"Good idea. So," she said with a grin when they stopped beside the passenger side. The closed doors and windows muffled Lainey's screeching and cursing, and both officers ignored her for the moment. "I heard from Dakota that you and Jenn are now an item." Dakota Swift was also on Tampa PD, the girlfriend of Logan Reese from the TS Omega Team, and a member of The Covenant. "About damn time you got your head out of your ass."

He opened his mouth to give a snarky retort, but then changed his mind. Despite their failed attempt at dating, he and Lynette were friends, and what she said was the truth. "Yeah, you're right. It was about time."

"She's good for you. Every time you look at her, there's love in your eyes. I'm glad it's working out for the two of you."

"Thanks. What about you? Anyone special in your life?"

"Maybe. I met someone a couple of weeks ago, and the first two dates went well." She shrugged. "We'll see how it goes."

Her partner handed Doug a card. "Here's the case number. Stop by tomorrow to give your statement and bring her file and any other evidence you've got." Many TPD officers had worked or trained with Trident Security employees before, so they were familiar with the company's practice of keeping detailed notes on every case.

"You've got it." Doug shook the man's hand and then Lynette's. "Sorry you got stuck with that nutcase."

She chuckled. "No worries. She seems like she'll be entertaining. It was a boring night before this. Take it easy, Doug."

"You too. Stay safe."

"Right back at ya."

As they got into the vehicle, Lainey's vitriolic rant grew louder before they shut the doors again. Doug returned to where Jenn and her friends stood, laughing as their gazes were glued to Yardley's phone. Jenn looked up and smiled at him. "Yardley's video is already viral. Lainey's going to lose a lot of followers after they see it."

Doug couldn't care less, but then again, he was kind of glad that karma was a bitch. He and his men had wasted almost two weeks protecting someone who didn't need it, all so she could post lies for views.

Spade approached. "So, does this mean we're officially off duty?"

"Yup. Although we have to go give our statements tomorrow."

"No problem." The man grinned and cocked his head toward the four women but directed his words to Doug. "Wanna stay for a drink?"

He was tempted to ask which one of Jenn's friends Spade was interested in, but decided not to interfere. Instead, he eyed his woman, finally noticing how hot she looked in a denim mini skirt, a blue tank top with a sheer white blouse over it, and cute navy-blue wedge sandals. She had a little bit of makeup on, and her hair was up in a ponytail. While he had complete faith she would never cheat on him, he sure as hell didn't trust any of the men in the club not to hit on her. "Oh, yeah. We're definitely staying."

CHAPTER TWENTY-SIX

"That was so much fun! I can't believe we did it!" Jenn's body still buzzed with excitement after spending an hour soaring above the Rio Grande Valley in New Mexico, suspended in a colorful hot air balloon just after sunrise. It was the perfect day for it—sunny, with a few white, puffy clouds and fair winds. The pilot had steered them over the Rio Grande River and lowered the balloon enough for them to skim over the water, allowing for a better view of the beautiful landscape. They'd spotted several bighorn sheep and a bull elk with a massive rack of antlers along the river banks. It was an exhilarating experience that Jenn would never forget. It was even more special that she got to share it with Doug.

After setting down at the landing zone a little while ago, they celebrated their flight with a complimentary glass of champagne and received a commemorative certificate. Then, they thanked the pilot and tipped him before hopping into a shuttle van that transported them back to their rental car at the company's main office.

Margie's memorial was two days earlier, and Doug had taken three days off from work so he could go with Jenn and make a long weekend out of the trip. The deceased woman's family loved that several volunteers who'd served with her had driven to or flown in for the service. The memorial was bittersweet, with many of Margie's former students and teachers also attending. A catered repast was held afterward at a local VMA hall that her brother belonged to in Albuquerque. Jenn was thrilled to see Tony and reintroduce him to Doug, who didn't act like a green-eyed oaf now that he knew the other man had no interest in her. Secretly, Jenn liked it when his jealousy emerged occasionally. It got her heart racing and her panties wet.

She'd been happy to learn Tony was in a new relationship and it was going well. However, his boyfriend, Tad Winslow, a police officer from Hazard Falls, was unable to make the trip because he had a mandatory K9 certification training scheduled on the same day as the memorial. Tony showed her some pictures of the guy, though, and she had to admit, he was damn good-looking, and they made a cute couple.

She hoped it worked out for them because Tony deserved to be loved by someone special.

Things were tense between Tony and Doug at the beginning of the trip—mostly a clash of alpha protector grunting—but they'd since managed to call a truce. Jenn might even go so far as to call them friends…on a good day. After having breakfast and spending a few hours sightseeing with the couple yesterday, Tony left to catch an evening flight home, promising to keep in touch.

The shuttle dropped them off, and as they approached their car, Doug unlocked it with a key fob and opened the passenger door for her. "I parachuted a few times in the Marines, but I think I prefer floating over falling. I really enjoyed it." He leaned down and gave her a swift kiss. "Although I think the beautiful woman in the basket with me had something to do with that."

"Hmm. Who knew you were such a sweet talker?"

"Only for you."

He kissed her again before closing the door and hurrying around to the other side to get in. As he started the engine, Jenn scrolled through dozens of pictures she'd taken on her phone before, during, and after the high-in-the-sky adventure. Selecting a few of her favorites, she posted them in the private family Facebook group. She would put them on her regular Instagram and Facebook profiles in a few days for her friends to see. One of the first things Uncle Brody insisted on when she moved to Florida was that she keep her social media profiles locked down, allowing only people she knew to view her content. Another was that she didn't post anything live that would indicate her current location. He'd told her how people's houses were burglarized because they announced to the world they were on vacation somewhere else, or how stalkers easily found their targets because they tagged their locations in posts. Jenn followed his rules because they made sense. Her family didn't post any photos of the kids either—those were sent by encrypted email only.

Speaking of tagging locations on social media, Lainey Hall experienced a massive dose of reality after several videos of her arrest, including Yardley's, went viral on the internet. She lost all her sponsors, collaborators, and hundreds of thousands of followers. Within a week, she took down all her profiles after a flood of hateful comments and mockery overwhelmed her previous posts. She attempted to crowdfund to cover her legal expenses for the charges she still faced, but the site removed the page since it didn't allow fundraisers for that purpose. Jenn didn't feel an ounce of pity for the woman—she didn't deserve it after the stunt she pulled.

Pulling out of the parking lot, Doug glanced at her. "Okay, Ms. Tour Guide, what's next?"

They still had another full day and a half before they had to head to the airport for their flight home. The TS jet had been needed for something, so Doug bought them first-class tickets on a commercial airline, to Jenn's surprise. She then insisted on paying for their hotel, which took a little persuasion on her part. They agreed to split the rest of their expenses, for meals and activities, after a brief argument. Jenn had to remind her lover that she now had a steady paycheck since starting her new job. She also had her savings from her parents' life insurance policies and the sale of their old house in Virginia, but she didn't like dipping into that unless it was necessary. Some of it was used for her college education, and a significant amount had been invested under Grandpa Chuck's guidance. She'd waited tables during college to earn spending money, not wanting to deplete her savings or rely on her uncles to cover her personal needs and activities. She was fortunate to live at the TS compound rent-free, which, in her opinion, was more than enough, while only paying for her phone, cable, and internet. Doug had savings and investments as well, and also owned his condo, but she refused to expect him to pay for everything if they went anywhere. She wanted them to contribute equally to their relationship in every way possible, including financially.

"Breakfast first. That muffin I had a few hours ago

won't sustain me until the pub crawl." She reached over and entered an address from her phone into the car's GPS. "Margie's niece recommended this place."

They'd done so much in only a few short days that she was certain both would sleep during the entire flight home. After Tony left last night, they'd gone to dinner and then taken a ghost tour around Albuquerque, visiting the most haunted places in the city. *Allegedly* haunted, as Doug had whispered to her more than once during the tour. While they hadn't encountered any paranormal activity, it was still fun. Despite his amused pessimism, they were both fans of the show *Paranormal Caught on Camera* on the Travel Channel, and he'd been just as excited as she was to take the tour.

He took her hand and squeezed it. "Sounds good. I'll go wherever you want me to."

Jenn giggled loudly as Doug attempted to get the key card in the slot to open their hotel door for the third time. Leaning against the wall, she tried to remember the last time she'd gotten this drunk. It had definitely been a while.

The pub crawl was a blast. The fourteen other people they'd been with were friendly, and the day was filled with plenty of laughter. Their guide, a man in his mid-twenties, entertained them by imparting trivia and folklore about Albuquerque's history, performing a few magic tricks, and telling jokes. A few of the bars had live music, and one had karaoke. Jenn and Doug were tipsy enough at that point to perform an off-key duet of "Summer Nights" from the movie *Grease*. Neither one had a great singing voice, but they didn't care because it was fun. At least the crowd cheered them on and sang along.

Despite noshing on a variety of food at each location, their entire group had gotten intoxicated. Thankfully, she and Doug had the foresight to take a ride-share to and from the event. A few others hadn't thought of that and needed to leave their cars at the start/end point and take taxis home.

"Stop laughing at me," Doug said, even though he was chuckling too. The key finally slid into the slot, and the light turned green. "There. Got it. Now, get your cute..." *Hiccup.* "...little ass in there."

"Yessss, ssssir!"

He followed her into the room. "Oh, God. Don't call me 'sir.' Ian will beat the shit outta me if he thinks we're doing any...any BSMD stuff."

"BSMD?" She flopped backward onto the king-size bed, with her arms splayed out to the side as the room spun a little. "You ding-a-ling. That's wrong." Lifting her head a few inches, she eyed him. "Isn't it?

"DSMB? Fuck. Whatever." *Hiccup.* "It means the same damn thing no matter what order they're in...the letters, I mean." After tossing the key card, his wallet, and his phone on the room's desk, he kicked off his shoes before crawling onto the bed and over her body. "Anyway, I'm not giving him any excuse to shoot me, so no calling me 'sir.' Got it?"

"What about Daddy?" she asked with a snicker as she wrapped her arms around his neck and pulled him down on top of her.

"Definitely not Daddy! Damn, woman, just call me by my name or give me a pet name for fuck's sake." *Hiccup.*

He nuzzled her neck, and she turned her head to the side to give him better access. "Okay, tinsel-twat."

Growling, he rolled to the side, taking her with him, and then began to tickle her. She shrieked with laughter. "Stop! Okay! Stop! No tinsel-twat!"

"No 'sir,' 'Daddy', or 'tinsel-twat.' Got it?"

"Yes! I got it! Now stop tickling me!"

Thankfully, he did. She collapsed on top of him, trying to catch her breath. After a few moments, she pushed off him. "Ugh, I've got to pee again. New rule —no tickling me when I've got a full bladder and I'm half-drunk."

"I hate to tell you, sweetheart," he said to her back as she staggered toward the bathroom. *Hiccup.* "But you're not half-drunk. I am, but not you. You're completely drunk."

She refused to admit he was right about her, but she also thought he was just as drunk.

After relieving herself, she removed her sundress, bra, and panties in the bathroom, then tried to seductively sashay back to the bed and her sexy man. She probably wasn't successful, though, since she couldn't walk a straight line, but Doug still perked up when he realized she was in her birthday suit. "Well, hello there, beautiful."

Stopping at the end of the bed, she tugged on the leg of his cargo shorts. "You have waaaaay too many clothes on. Get nek-kid for me."

"Nek-kid?"

She nodded her head once, emphatically. "Yup. Nek-kid. Now, mister."

"Wha—? Ugh. For a second there, I thought you said..." *Hiccup.* "...master."

"Oh, hell no." She tugged his shorts again. "Get nek-kid and ravish me."

A slow grin spread across his face as his gaze drifted down her body. "Ravish? Is that an order?"

"Damn right, it is."

Hiccup.

Another giggle slipped past her lips. "You've got the hiccups."

Rolling off the side of the bed, he got to his feet and

swayed to the side, slapping his hand against the wall to steady himself. "Great observation, Captain…" *Hiccup*. "Captain Obvious."

When the room began to spin again, Jenn crawled onto the bed as Doug headed toward the bathroom. Hopefully, he'd come back out *nek-kid*. Even though she was drunk, she was also horny.

Just thinking about having sex with Doug made her aroused. Not bothering to wait for him, she skimmed one hand over her breasts and the other down her torso to where her clit throbbed. She was already wet with desire.

"Mmm. That's so fucking hot."

Her eyes flew open—she didn't remember closing them—and she grinned at him. He'd stripped his clothes off and now stood next to the bed with his cock half hard. He licked his lips while his gaze was glued to where she pleasured herself. "Keep going."

She did as requested while he put one knee on the bed and wrapped his hand around his shaft. A few strokes were all it took for him to be fully erect. Clearly, Doug wasn't too drunk that he couldn't perform. Thank fuck for that because she wanted him inside her. But first…

Getting onto her hands and knees in front of him, she batted his hand out of her way, then lowered her head, and took his cock into her mouth. He grabbed her hair, sending a delicious shiver down her spine.

"Oh, fuck, sweetheart! Yes!" He brushed his thumb over her cheek. "Love you so much."

She licked and sucked from root to tip before taking him to the back of her mouth and swallowing, drawing a hiss from him. It was then she noticed his hiccups were gone, which made her laugh and nearly choke on his cock. He pulled out and released the grip on her hair. "Are you okay?"

After coughing a few times, she nodded. "Yup. Fuck me."

He tilted his head and stared at her. "Was that a request or a statement, like fuck me, your dick is so big, it choked me?"

That made her laugh even harder as she fell back onto the bed. Who knew drunk sex could be so much fun? She sure as hell hadn't, but then again, this was her first time.

She wiggled the fingers of both hands at him in a "come here" gesture. "The first one, although the second one is true too."

Grinning, he got onto the bed, spread her legs, and settled his body between them. "Good to know."

Before she could say or do anything more, his head dipped, and he speared her pussy with his tongue. She squirmed and moaned as he ate her with fervor while two of his fingers massaged her clit. It wasn't long before she gasped for air and pleaded for him to make her come.

He stopped teasing her only long enough to say, "Play with your nipples. Tug on them."

She followed his command, and it was like an electric shock shot through her body, directly down to her clit, making it even more sensitive to his ministrations. An orgasm rose within her, barreling fast and hard until she couldn't hold back anymore. She screamed as wave after wave of pleasure careened through her, and she didn't care if anyone else heard her. Let them call the hotel's security—she would tell them how the man she loved took her to titillating heights she'd never been before.

She was still coming down from her climax when Doug plunged his cock inside her with one thrust.

"So fucking tight. God, I love you." He didn't sound as if he still felt the effects of the alcohol, and Jenn realized her mind wasn't as fuzzy as it'd been earlier. He drove into her harder and faster, and she felt another orgasm threaten to overtake her. Not that she minded at all.

Running her hands down his torso, she made a V with her fingers over her slit, on either side of his cock, letting it brush against them. His eyes widened. "Shit, that feels good. A little tighter. Oh, yeah. Like that. Stay there."

Sweat dripped from his brow onto her chest before he leaned down and sucked one of her nipples into his mouth. When he bit down lightly, the orgasm hit her, and she screamed again. Seconds later, Doug gave his hips one final snap and stilled as he came inside her. "Fuck! Oh, fuck!"

The tension left his body, and he held himself over her, leaning on his forearms. They both struggled to replenish their lungs with much-needed oxygen. After several moments, he slid out of her and rolled onto his side, pulling her close against him. The only sound in the room was their heavy breathing and the hum of the air conditioning.

No, that wasn't right. A rhythmic thumping caught their attention, and they stared at each other in confusion. She opened her mouth to ask what the noise was, but stopped when they heard a man and a woman howl in ecstasy—it came from the room next door.

Doug's and Jenn's eyes grew in amusement, and then they burst out laughing. It took a bit to get themselves under control again. When they finally did, Doug nuzzled his nose against hers. "Think we inspired them?"

"Mmmaybe. Want to test that theory in a little while with round two?"

He snorted, then grinned. "You're going to be the death of me, woman."

"But what a way to go, right?" She kissed him until they needed to come up for air again. "I love you."

"I love you too."

She brushed her fingers over his eyebrows, and her tone grew serious. "You know, I waited for what seems like forever for this. Don't ever leave me."

Grasping her hand, he brought it to his lips and kissed her fingertips. "Not a chance in hell, sweetheart. I'm here for the long haul."

"Good because so am I."

EPILOGUE

One year later...

Doug stood up from his office chair, then sat back down again. It was the fourth or fifth time he'd done that while trying to summon up the courage to knock on Ian's door. He honestly didn't think the man would turn him down, but he was still scared shitless.

He covered his face with his hands in frustration, but a loud knock had him dropping them again. Jake stood in the open doorway with his arms crossed, glaring at him. "What the fuck is up with you? I'm in my office trying to get some work done, and you're over here, standing, sitting, standing, sitting, standing, sitting, and looking like you want to puke. If you're going to hurl, take it outside or something. Don't mess up the bathroom."

Their offices were across the hall from each other, so it was no surprise that the other man noticed Doug's inane antics. "I'm not sick. I'm just...I need to go talk to Ian and...Shit, I don't know why I'm so nervous."

Jake stared at him for a few moments before a slow grin spread across his face. "Ah. I get it. Don't worry about it. You're doing the right thing. I think he's been expecting you to ask if you can marry Jenn."

"Yeah? Really?"

"The women have been gossiping lately, wondering when you're going to propose. Ian caught wind of it and blew his top before Angie calmed him down. Now that he's had some time to come to terms with it, I think you're good to go. I mean, you're already living with her, so he had to know a ring was coming at some point."

He moved into Jenn's apartment a few months ago, after they'd discussed it for a bit and decided that living at the compound instead of his place made sense. He no longer had to drive to work, and it was closer to her job than the condo, which he eventually rented out to one of the married bodyguards who worked for him. Jenn was also able to hang out with her aunts in the she-shed or see her nieces and nephews whenever she wanted. Of course, her uncles had to chime in and proclaim it was safer for Jenn to live at the compound. That had been the final tipping point for Doug when he thought about all the danger that had and could still come her way because of her association with everyone at Trident. Surprisingly, her uncles hadn't given him a ton of shit about him moving in with her—there'd been some, but as usual, Jenn shut that shit down quickly.

Doug flopped his head back against the chair. "What if he's just waiting for me to ask so he can say no?"

Leaning against the door jamb, Jake shook his head. "If he wasn't okay with you two being a couple and living together, you'd be shark food by now. I know we all gave you a hard time in the beginning, but that's what happens when you've known a woman you consider family since she was born and watched her grow up. Even before everything that happened with her folks, we were all overly protective of her. I'll be the first to admit that, but given our military backgrounds and the lifestyle we're in, it's to be expected. But to Ian, she's more like a daughter than a niece. He'll be the same way when Peyton is old enough. I feel bad for any little high school shit who wants to date her. Poor guys will show up to take her out, and he'll be sitting there, cleaning his guns, and making them piss their pants."

Doug snorted. "And Nick'll be sitting on the couch with a bowl of popcorn, cackling his ass off, I'm sure."

A boisterous laugh erupted from Jake. "You got that right. I might sit right next to him to enjoy the show." He paused for a moment. "Seriously. You and Jenn are good for each other. You make her happier than I've seen her since before her folks died, maybe ever. If this is the only thing holding you back from proposing, just go talk to him. I think he'll surprise you."

Although not entirely convinced, he forced himself to stand. "You're right. He's had plenty of time to kill me before now, and I haven't given him any reason to say no, right?"

"Right."

Jake moved out of Doug's way so he could exit the office, but then the man followed him down the hall toward the reception area. Doug glanced over his shoulder. "Where are you going?"

"To find Junior. He's helping Stefan with the new class. For once, I've got some hot gossip before my husband, and I can't wait to throw it in his face."

Doug chuckled and shook his head. "Just tell him to keep his trap shut until I actually do this."

"No problem."

They separated by Colleen's desk, with Jake slapping Doug on the back before striding toward the door to the parking lot. "Good luck."

"Thanks." He stopped beside Colleen. "Is Ian busy?"

She smiled up at him. "Just signing everyone's paycheck. He's not on the landline, but he could be on his cell, so knock first."

"Thanks."

He moved to stand in front of the closed office door. His heart pounded, and his mouth went dry, forcing him to swallow a few times, then clear his throat. "Just fucking do it," he silently told himself.

Lifting his fist, he paused for another few seconds before knocking three times.

"Enter!"

He turned the knob and pushed the door open to find Ian behind his desk, scribbling his signature on the top page of a stack of papers. For some unknown reason, the man refused to have a stamp made of his signature, which would have been faster. "Got a minute, Boss-man?"

"Yeah, come on in." Ian dropped his pen on the desk and leaned back in his chair as Doug closed the door behind him and took a seat. "What's up?"

Despite the building's air conditioning, Doug was sweating bullets, and nausea flooded his gut again. He took a deep breath and let it out before meeting Ian's intense gaze. "I...um. Look. I know I got off on the wrong foot with you by not telling you Jenn and I were dating right away, but I want to rectify that in a way."

Cocking his head to the side, Ian remained quiet.

"Um…" Fuck. He knew this wouldn't be easy, but he just needed to spit the words out. Taking a deep breath, he released it and then blurted, "I want to ask for your permission to propose to Jenn."

Silence hung in the room like a weighted blanket. Seconds ticked by while the two men stared at each other. If Doug's nausea got any worse, he'd puke all over the desk. Not fun.

Finally, Ian leaned forward. "Tell me you didn't buy a ring yet."

What? That was the last thing he expected his boss to say, and his heart sank. The man was going to say no. *Shit.* "I…uh…"

Ian slammed his hand on the desk. "Answer me, tinsel-twat! Did you buy the fucking ring yet?"

"N-no. Not yet. I-I looked at some rings the other day but didn't find anything I thought she'd like. Besides, I wanted to wait until after I spoke to you about it. Listen, i-if you want me to wait a little while longer, I will. But I love—"

"Get up," Ian interrupted as he stood and snatched his cell phone from where it sat on the desk.

Confused, he obeyed the man. "What—"

His boss circled the desk and headed for the door. "Come with me." When Doug just stood there, staring at the man's retreating back, Ian stopped and glared at him over his shoulder. "Hey, doofus! Move it."

Scrambling around the chair, Doug hurried after the man. He had no idea what was going on, and Ian didn't seem inclined to clue him in. Doug didn't catch up to him until he was halfway across the parking lot, purposefully stalking toward the apartment building. He followed Ian into the man's downstairs unit.

"Boss-man, what are we doing here?"

Ian didn't respond or stop as he strode down the hallway to the primary bedroom and disappeared into a walk-in closet, flipping on the interior light. Since he didn't say to follow him in there, Doug stayed in the bedroom, more confused than ever. Against the back wall, Ian moved something on a shelf, exposing a scanner like the ones that opened most of the doors around the compound. When he placed his hand on it, a concealed panel in the wall popped open, revealing a large safe. He hit a bunch of buttons on a keypad, opened the door, and then reached inside to grab something. Doug couldn't see what it was, but it was small enough to fit in the man's fist as he shut the safe and put the panel back in place.

Exiting the closet, he stopped in front of Doug. "I know you love her. And I know you'll take care of her and treat her like she's the most cherished woman on this planet. I've watched you do that for the past year."

Ian lifted his hand. In it was a red velvet ring box. When he opened it, Doug's breath caught in his chest. Nestled inside on a white satin pillow was a stunning emerald-cut diamond and platinum ring. "This was Jenn's mother's engagement ring. Before the caskets were closed, I had the funeral home take it off her because it was what Lisa asked me to do. She and Jeff each gave me updated 'just in case' letters every year since Jenn was born."

Doug knew what those were. Everyone in the military did. It would contain final words and instructions for whoever it was addressed to in the event of someone's untimely death. Some members of the military wrote them, while others opted not to or had a will drawn up instead, depending on their personal preference. Doug had known a few Marines who thought the letters would jinx a mission or tour, but he had written one to his family and given it to a trusted teammate to deliver—just in case.

"One of the things Lisa wanted was for Jenn to have this. She doesn't know I have it." Ian smiled sadly. "She always loved trying it on while growing up, and Lisa told me to give it to the man who won her daughter's heart when he was ready to propose, as long as I approved." He handed the box to Doug, who couldn't stop staring at the ring as he accepted it. "I approve, Doug. While I wasn't happy about you and her in the beginning, you've since proven to me that I can trust you with her heart. You have my blessing."

While blinking back tears that threatened to fall

and swallowing a thick lump in his throat, Doug transferred the box to his left hand and held out his right to the man he would soon consider his father-in-law. "Thank you, Ian."

Ian grasped Doug's hand and pulled him into a fatherly embrace, slapping him on the back several times. "You're welcome, son."

Doug couldn't stop the tears from falling after that, even if his life depended on it.

It was a beautiful, sunny Saturday as the boat gently swayed a few hundred yards offshore in the Gulf of Mexico. A mild breeze, the pink bikini Jenn wore, and the U of T baseball cap on her head kept her from getting too hot. After they'd dropped anchor, Doug removed his T-shirt, showing off his tanned, muscular physique. His blue swim shorts hugged his hips, and she eyed his taut ass whenever he bent over. Damn, the man was fine, and he was all hers.

Last night, when he asked if she wanted to go fishing, she agreed immediately. She loved being out on the water. Sometimes, they went out on Grandpa Chuck's larger boat with family and friends or invited a few people to join them on the *A Salt Weapon*, but mostly, it was the two of them. One day, she hoped they could teach their children how to fish. Even if they didn't catch any keepers or anything at all, it was still fun.

Over the past year, they'd talked about marriage and kids several times, but she never pressured him into proposing. She suspected that when the time was right, he would, but a ring and a piece of certified paper wouldn't make that much of a difference to her. She already had everything she needed. Every day and night, he showed her how much he adored, cherished, protected, and loved her, and she returned each sentiment as best she could.

"Hey, Jenn. Put on a little more sunscreen. Your nose is getting pink."

Case in point. He always looked out for her, yet still let her have the freedom to spread her wings. He treated her like she was his equal, and instead of fighting her battles for her, he stood beside her, ready to step in only if necessary.

Any serious arguments they had over the past year could be counted on one hand and never lasted long. There hadn't been a single instance when they'd gone to bed mad at each other.

A few weeks after everyone knew they were dating, Tahira Knight, wife of Omega Team member Darius Knight and the princess of Timasur, a small north African country, was at the compound for a barbecue.

Her face lit up as soon as she saw Doug and Jenn together. The woman was a firm believer in soulmates and could supposedly see people's auras. Jenn wasn't convinced about the latter, but if what Tahira had said was true, about seeing reds, pinks, purples, oranges, and yellows surrounding the couple, she was all for it, even though it sounded like a tarot card reading. According to Tahira, reds meant passion and vitality. Pinks were for love and compassion. Purple symbolized unconditional love and spiritual connection. Orange suggested a sense of sexual vibrancy and excitement about life. And finally, yellow depicted joy. All described exactly what Jenn felt being in Doug's arms.

After putting more sunscreen on herself, she gave him the tube of lotion for his face and then applied the protective spray to his back, chest, shoulders, arms, and legs. As she rubbed it into his skin, she felt a little frisky and ran her hands up his legs under the hem of his shorts to squeeze his tight ass cheeks.

He jerked and moved away. "Hey! I told you. No nooky until we catch dinner."

Standing, she tossed the can and tube back into her tote bag. "Fine. Fish first, but then I'm taking you down into the bunk and attacking you." She could've jumped his bones right there on the deck, but several other fishing boats were close enough to see the occupants, but far away enough that they couldn't hear them or get their lines tangled. Neither she nor Doug was an exhibitionist, so they would take their sexy time below, away from curious eyes.

Returning to her fishing pole that was in a holder attached to the boat, she was about to reel in the line to see if there was still bait on her hook when she felt a bite. The rod bent and the line went taut, suddenly heavy. Whatever was caught on the hook made the tip of the rod bob up and down. "I've got one!"

"Reel it in!"

Excitedly, she started to bring the fish up, increasing and then releasing the tension as she spun the reel's handle. About halfway up, the line snapped and sent her stumbling back a few steps, but Doug grabbed her arm to steady her.

"Darn it!" Not only had she lost the fish, the lure, and the hook, but she hadn't won their bet—yet. It'd become a game for them every time they went fishing—the first person to bring up a keeper didn't have to clean what was caught later for dinner.

Doug set his pole in a holder as she reeled in the now-slack line. When she was done, he took the rod from her, grabbing hold of the line flying in the wind. "I'll fix it for you. Do me a favor? In the outer pocket of my duffel bag, there's a new box of lures I picked up because Chuck recommended them. He said he caught some nice-sized fish with them last time he went out. Get the box for me, please?"

"Sure."

She turned toward the passenger seat in the cockpit, where his duffel was lying on the ground beneath it. Lifting it, she set it on the seat and opened the zipper of the bag's front pocket. Her eyes narrowed in confusion. Instead of a box of lures, the only content was a small, red velvet box. Her hand trembled as she reached for it. A box like that could only contain one thing. Her breath caught as she picked it up. Instead of opening it, she spun back to face Doug, only to find him down on one knee. He took the box from her and opened it. Her right hand flew to her mouth when she saw her mother's engagement ring nestled inside, recognizing it instantly. She thought it was buried with her mom, along with her wedding ring. How had Doug gotten it?

Tears flowed down her cheeks in rivulets as Doug took her left hand. "Jenn, you're a part of me that I never knew was missing. But then you made me open my eyes to see what was right in front of me all along. You're my lover, my best friend, my fishing buddy, my confidant, and now, I want you to be my wife. I want to have children and grandchildren with you. I want to grow old with you. When I asked Ian for permission to propose to you, he gave me this. He said your mother left instructions for him to save it and give it to the man who won your heart. I hope that man is me. Will you marry me?"

She nodded enthusiastically before he finished the question, as her body shook from a combination of shock, exhilaration, and pure love. "Y-yes! Absolutely, one hundred percent yes!"

As he released her and removed the ring from the box, she dropped to her knees. He retook her left hand, holding it steady as he slipped the ring on her finger. It fit perfectly. Cupping her jaw, he drew her close and kissed her. "I love you. Thank you for waiting for me to get my head out of my ass."

"I love you, too, and I would've waited forever."

But wait!
There's more!

Get Jenn and Doug's wedding story at
dl.bookfunnel.com/s87fsf26g1

Looking for more steamy romance? Check out the Hazard Falls series, starting with *Don't Fight It*!

Want to know what's coming next? Join my Facebook Group -
Samantha Cole's Sexy Six-Pack's Sirens
or sign up for my newsletter -
www.samanthacoleauthor.com/newsletter-signup

WHO'S WHO AND THE HISTORY OF TRIDENT SECURITY AND THE COVENANT

***While not every character is in every book, these are the ones with the most mentions throughout the series. This guide will help keep readers straight about who's who.

Trident Security (TS) is a private investigative and military agency, co-owned by Ian and Devon Sawyer. With governmental and civilian contracts, the company got its start when the brothers and a few of their teammates from SEAL Team Four retired to the private sector. The original six-man team is referred to as the Sexy Six-Pack, as they were dubbed by Kristen Sawyer, née Anders, or the Alpha Team. They, along with Ian and Devon's brother, Nick, are now shareholders in the business. Trident had since expanded and former members of the military and law enforcement have been added to the staff. The company is located on a guarded compound, which was a former import/export company cover for a drug trafficking operation in Tampa, Florida. Three warehouses on the property were converted into large apartments, the TS offices, gym, and bunk rooms. There is also an obstacle course, a Main Street shooting gallery, a helicopter pad, and more features necessary for training and missions.

In addition to the security business, there is a fourth warehouse that now houses an elite BDSM club, co-owned by Devon, Ian, and their cousin, Mitch Sawyer, who is the manager. A lot of time and money has gone into making The Covenant the most sought after membership in the Tampa/St. Petersburg area and beyond. Members are thoroughly vetted before being granted access to the elegant club.

There are currently over fifty Doms who have been appointed Dungeon Masters (DMs), and they rotate two or three shifts each throughout the month. At least four DMs are on duty at all times at various posts in the pit, playrooms, and the new garden, with an additional one roaming around. Their job is to ensure the safety of all the submissives in the club. They step in if a sub uses their safeword and the Dom in the scene doesn't hear or heed it, and make sure the equipment used in scenes isn't harming the subs.

The Covenant's security team takes care of everything else that isn't scene-related, and provides safety for all members and are essentially the bouncers. With the recent addition of the garden, and more private, themed rooms, the owners have expanded their self-imposed limit of 350 members. The fire marshal had approved them for 500 when the warehouse-turned-kink club first opened, but the cousins had intentionally kept that number down to maintain an elite status. Now with more room, they are increasing the membership to 500, still under the new maximum occupancy of 720.

Between Trident Security and The Covenant there's plenty of romance, suspense, and steamy encounters. Come meet the Sexy Six-Pack, their friends, family, and teammates.

The Sexy Six-Pack (Alpha Team) and Their Significant Others

- Ian "Boss-man" Sawyer: Devon and Nick's brother; retired Navy SEAL; co-owner of Trident Security and The Covenant; husband/Dom of Angelina (Angel); father of Peyton Marie.
- Devon "Devil Dog" Sawyer: Ian and Nick's brother; retired Navy SEAL; co-owner of Trident Security and The Covenant;

husband/Dom of Kristen; father of John Devon "JD."
- Ben "Boomer" Michaelson: retired Navy SEAL; explosives and ordnance specialist; husband/Dom of Katerina; son of Rick and Eileen.
- Jake "Reverend" Donovan: retired Navy SEAL; temporarily assigned to run the West Coast team; sniper; husband/Dom of Nick; brother of Mike; Whip Master at The Covenant.
- Brody "Egghead" Evans: retired Navy SEAL; computer specialist; husband/Dom of Fancy.
- Marco "Polo" DeAngelis: retired Navy SEAL; communications specialist and back up helicopter pilot; husband/Dom of Harper; father to Mara.
- Nick "Junior" Donovan (nee Sawyer): Ian and Devon's brother; current Navy SEAL; husband/submissive of Jake.
- Kristen "Ninja-girl" Sawyer: author of romance/suspense novels; wife/submissive of Devon; mother of "JD."
- Angelina "Angie/Angel" Sawyer: graphic artist; wife/submissive of Ian; mother of Petyon Marie.

- Katerina "Kat" Michaelson: dog trainer for law enforcement and private agencies; wife/submissive of Boomer.
- Millicent "Harper" DeAngelis: lawyer; wife/submissive of Marco; mother of Mara.
- Francine "Fancy" Maguire: baker; wife/submissive of Brody.

Extended Family, Friends, and Associates of the Sexy Six-Pack

- Mitch Sawyer: Cousin of Ian, Devon, and Nick; co-owner/manager of The Covenant, Dom to Tyler and Tori.
- T. Carter: US spy and assassin; works for covert agency Deimos; Dom of Jordyn.
- Jordyn Alvarez: US spy and assassin; member of covert agency Deimos; submissive of Carter.
- Tyler Ellis: Stockbroker; lifestyle switch—Dom of Tori; submissive of Mitch.
- Tori Freyja: K9 trainer for veterans in need of assistance/service dogs; submissive of Mitch and Tyler.
- Parker Christiansen: owner of New Horizons Construction; husband/Dom of Shelby; adoptive father of Franco and Victor.

- Shelby Christiansen: stay-at-home mom; two-time cancer survivor; wife/submissive of Parker; adoptive mother of Franco and Victor.
- Curt Bannerman: retired Navy SEAL; owner of Halo Customs, a motorcycle repair and detail shop; husband of Dana; stepfather of Ryan, Taylor, Justin, and Amanda. Lives in Iowa.
- Dana Prichard-Bannerman: teacher; widow of retired SEAL Eric Prichard; wife of Curt; mother of Ryan, Taylor, Justin, and Amanda. Lives in Iowa.
- Jenn "Baby-girl" Mullins: college student; goddaughter of Ian; "niece" of Devon, Brody, Jake, Boomer, and Marco; father was a Navy SEAL; parents murdered.
- Mike Donovan: owner of the Irish pub, Donovan's; brother of Jake; submissive to Charlotte.
- Charlotte "Mistress China" Roth: Parole officer; Domme and Whip Master at The Covenant; Domme of Mike.
- Travis "Tiny" Daultry: former professional football player; head of security at The Covenant and Trident compound; occasional bodyguard for TS.

- Doug "Bullseye" Henderson: retired Marine; head of the Personal Protection Division of TS.
- Rick and Eileen Michaelson: Boomer's parents; guardians of Alyssa. Rick is a retired Navy SEAL.
- Charles "Chuck" and Marie Sawyer: Ian, Devon, and Nick's parents. Charles is a self-made real estate billionaire. Marie is a plastic surgeon involved with Operation Smile.
- Will Anders: Assistant Curator of the Tampa Museum of Art Kristen Anders's cousin.
- Dr. Roxanne London: pediatrician; Domme/wife (Mistress Roxy) of Kayla; Whip Master at Covenant.
- Kayla London: social worker; submissive/wife of Roxanne.
- Grayson and Remington Mann: twins; owners of Black Diamond Records; Doms/fiancés of Abigail; members of The Covenant.
- Abigail Turner: personal assistant at Black Diamond Records; submissive/fiancée of Gray and Remi.
- Chase Dixon: retired Marine Raider; owner of Blackhawk Security; associate of TS.

- Reggie Helm: lawyer for TS and The Covenant; Dom/husband of Colleen.
- Alyssa Wagner: teenager saved by Jake from an abusive father; lives with Rick and Eileen Michaelson; attending nursing school.
- Dr. Trudy Dunbar: Psychologist.
- Carl Talbot: college professor; Dom and Whip Master at The Covenant.
- Jase Atwood: Contract agent/mercenary; Lives on the island of St. Lucia; Dom of Brie.
- Brie Hanson: Owner of Daddy-O's in St. Lucia; submissive of Jase.
- Stefan Lundquist: Lieutenant Commander US Coast Guard; Dom; Shibari Master.
- Cassandra Myers: Cardiac Rehabilitation Technician; attending nursing school; submissive.

The Omega Team and Their Significant Others

- Cain "Shades" Foster: retired Secret Service agent.
- Tristan "Duracell" McCabe: retired Army Special Forces.

- Logan "Cowboy" Reese: retired Marine Special Forces; former prisoner of war. Boyfriend/Dom of Dakota.
- Valentino "Romeo" Mancini: retired Army Special Forces; former FBI Hostage Rescue Team (HRT) member.
- Darius "Batman" Knight: retired Navy SEAL.
- Kip "Skipper" Morrison: retired Army; former LAPD SWAT sniper.
- Lindsey "Costello" Abbott: retired Marine; sniper.
- Dakota Swift: Tampa PD undercover police officer; submissive girlfriend to Logan.
- Tahira: Princess of Timasur; wife of Darius.

Trident Support Staff

- Colleen McKinley-Helm: office manager of TS; wife/submissive of Reggie.
- Tempest "Babs" Van Buren: retired Air Force helicopter pilot; TS mechanic.
- Russell Adams: retired Navy; assistant TS mechanic.
- Nathan Cook: former computer specialist with the National Security Agency (NSA).

Members of Law Enforcement

- Larry Keon: Assistant Director of the FBI.
- Frank Stonewall: Special Agent in Charge of the Tampa FBI.
- Calvin Watts: Leader of the FBI HRT in Tampa.
- Colt Parrish: Major Case Specialist, Behavioral Analysis Unit.

The K9s of Trident

- Beau: An orphaned Lab/Pit mix, rescued by Ian. Now a trained K9 who has more than earned his spot on the Alpha Team.
- Spanky: A rescued Bullmastiff with a heart of gold, owned by Parker and Shelby.
- Jagger: A rescued Rottweiler trained as an assistance/service animal for Russell.
- FUBAR: A Belgian Malinois who failed aggressive guard dog training. Adopted by Babs.
- BDSM: Bravo, Delta, Sierra, and Mike, two Belgian Malinoises and two German shepherds, the guard dogs at the Trident compound: Ian named them using the military communication's alphabet.

OTHER BOOKS BY SAMANTHA COLE

***Denotes titles/series that are only available on select digital sites. Paperbacks and audiobooks are available on most book sites.

THE TRIDENT SECURITY SERIES

Leather & Lace

His Angel

Waiting For Him

Not Negotiable: A Novella

Topping The Alpha

Watching From the Shadows

Whiskey Tribute: A Novella

Tickle His Fancy

No Way in Hell: A Steel Corp/Trident Security Crossover (co-authored with J.B. Havens)

Absolving His Sins

Option Number Three: A Novella

Salvaging His Soul

Trident Security Field Manual

Torn In Half: A Novella

***Heels, Rhymes, & Nursery Crimes Series
(with 13 other authors)

Jack Be Nimble: A Trident Security-Related Short Story

***The Deimos Series

Handling Haven: Special Forces: Operation Alpha

Cheating the Devil: Special Forces: Operation Alpha

The Trident Security Omega Team Series

Mountain of Evil

A Dead Man's Pulse

Forty Days & One Knight

The Doms of The Covenant Series

Double Down & Dirty

Entertaining Distraction

Knot a Chance

The Blackhawk Security Series

Tuff Enough

Blood Bound

Master Key Series

Master Key Resort

Master Cordell

HAZARD FALLS SERIES

Don't Fight It

Don't Shoot the Messenger

THE MALONE BROTHERS SERIES

Her Secret

Her Sleuth

LARGO RIDGE SERIES

Cold Feet

***ANTELOPE ROCK SERIES

(CO-AUTHORED WITH J.B. HAVENS)

Wannabe in Wyoming

Wistful in Wyoming

AWARD-WINNING STANDALONE BOOKS

Where the Broken Bloom

Scattered Moments in Time: A Collection of Short Stories & More

***THE BID ON LOVE SERIES

(WITH 7 OTHER AUTHORS!)

Going, Going, Gone: Book 2

***THE COLLECTIVE: SEASON TWO

(WITH 7 OTHER AUTHORS!)

Angst: Book 7

SPECIAL COLLECTIONS

Trident Security Series: Volume I

Trident Security Series: Volume II

Trident Security Series: Volume III

Trident Security Series: Volume IV

Trident Security Series: Volume V

Trident Security Series: Volume VI

ABOUT SAMANTHA COLE

USA Today Bestselling Author and Award-Winning Author Samantha Cole is a retired policewoman and former paramedic. Using her life experiences and training, she strives to find the perfect mix of suspense and romance for her readers to enjoy.

Awards:

Wannabe in Wyoming (co-authored by J.B. Havens) won the bronze medal in the 2021 Readers' Favorite Awards in the General Romance category.

Scattered Moments in Time, won the gold medal in the 2020 Readers' Favorite Awards in the Fiction Anthology category.

The Road to Solace (formerly *The Friar*), won the silver medal in the 2017 Readers' Favorite Awards in the Contemporary Romance category.

Samantha has over thirty-five books published throughout several different series as well as a few standalone novels. A full list can be found on her website.

Sexy Six-Pack's Sirens Group on Facebook
Website: www.samanthacoleauthor.com
Newsletter: www.samanthacoleauthor.-com/newsletter-signup

- facebook.com/SamanthaColeAuthor
- instagram.com/samanthacoleauthor
- bookbub.com/profile/samantha-a-cole
- goodreads.com/SamanthaCole
- amazon.com/Samantha-A-Cole/e/B00X53K3X8

Printed in Dunstable, United Kingdom